THE PICTURE ON THE FRIDGE

IAN W. SAINSBURY

Cover by

Good Cover Design

https://www.goodcoverdesign.co.uk

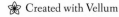 Created with Vellum

For Ruth

CHAPTER ONE

Mags crouched behind the log pile, waiting for a murderer.

It wouldn't be a long wait. Before leaving the cabin, she and Tam had watched a dark shape stumble up the icy slope towards them.

She looked at her daughter. Tam's dark hair had stuck to her forehead. She was breathing too quickly, taking short gulps of air, each exhalation puffing out clouds into the freezing morning. Mags thought of the Thomas the Tank Engine episodes from when Tam was in kindergarten, seven years ago. It felt like decades.

Thomas the Tank Engine puffed into the station. The Fat Controller was waiting for them and he looked angry. Very angry.

Mags didn't know if the murderer was fat, but she knew he was angry. She didn't know if he was thin, tall, short, old or young. He might be an office worker, or a taxi driver. He could be a drifter, a carpenter, a teacher. Tam couldn't tell her mother if he was black, white, or Asian. She only knew what he had done to reach them, and what he wanted now.

And what he wanted now was Tam. Which meant he'd have to kill Mags, because she didn't care if the murderer was built like a bear, she was going to stop him. Mags shook her head in mute fury and despair. The odds of her walking away from this encounter were close to zero.

"He'll find us, Mum."

Tam's face was rigid, her eyes staring. Mags turned to her, taking both her hands in hers, squeezing. She pulled her daughter's wool hat down over her ears and stroked her cold cheeks.

The last time I'll touch her.

"You remember the path we saw through the trees?"

Tam nodded.

"It leads to the next town. When I tell you to run, do it. Okay, Tam-Tam? Run as fast as you can."

Tam shook her head. She didn't speak. Not even to object to being called Tam-Tam. Her lips were pressed tightly together, white lines on a pale face.

Mags looked into her daughter's eyes and lied to her.

"I'll be right behind you. We don't have time to argue."

They both heard it. The crunch of snow at the front of the cabin, the laboured breathing. For a few seconds, nothing. Then footsteps climbed the steps to the porch.

Mags released her daughter and placed her right hand on her chest, pushing her away.

"Run, Tam. Run. Now."

A moment's hesitation, an agony of indecision before Tam turned and ran for the trees. Mags watched the tuft of hair below her hat, and the inch of skin beneath it until she was out of sight. Tam didn't look back.

Good girl.

At the front of the cabin, the murderer rattled the door. When he stopped, Mags held her breath. She let the air out in a rush at the sound of glass breaking, and a window being pulled up.

Not long now.

Keeping the logs between her and the back of the cabin, she shuffled across to where she'd hidden the axe. Mags found the gap in the logs and slid her hand into the pile of snow-soaked leaves. She patted the frozen ground beneath, stretching out for the handle.

It wasn't there.

Her own breathing quickened now. She felt light-headed.

No. No. It had to be there.

She scanned the immediate area and saw another gap, a few feet away. Mags leaned across, her body flat against the cold, hard soil. She stretched as far as she could, her fingers going numb.

"Oh, Christ, come on. Please."

The back door opened. She stopped moving. She stopped breathing.

Footsteps. A voice. Bland, unremarkable. What had she expected?

"You should go. I'm here for her, not you."

Fingers touched the rubber grip, nails dug in. She clawed it into her fingers. Once the axe was in her hand, all thoughts, even those of Tam, dropped away.

Mags stood up. Faced him. Lifted the axe.

"Come on, then."

Her voice sounded hoarse. Shaky. She screamed her next words.

"Come on, you fucker, COME ON."

CHAPTER TWO

SEVEN MONTHS EARLIER

Mrs Matlock called Mags back just as she reached the school gate. Beside her, Tam stiffened with embarrassment. Mags had promised she could walk to school on her own after Christmas. Tam would be one of the last in her year to do so. Mags knew her daughter thought her over-protective. She was right, of course.

"Mrs Barkworth! Mrs Barkworth!"

Mags turned and acknowledged the teacher with a wave, before making her way across the playground against the tide of parents and children.

Tam grabbed for her hand and slowed her down, pulling her closer. "I got my period," she whispered. "I was going to tell you at home."

Mags had put together a small bag with sanitary pads and a spare pair of knickers for Tam to take to school, but it was still in a bedroom drawer. Her own first period hadn't arrived until she was thirteen. She shook her head at her stupidity.

"I'm sorry, Tam, I—"

"It's all right, Mum. Jas lent me a pad."

"Thank goodness. And you're okay?"

"I'm fine."

Mags touched Tam's cheek. She looked a little paler than usual, her eyes even darker in contrast. Without the freckles, her face might be an adult's. Mags had a glimpse of a daughter she didn't know yet, the daughter who would go out into the world one day, and leave her. The lurch of pride and panic felt like a premonition.

Mrs Matlock waited in the doorway of the classroom. Her dense grey curls were half-tamed by a hairband.

Tam kept her head down as they followed her in. The teacher stopped at the far side of the room, her back towards them. Mags and Tam waited, unsure of what to do. The older woman looked over her shoulder and waved them forward.

"Well? What do you think?"

They joined Mrs Matlock in front of a wall of pencil sketches. Tam enjoyed art, although she had no particular talent for it. Mags scanned the pictures, hoping she could pick out her daughter's. She wasn't optimistic. All the pictures showed buildings: houses, skyscrapers, factories, farms, garages, train stations.

"This afternoon, the children sketched buildings," said Mrs Matlock, an eyebrow raised as if expecting some comment other than the obvious, "no shit." Mags nodded, checking the names in the corners of the drawings. Tam didn't have a recognisable style. She had crayoned stick figures with balloon hands and three fingers as a toddler before graduating to the standard four-windowed square house with a corkscrew of smoke curling from a chimney.

Then she saw it.

Near the top of the wall, just off centre, one picture stood out. It was so detailed, it might have been traced from a photograph. Its simple, but faithful, representation of everything in view reminded Mags of a documentary she'd watched about an autistic boy who drew intricate city skylines.

She took a step closer, then looked back at her daughter. Tam's face was unreadable, her expression blank.

"You drew this, Tam?"

The faintest nod in response.

"Don't be shy, Tamara," said Mrs Matlock. Tam hated Tamara even more than Tam-Tam. "What an amazing piece of work."

Mags turned back to the picture. The building portrayed was a big, detached house, unlike anything in their North London neighbourhood. The Barkworth's street comprised Victorian semis, Edwardian terraces, and a few modern glass and zinc-topped statements.

Nothing like this. The exterior walls were clapboard, the shingled roof boasted a single chimney. A wooden deck led to a screen door. Tam had, apparently, drawn from the perspective of an insect, because grass, leaves and branches obscured some of the building.

The artist's attention to detail was remarkable. One board, close to a gable, sagged, and an enterprising bird had nested in the resulting gap. Tendrils of ivy curled round a corner. On the decking, an old bicycle stood where Mags might have put a porch swing. In a basket on its handlebars, tightly shut flowers were just visible. Mags thought they might be tulips.

"I've never seen her so focused," said Mrs Matlock. She put a hand on Tam's shoulder. "Completely absorbed, she was. Wouldn't have noticed if the fire alarm had gone off, would you, Tamara?"

Tam said nothing. She was pale, tired-looking. Mags remembered about her period.

"Amazing," she said, smiling at Mrs Matlock, who was still talking.

"I've seen nothing of that standard in fifteen years of teaching. A talent like that, well..."

Tam squeezed Mags' hand and pulled her away.

"Yes, yes, you're right," said Mags, as they walked to the door. "Thanks again."

At home, with the kettle on, and Tam halfway through a glass of orange juice, Mags put an arm around her, pulling her close.

"My little artist," she said. "What's up? Is it your period? Are you tired? Does your tummy hurt?"

Tam raised her pale face to look at her. "It's the drawing, Mum."

"What about it, darling?"

Tam looked glum. "I don't remember doing it. I don't remember anything at all."

"When's Dad home?"

They sat at the kitchen table. The kitchen was still Mags' favourite room. House-hunting while pregnant, the open space and the clean modern kitchen made her grip her husband's arm when they'd first walked in. Then she'd fallen in love with the high, Victorian ceilings, the en-suite bathroom, the huge basement study for Bradley, and the glass box jutting into the garden at the end of the kitchen. The architect selling it had added that last feature; a sun trap in the summer, and the only spot where you could read without a lamp on a winter morning.

The shutters were still open at eight in the evening. Light from the sinking sun slatted across the wooden floor, striping the boards orange and umber. Birdsong added its exuberant counterpoint to the classical soundtrack on the bluetooth speaker.

Tam sipped milk and ate a cookie. Mags had insisted on referring to the snack as a biscuit for a few months after Tam first started talking, but she couldn't compete with an American husband and a daily helping of Sesame Street.

The milk and cookie ritual before bed was one American import she had been happy to adopt. Milk and cookie, teeth-cleaning, bed, story, reading time, lights out. A pattern unbroken since Tam was a toddler. The fact that she still occasionally wanted a bedtime story at eleven-and-a-half thrilled Mags, but she tried not to show it. Maybe it was an only child thing. Maybe it was because her father worked away so much. Whatever it was, Mags didn't care.

"His flight gets in early on Saturday. Very early. He'll be here for breakfast, honey."

Honey was another Americanism that had crept in. It didn't sound strange on her lips anymore. It had only taken fourteen years of being with the Man from Massachusetts to get used to it. The language may have taken years to absorb, but Bradley himself had been a whirlwind. They'd gone from *shooting the breeze* and *hanging out* to *dating* and *getting hitched* within three months. Her friends and family had been incredulous at such impulsive behaviour. Well, the ones who hadn't seen Bradley had been incredulous.

"Only two nights," said Tam, finishing her milk, leaving a bright white moustache behind.

"That's right." Mags wiped a tissue over Tam's top lip before clearing away the glass and plate.

"Mum." Tam took the tissue from her. Mags gave her the plate, and she put it in the dishwasher, holding out a hand for the glass. "I'm not a child."

Mags almost smirked at the solemn way she said that, but kept her expression neutral. And Tam had a point. In some cultures, today was the day she became a woman.

"Does it hurt? Your stomach, I mean. Is it uncomfortable?"

Tam leaned against the dishwasher. Her new haircut—short, but still, somehow, untidy—shone in the last of the sunlight, fine golden tips a reminder of the blonde curls she had as a baby. Her hair was brown now, but lighter than those dark, intense eyes of hers. The recent run of hot weather brought out her freckles. Tam hated her freckles. Mags loved them.

"I'm fine, Mum. You gave me all those books to read. I know more than most doctors. I am now an expert on ladies' plumbing."

"Two books. I gave you two books." Mags smiled. "I just want to make sure you're okay. You don't know how your period will affect you until it happens."

"Well, it's happening, and I'm fine. So stop worrying."

"And what about that picture?"

"What about it?"

Tam was reluctant to say much more about her episode of artistic genius. She was half-convinced she had fallen asleep in class, although part of her remained aware of the pencil in her hand, the pressure of the nib on the textured paper. But Tam didn't know the house she'd drawn, or even if it was a real house. She was as surprised as Mrs Matlock by what she had produced.

"Well..." Mags didn't want to push her. Tam wasn't keen to talk about it. A strange episode, but not worth getting upset about. She'd wait until she'd discussed it with Bradley. He always wanted every detail about what Tam had been up to.

In bed, with another chapter of Oliver Twist finished— and Mags as horrified at the appalling sufferings of Oliver as Tam was fascinated—she kissed her daughter goodnight. Tam had already picked up her copy of *What Ho, Jeeves*.

"You're reading that *again*?"

"It's a classic, Mum."

Mags was already in the hall when Tam called. "Mum?"

She put her head around the door. Tam's expression was serious.

"The picture," she began. She looked off to one side, as she often did when thinking. "When I finished, it..." Eyes to the side again. "It was like waking up from a dream. But... not a nice dream. A nightmare."

"Oh, honey," said Mags. Tam shook her head.

"I'm fine. But I didn't like it. I don't want it to happen again."

Mags gave her the smile that parents give their children when they're about to reassure them on a subject about which they know little, or nothing.

"I'm sure it won't," she said. "Goodnight."

CHAPTER THREE

Heathrow Airport, at 7:20 on a Saturday morning, was already bustling, although there was a muted quality to the buzz of conversation, as most of those checking in had got up in the early hours. They trailed towards the desks in a daze, dragging large cases and small children behind them.

Mags and Tam went to the arrivals hall. Half a dozen transatlantic flights were due in time for breakfast. The stream of faces emerging from customs had spent hours with hundreds of strangers in a tin box hurtling across the sky, most of them eating peanuts and drinking too much. They looked in shock; movements slow, expressions blank.

Bradley stood out. Not just because he looked alert, and rested, but because Bradley always stood out.

Kit, Mags' brother, had taken her aside when she'd first brought Bradley round to show him off. "My gaydar is off the scale with this guy. Nobody is that good-looking, dresses that well, and is straight. Nobody." He didn't add that Bradley was in a different postcode, looks-wise, to Mags. She was his twin. He didn't have to. But he'd put a hand on her shoulder, looked her in the eye, and said, "I always thought I was the best lover in Britain, but I suppose I'll have to hand you the title. I mean, seriously, what else can it be? It's not like your personality is anything to write home about." She had punched him on the arm. Hard.

Looking at Bradley now, in those few seconds before he spotted her and Tam, she felt that familiar sense of dislocation, of being the wrong person in the wrong place, waiting for the wrong man. She had spent half an hour on her make-up this morning, wanting to be sure she looked her best after ten days apart. But, looking in the full-length bedroom mirror, she noticed the weight around her hips, the tired-looking eyes, the roots of her blonde hair greying. She was forty years old, and she looked it. But Bradley was thirty-eight and looked like a movie star. Not in a pretty-boy way. His face was too interesting to be pretty. His eyes were Paul Newman blue, but his nose was too big. Somehow, that just made him sexier. He kept his dark hair short, but scruffy. That detail, on a man who otherwise took pride in his appearance, had been the grit in the oyster for Mags when they'd first met.

"Dad!" Tam ran to her father, who swept her up and hugged her. Mags hung back, letting them have their reunion. Ten days was a long time for an eleven-year-old.

"Mum, Mum, look, Dad bought me a book." She waved an old hardback, dark brown. *The Adventures Of Huckleberry Finn, by Mark Twain.*

Bradley leaned down and kissed the top of Mags' head, then cupped the side of her face in his palm until she looked at him. He smiled.

"PG Wodehouse is okay, I guess," he said. "But it's about time she read a *real* classic." His Boston accent was always stronger when he'd been back there.

"Clarssic," she said, trying to mimic the sound. She had no gift for it, could never get the flat sound of the *vowels* right. "Claaahsic."

"Nope," he said, still smiling. "Nowhere near."

Tam butted in. "Hey, Dad, when you were in Boston, did you pahk your cah in Hahvahd Yahd?"

He wheeled on her, eyebrows raised in mock-astonishment. "Hey, that's not bad for a half-Brit."

"Hahf Brit."

"Right, you asked for it."

"Ahsked." Tam giggled as Bradley lunged for her and started tickling. She could hardly breathe for laughing, but still worked her Boston impressions into her protestations. "Stowap! Nowat fair! Nowat fair!"

"Okay, Tam-Tam, spill the beans. What's been going on?"

Tam folded her arms and looked out of the window of the car. Bradley shuffled round in the front seat and looked at her. "Oops. Sorry, sweetheart. It's hard for me to stop calling you Tam-Tam, so I might screw up now and then. Will you accept my humble apology, Miss Barkworth?"

Tam snorted. In the rearview mirror, Mags saw her turn back to her father and smile.

"Actually, Dad, you're right. I'm not a child anymore. I got my first period."

Tam shared everything with her father as easily as she did with Mags. Ever since she could talk, Bradley had asked questions about how Tam was feeling, what she was thinking, taking a keen interest in everything she said and did. Family and friends often commented on the closeness between father and daughter.

"Wow. That's great, honey. Is it uncomfortable? Do you feel ill? Any headaches, or nausea? Any other changes you want to talk about?"

Mags prodded her husband's leg. "What is this? Twenty questions?"

"Sorry. Just interested, is all. Our daughter is becoming a woman. What kind of father wouldn't want to hear all about it?"

"Right, but you're her father, not her doctor."

Bradley nodded and stretched a hand back to Tam. "Thanks for telling me. We'll talk about it later."

The traffic on the north circular was dense and still building as rush-hour got into full swing. The final mile-and-a-half took twenty-five minutes, but eventually they were at the kitchen table, croissants warming in the oven, a pot of coffee bubbling on the hob. Tam told her dad about the auditions for the school play, her essay on the Battle of Britain, and that most of the class were ignoring Morag Wilkinson because she was a bigot. Mags saw Bradley nod with satisfaction at his daughter's vocabulary.

Bradley answered questions about his trip, with few details. He always spoke of his work in general terms, joking that it was boring for anyone who didn't have a degree in genetics. He'd worked for his father since graduating. Edgegen Technology was a genetic research specialising in new treatments for debilitating neurological conditions. Mags didn't know much more than that. Most of Bradley's work was covered by nondisclosure agreements.

"I spent far too much time indoors, running tests and going over the results again and again,". He topped up his coffee, offering the jug to Mags. She declined. A cup and a half per day was the limit. More than that and her pulse would quicken, and her skin tingle, reminding her of the onset of the panic attacks that had plagued her after Tam was born. Her daughter's birth had been both the happiest and saddest moment of her life. Just the thought of it produced that familiar vertigo, the sense of walking on the edge of an abyss.

Mags glanced up at the calendar on the kitchen wall and looked for the next red sticker. Monday afternoon. She wondered if she would ever stop needing therapy. She tuned back into the moment. Bradley was still talking.

"I meant to get out on the lake, but I was too busy. Anyhow, I'm back for a while this time. I have three sets of trial results to go through. It will take six to eight weeks at least."

"Promise?" said Tam.

"Promise." They fist-bumped. "Now, is that all the news?"

"That's it," said Tam with a smile. "Can we see a movie this afternoon?"

"Sure. How about a documentary on the economy?"

"Da-ad."

Mags cleared away the plates and loaded the dishwasher. Tam hadn't said a word about the picture.

Later, while Bradley brushed his teeth, Mags considered not telling him about the picture. She thought of the look on her daughter's face as she described drawing the house. Tam hadn't mentioned it since, and was keen to forget about it.

But not telling Bradley felt wrong. Ria, her therapist, insisted she needed to keep their lines of communication open.

"Relationships only break down when you stop talking,"

the therapist had argued. "Communication is everything. Even if you still can't tell Bradley how your anxiety affects your view of him, tell him everything else. Stay in the habit of talking to each other. In time, you'll be ready to open up about your trust issues."

Mags closed her book as Bradley came out of the bathroom. She had stared at the same page without reading a word for five minutes. She put it on the bedside table and watched him cross the room. He wore drawstring pyjama bottoms. His upper body was lightly muscled and lean. He ran most days and went to the gym three times a week. Her occasional attempts to do the same inevitably ended after a week or two, but he insisted the additional few pounds she'd gained made no difference to him.

"Tam did an amazing drawing," she began. Bradley had been about to slide into bed next to her. He stopped, one hand on the corner of the duvet.

"Really? She's never been interested in art before."

Mags nodded. "I know. I could hardly believe it was Tam's."

"What was so amazing about it?"

Mags shrugged. "It was so realistic. Like a photograph."

"Can I see it?"

"It's at school. Mrs Matlock said they would display it in the hall. But—"

She stopped. Bradley's eyes narrowed, his attention on his wife's face. "But what?"

And there it was: he looked at her as if she meant nothing to him. The moment passed, and his expression softened. *Projection,* Ria would have called it. Not real. Mags shrugged a second time. "It's not important."

Bradley sat down on the bed, smiled, and took his wife's

hand. "Tell me what were you going to say. I'll be the judge of whether it's important or not."

Now he was patronising her, the scientist in him coming out. She felt like a test subject, answering questions that would be examined later, before her score was graded.

Bradley sensed her withdrawing. "I'm sorry. I'm just interested. She's our daughter, and if she's showing talent in any area, I want to hear about it." He rubbed his thumb along her wrist, and kissed her hand. "Please. Tell me."

Mags squeezed his fingers, reminded herself to stay present, not to judge Bradley by the paranoia produced by her anxiety. As always, she thought back to the first few months of their relationship, before they got married, before she fell pregnant. The excitement, the desire, an easy sense of love given and received. "Tam says she doesn't remember doing it. She didn't want to talk about it afterwards." Mags told Bradley about the house in the picture, about Tam's strange sense of being disengaged, of waking up as if from a bad dream. "She hasn't mentioned it since. You might need to give her some space."

Bradley let go of her hand. "When did she draw it?"

"Wednesday, or Thursday."

"Which is it?"

What does it matter? Right, fine, it was Thursday."

"You sure?"

"Yes, I'm bloody sure. The same day she started her period." Mags picked up the book again. "Which is what you should be interested in. She is coping brilliantly, thanks for asking."

Bradley sighed and sat down. "I'm sorry, honey. Jet-lagged, I guess. But that doesn't excuse me snapping at you. Seriously, I'm sorry. Forgive me?"

Those guileless blue eyes could still melt her. Mags

reminded herself of Ria's advice. Her anxiety, despite being far more under her control now, coloured her view of her husband. He was a good man, an attentive father, a willing and sensitive lover. She needed to acknowledge that. She pulled him towards her and they kissed. As his hands moved over her body, Mags brought her attention into the moment, using Ria's mindfulness technique. She counted to six while breathing in, and, when she exhaled, she brought her attention to the parts of her body he was touching. The third time she did it, she lost count, giving herself up to pleasure.

She opened her eyes at 3am and reached for a glass of water. Bradley's side of the bed was empty, the adjoining bathroom dark and silent. He often woke in the night and spent an hour or two in his basement office. She knew Bradley's work provided a beautiful house, holidays in the tropics, and a decent amount in the bank. She shouldn't resent that.

Mags smoothed one hand across the dent in his pillow.

He did everything right. He always had. So why didn't she trust him?

CHAPTER FOUR

I forget who I am for a few seconds. My skull hums, vibrating. It makes my teeth hurt. I half-open my eyes. Glass, rain, blackness. Then a sweep of light across my face from above. I sit up, take my head off the glass, look back at the light. It falls from a sign over the freeway. I turn around in my seat again. I'm on a bus. Just can't remember where I'm going. Or where I started out.

The bus is half-empty. Most folk are sleeping. I like that. It feels good to be here. We are between cities, somewhere in the mid-west. Before the treatment, I never left Florida. When I found out about the program, I went north for the first time. I travelled on buses like this one. I didn't enjoy it. I didn't enjoy being away from home. There was no purpose to my life back then.

They thought they could cure me. They said one operation might do it. No one likes to think of their head being cut open, but if it meant I could sleep after, I said they could take my whole head off. They laughed when I said that. It wasn't a joke.

They didn't cure me. The last time I slept properly was

when I was under the knife. It's as bad now as it's ever been. I nap for one minute, maybe two, then I'm awake again.

The drug-trial doctors thought they had failed. Maybe, for them, it was a failure, because I still have insomnia. But everything is different now.

I bring my hand up to the scar. My hair has grown back, but I can trace it still, the rough raised skin behind my ear running up and across to the top of my forehead. It's like a staircase, the way it jigs and jags. That's one of the two things the docs gave me. The scar. They also gave me a reason to live. They don't know that, of course. I didn't know it myself for a while. It was days, maybe weeks, later. I realised the operation had given me something extra. Something much better than sleep.

I look around the bus again. I count eleven heads. All sleeping, apart from some Hispanic old lady, who looks at me then turns away.

I look forward again. My eyes flick to the mirror at the front of the bus. The driver is staring right at me. I look down; realise I've been speaking out loud. I need to watch that. If I draw attention to myself, I won't be able to do my work. I have to be able to work. There are so few of us blessed with a purpose.

It's another couple hours before we reach the next stop. I miss the sign saying where I am, but I get off anyway. The bus pulls away. There's a gas station and an overnight truck stop. Good. I've been on the move for a day or two, I think.

I go to the gas station, ask about showers. I pay the guy five bucks for a token and walk round the back. The water is warm so I turn it down until bumps appear on my skin and my hands shake. I wash and change into the new clothes I have in the bag. I leave the old clothes hanging on the pegs outside the shower. Someone will take them. They always do.

It's only been a week since the last time. But I was given a sign. A sign that someone is watching over me.

From the edge of the gas station I see the lights of a town less than a mile away. If I cut across the fields, no one will see me. It won't be light for an hour or two.

I take one last look around me. No one is looking, no one sees, everyone is half-asleep. The guy in the gas station is hunched over his phone, playing some game.

If he knew who I was, what I can do, he would ask for my help. He would beg for it. If folk understood what I'm offering, everyone would want it.

No need to be half-asleep, or half-awake, any more. When I help you, you can sleep. You can sleep.

CHAPTER FIVE

Ria was Mags' fifth therapist in a decade, and the only one she had stayed with for more than three sessions. If pressed, Mags might have struggled to explain what it was she liked about Ria. On the surface, the evidence suggested she might need counselling herself, rather than giving it to others. Her basement flat—in one of the roads that extended like spider's legs from Hyde Park—was always in chaos. More than once, Mags had passed a dazed male in the doorway. Ria only took female clients, so these men, as she unblushingly pointed out, were conquests.

There was no man this time. Mags followed Ria through the usual obstacle course of discarded clothes, wine bottles, and books.

Ria's office was so different to the rest of her living space, it might have belonged to another person. There was a simple desk with a keyboard and monitor, plus a notepad and pen. On a shelf next to the high, wide window was a jug of water, glasses, and a box of tissues. Ria poured them a glass each and sat down in her swivel chair, tapping the spacebar to bring up the record of their sessions, then picking up pen and paper.

"What's on your mind?"

Ria opened every session the same way. The first time, Mags had thought it was glib. But by the end of that first hour, she knew she had found a kindred spirit, someone who wasn't feigning interest, someone who never suggested cookie-cutter, one-size-fits-all solutions.

"Bradley's back for a month or two."

Ria nodded. She was, Mags guessed, in her early fifties. She must have been at least a stone heavier than Mags, a few inches shorter than her own five-foot-five, but she carried the weight as if it meant nothing to her. Judging from the semi-regular stream of happy looking men leaving the flat, it wasn't an issue for anyone else either. Ria said Mags' concern with her own fluctuating weight was a deflection, a way of avoiding more important issues. She was probably right, but Ria's air of self-assurance suggested she'd never experienced the burst of happiness at getting into a new outfit after a crash diet, or spent a morning crying after catching sight of her belly spilling over the top of her jeans.

"Have you spoken to him?"

Mags didn't need to ask her to clarify. It was the same question every session, and she always answered it the same way.

"No." Mags spread her hands in a gesture of appeal. "How can I? Where would I start? You always make it sound so easy, but it isn't."

Mags never talked about her marriage in their sessions until she had spoken about Tam. Her concerns, her fears, the irrational thoughts she sometimes entertained when Tam was at school. Talking therapy helped. Mags knew her relationship with her daughter was far stronger now, because of the way Ria showed her the pitfalls of her over-protective behaviour. Mags would never find it easy to give Tam her own space, to let her go on school trips, to drop her off at a friend's house and drive away, but now she had strategies to deal with her reluctance to do any of these things. And, as Ria had promised, the mother-daughter relationship had become stronger. One day, Mags thought, she would be able to tell Tam why she found it harder than most mothers to grant her daughter some independence.

What hadn't improved was Mags' relationship with Bradley. Mags couldn't explain why she could make no headway with her feelings about her husband.

"Rationally, logically, you accept Bradley is what he seems to be: a good father and husband." Ria doodled as she spoke. "He's intelligent, attractive, and he works hard in a vocational job which gives him great professional satisfaction." It wasn't a question, not really. Both Ria and Mags knew the answer. She made a face anyway.

"Don't make him sound perfect. My family and friends do quite enough of that."

"I didn't say he was perfect."

"Fine. Yes, all right, I accept that. Makes no difference. It's just..." Mags sat forward, put her elbows on her knees, and pushed her fingers through her hair, massaging the sides of her head as she did so. "For whatever reason, I still feel the same way. I know it's crazy."

That was something else Mags liked about Ria. She never discouraged the use of the word crazy. She even used it herself. "Yeah," Ria agreed, "it is crazy, Mags."

"I can't understand why I'm getting nowhere."

"This is a major sticking point for you. You've seen progress in other areas, you will see progress in this too. It'll take as long as it takes, that's all. Some issues take time to be resolved."

"But how long? This has been going on ever since, ever since," she stopped speaking. Ria waited, without comment, until she could finish the sentence. "Ever since Clara died."

Ria nodded. "Good. You know when this distrust of Bradley began, but you have been unable to untangle the reasons why. Clara's death and your problem with Bradley are inextricably linked. You still feel you haven't achieved closure regarding Clara. Because of how it happened, you were never able—" She fell silent. "Well, I won't say it for you. That costs extra."

Mags gave her weak smile. "I never said goodbye, I never saw her. I never held her. But I never will, will I? I can't change those things. How can I have closure now?"

Ria finished the last of the water in her glass. "You both lost a daughter that day, Mags. You get closure by talking to Bradley about it." She pointed her pen at the clock.

Mags stood up. The time always passed so quickly. "I knew you would say that. See you next week."

CHAPTER SIX

M ags used the therapy session in the centre of town as an excuse to catch up with some clothes shopping. A sandwich and an iced coffee on the steps to the Royal Festival Hall gave her the opportunity for people-watching from behind newly purchased sunglasses.

She got off the tube a stop early and walked the last half-mile home. Spring was yielding to summer in London, which meant every patch of grass, however small, and however close to a busy road, boasted a group of semi-naked bodies. The sun lifted her mood. Bradley would have said it was because of her absorption of vitamin D. Mags didn't care about the science, she just enjoyed the optimistic buzz of the city, the ready smiles and nods that went with shorts and skirts after the wrapped-up hibernation of winter.

Her mood was still good when she rounded the back of the house. Bradley and Tam were at the table, laughing together. She walked past the back door and was about to tap on the window when she saw it.

Tam's picture from school was on the fridge.

Tam noticed her peering in and ran to open the door,

hugging her mother. Her unique smell, the one she'd had as a baby, might be harder to detect these days, but it was there. When Mags nuzzled the base of her daughter's neck, Tam squirmed, wriggled free, and skipped away. Mags followed her over to the table where Tam and Bradley had been studying something. It was a letter from the Guides, which Tam had joined just over a year before. There was a form for a residential weekend in Norfolk, and Bradley had already signed it. Mags felt a brief twist of betrayal and anger. Tam had never stayed more than one night away, and only with family. Norfolk was a three-hour drive, and the thought of a whole weekend not knowing what Tam was doing and whether she was safe, filled her with panic. She gripped the side of the table, the familiar prickling on her arms alerting her to a possible panic attack. She breathed deeply and deliberately, aware that Bradley had stood up. Her shoulders shook as he put his hands on them. She wouldn't meet his eye.

Tam looked up in concern. "You okay, Mum?"

"She's fine, Tam," said Bradley. "Can you get a glass of water, please?"

When Tam came back with a large mug, Mags managed a smile. It didn't seem that long ago when the beginnings of a panic attack meant an hour or two of torture. But Ria's strategies, and her own awareness of her triggers, meant she caught the signs early. "That's better," she said, taking a sip. "Too many clothes for this weather. Got overheated."

She allowed Bradley to slip her jacket off and hang it on the back of a chair. "What's this about Norfolk?"

Tam slid the form across the table. "Mrs Greaves gave me this at school. Amelia is going. So is Holly. And Connie. I can't wait. Beth says it'll be epic. Dad said I could go."

Bradley mussed his daughter's hair. "That's not quite what I said, honey. I said we should talk to Mom first."

"Yes, but it's fine, isn't it, Mum? Everyone will be there. Guides are going from all over London. There's archery, and the climbing wall, and canoes. Beth went last year. She said rabbits come out on the lawn every night. I can go, Mum, can't I?"

Mags exchanged the *we'll talk about this later* look with Bradley. "Yes, you can go. It sounds brilliant."

Tam hugged her tight, almost squeezing the breath out of her. "Thank you Mum, thank you thank you thank you."

Bradley picked Tam's schoolbag off the floor. "Any homework in here along with that letter?"

Tam didn't roll her eyes for once, still too excited about the trip.

"Yes, maths and guided reading." She looked from her mum's face to her dad's and drew her own conclusions. "I'll just pop upstairs and do that now, shall I?"

Bradley nodded. "Good idea, sweetheart. Why don't we go out for pizza tonight?"

"What an excellent idea, Father. First rate, and tip top." Tam's PG Wodehouse obsession showed no signs of abating. Bradley smirked. Tam pulled her mum's head towards her and planted a kiss on her cheek. "Thank you, Mum," she whispered. She grabbed her bag and disappeared.

"I'll make tea," said Bradley, filling the kettle and opening a tin of loose leaf Assam.

"I'm not so easily bought."

He warmed the pot, spooned in the tea, poured the water, replaced the lid. It had taken a few years to train Bradley in the art of tea making, but he had mastered it, eventually. "Look, I'm sorry," he said. "She kinda sprung it on me, and she was so excited. I couldn't say no. Besides..."

He poured the tea into a china cup through a metal strainer, adding the milk last. Mags had once told him that was how the Queen prepared her tea, and he had never questioned it. He brought the cup over and pushed it in front of his wife, sitting down next to her.

"Besides?" Mags raised her eyebrows. Bradley took her hand.

"Besides," he continued, "you seem to be doing so well with therapy. I hoped you were ready to let Tam take this step. We don't want her to miss out on bonding with her peers."

Mags was still angry with him for deciding without her.

She pointed at the fridge. "Explain."

"You were right," he said. "When I tried talking to Tam about the picture this morning, she clammed up. Then she said she was embarrassed because she didn't remember drawing it. And she admitted that—when she saw what she had drawn—she was scared."

Mags said nothing.

"I know, I know, that's what you said. But I wanted to hear it from her. I'm not sure she was scared by the process itself. I think she's worried that she can produce something so amazing without being aware of how she did it. I looked online. What she experienced is rare, but not unheard of."

Mags couldn't stop herself snorting. With Bradley, the scientist always rose to the top. When Tam had been a baby, he had kept a notebook with observations, updated every few hours. When she confronted him, suggesting he give her some support, rather than treating their baby like a research project, he had capitulated. That was the last time she'd seen the notebook, but that didn't mean he had stopped. Bradley saw the world a certain way. He dealt with problems by categorising, by measuring, by comparing. He argued that his need to understand didn't make him cold. Mags had never completely bought it. Watching him scribble in that notebook, standing over the crib, just weeks after Clara...

"Look, Mags, I just want to understand how a talent like that could manifest itself with no previous warning. And I find it comforting that it's happened to other people."

Mags pointed at the fridge again. "How did that get here?"

"I phoned the school, and met Mrs Matlock while the kids were at lunch. I wanted to see the picture, and once I had seen it, I thought it was important to show Tam we are proud of what she has accomplished."

"And you didn't think about discussing this with me?" The argument was slipping away from her. Subtle, but familiar, the way Bradley's rational approach undid her objections before she could make them. These were familiar, well-worn pathways. He retreated into logic, she felt emotional, weak, and intellectually outmatched. Patterns set in place over many years were not easily changed.

"When Tam came home, I talked to her about artists, composers, and scientists who have come up with their best work in a mental state where they gave up conscious control. Once you understand something, there's no need to fear it. I told her she should own her talent,"

"Bloody American," muttered Mags.

"I am a bloody American. Bit late to complain about that, don't you think? Anyway," he poured her cold tea down the sink and replaced it with a fresh cup, "it helped her. When it happens again—"

"—if it happens again—"

"When. This isn't a one-off, Mags. If this talent for art has been lurking in her subconscious and has found an outlet, there will be more pictures. We can help her accept the strangeness of the process and encourage her creativity."

Mags looked at the picture again. It really was remarkable. Not only the details, but the unusual point of view. The way the building was partially obscured, as if the artist was lying in the grass, looking up. The effect was striking. Mags was still doubtful, though. Tam had always loved books, the sound of words, the momentum of a story well told. She had never shown the slightest bit of interest in the visual arts.

They might have spoken more, but Tam reappeared, Bradley's old smartphone in her hand. She couldn't make calls with it, but the phone connected to the Wi-Fi, and she was as adept as the rest of her generation with Google.

"Documentary at the Picturehouse," she said, holding up the phone. "Some chap climbing a mountain with no safety equipment. Not sure if he falls off and dies or not. The reviews don't say. Sounds amazing. Can we go?"

"Watching a guy fall off a cliff in high definition? Yeah, sounds perfect." Bradley held his hand palm up for a high five, and Tam duly obliged, accompanying it with, "'Top hole."

Mags drained the last of her tea. "And you've finished your homework?"

Tam made a non-committal sound, her eyes not meeting her mother's.

"Tam?"

"I've done the guided reading," she said, as if that closed the subject.

"And the math?" said Bradley.

"Maths." Mags and Tam corrected him at the same moment. Bradley had heard it too many times to react. Tam retreated. "Back in ten minutes."

"Don't rush," Mags called after her.

"Are we okay?" Bradley raised his eyebrows and fixed those disarming blue eyes on hers.

"Yes. We're okay."

He put a hand on her shoulder and squeezed. "I'll just tidy a few loose ends in the office, answer an email or two. Give me half an hour. Then we'll go get pizza."

After he'd gone, Mags sat and stared at the picture. What Bradley had said made perfect sense, but as Mags looked at the scene, wherever it was, she shivered. It was nowhere her daughter had ever been. She was sure. Where had she seen that house? And how could she reproduce it in such detail?

CHAPTER SEVEN

It takes a long time to find them. Weeks, actually, and when I do find them, for a while I'm still not sure they're right. I know why I hesitate. It's the children.

I see them for the first time in a parking lot. There are two shopping malls in the town, and I'm careful to pick different times of day to get my food so I'm not remembered. I guess I'm lucky that way, though. I have one of those faces people struggle to place. Even at home, even where I grew up, I'd sometimes meet people I had been in high school with, and they'd stare right through me. Not that I want to talk to them, anyway. But it hurts when people don't acknowledge you even exist. Or, at least, it used to hurt. Now, of course, I know there's a reason I am forgettable. It's a strength, not a weakness. The longer I move among them, with no one having any clue who I am, the clearer it becomes that I am chosen. I'm like a guardian angel. Invisible.

I follow them home that first day, find a place I can watch them from. I take a risk, watch for a week. Not every day, and I'm real careful. I want to be sure. I see them coming in and out of their house. The kids waiting for the school bus. Mom driving off to work in the morning. The dad stays home, stares at his computer screen all day in the office over the garage. I watch him rub his eyes, yawning.

They have a dog, a big mongrel. He has the run of the yard, and when the dad goes to the bathroom, I call the mutt over, feed him some treats I bought. The third time I do it, his tail wags as soon as he sees me.

This morning, real early, I get a scare. I'm in the woods behind their yard when I feel fingers on my back. I freeze, panicking. I think it's all over. For a second, I could cry. I know nobody will understand, nobody will believe me if I tell them I'm helping. I see my future disappearing.

I'm kneeling on the hard earth. If it's a cop, I hope he just blows my head off and is done with it. But I know he won't. I know he'll lock me up.

I get ready to run. Then he'll have to shoot.

The fingers move up to my shoulder. I turn my head, real slow. Then I see it. A mouse. It's washing its face, sitting on my shoulder like some freaking parrot or something. I was so still it didn't even know I was there. I laugh and it runs, scampering into a hole at the base of the nearest tree.

I nod to myself. I remind myself how important it is to look out for signs, to recognise them when they appear. This is the universe getting in touch, through one of its smallest creatures, reaching out, telling me I'm okay. Telling me to go ahead.

I stand up. It's only just getting light. Saturday. I guess it'll be a while before anyone stirs. In the house, they are asleep. At least, what passes for sleep. Not the real thing. Not peace. Not the sleep I can give them.

I brush the dirt from my knees, pat down my pockets. I have everything I need. I walk towards the silent house.

Before most folk are awake, I'm on a bus out of town. I picked this route a few days back, when I saw how busy it gets with factory workers, janitors and the like, heading into the city. Best way not to be noticed is to join a crowd of tired, poor people.

I'm dressed like they are. Overalls and an old T-shirt. Earbuds. Mine aren't plugged into a phone, though. They're just part of the camouflage, and a reason not to talk to anyone. When the cops get around to checking the bus routes out of town, nobody will remember me.

I look through slitted eyes, pretending to be asleep. There are so many people I could help here. But I know I have to be careful, have to stay hidden, until my purpose is fulfilled and I can rest.

Ten minutes into the bus ride, a miracle happens. I sleep. It happens so naturally. I just shut my eyes and let everything fall away. When I wake up, I've been asleep for ten minutes. Haven't slept that long since I was a kid. Hot tears well up at this blessing, and I rest my cheek on the dirty window. My tears leave a clean stream through the dust and grime on the glass.

I know how to recognise a sign, and this is big. It's a billboard, a flashing neon sign, and it says, YOU 'VE DONE GOOD SO FAR. YOU KEEP ON GOING. BRING THE PEOPLE REST.

I smile as the outskirts of the city spring up around me. I'm doing the will of the universe. The quiet neighborhoods, the neat suburbs. My work awaits.

CHAPTER EIGHT

B radley was back in Boston the weekend Tam went to Norfolk, so it fell to Mags to do the driving. She had passed her test twenty years ago, but living in London meant she rarely got behind the wheel. As usual, the first half hour was an ordeal, as she reminded herself of every action she needed to take while driving. Left foot on the clutch, find the biting point, check the mirror, look over her shoulder, accelerate, indicate, change gear, look for a gap in the traffic. She headed out of London into unfamiliar terri-tory and was glad of the satnav. The blue line drew her north.

The ordeal wasn't made any easier by the four eleven-year-old passengers. For the first twenty minutes, the constant stream of inane chatter was as predictable as it was distracting, but the girls were still going strong two hours into their trip.

They stopped for lunch at a McDonald's. Mags watched her daughter with her friends. She noticed Tam dumbed down her vocabulary when she was with her peers.

When Tam caught her eye, she winked. Tam smiled at her around a mouthful of fries.

Mags had volunteered to drive the girls both ways, and their parents had been quick to accept. She had booked a hotel in Norwich for the weekend.

There was a lull in the conversation after their stop, but once they crossed into Norfolk, the volume built to a new peak. Mags vicariously enjoyed the girls' excitement as they contemplated the adventure ahead. They were thrilled about the prospect of sleeping in dormitories, six to a room, and were already negotiating who should have the bed nearest the window.

By the time they arrived, the car's tyres crunching up a curved gravel drive, it was nearly dark. Mrs Greaves, the Guide leader, came out to meet them, checking them off as they filed in, dragging prime-colour suitcases.

"Amelia, Holly, Beth, Tam. Everyone else is here, but we put you all in the same bedroom. Two floors up on the right."

There was a chorus of whoops, and the girls stampeded, heading upstairs. For a moment, Mags thought Tam had forgotten, but she skidded to a stop at the foot of the staircase, dropped her case, and ran back. Their hug was brief. "Love you, mum. See you after lunch on Sunday."

"Yes, see you then. Have a brilliant time."

Tam kissed her cheek. "I will." Then she was gone.

Something in Mags' expression must have alerted Mrs Greaves. The older woman stepped forward, put a hand on her arm. "We've been coming here for nearly twenty years. It's a brilliant centre. Very safe. She will have a lovely time."

Mags felt the first tear spill from her lashes and roll down her face. "I know she will," she said.

The weekend in Norwich turned out to be a good idea. If Mags had stayed home, she would have rattled round the house and driven herself crazy. Being in a hotel, in a city she had never visited, where no one knew her, was perfect. She felt like a ghost, drifting around the streets in perfect anonymity. Her thoughts drifted to her daughter, but she could relax knowing she was only a twenty-minute drive away. Not that anything would happen, she told herself, despite knowing logic could never overcome the implacable force of a mother's fear.

Mags knew how it felt to lose a daughter.

Bradley called once, on the first evening. Mags had never enjoyed talking to him on the phone. She needed to see his face. The unfounded suspicions she had worked to quell in years of therapy were more likely to come back when she couldn't look into his eyes. He asked all the right questions, was solicitous as to her health and state of mind, but it was as if he were working his way down a checklist. She was glad when the call ended, then felt guilty at her sense of relief.

She only called the Guide centre once, although her finger had hovered over phone at least a dozen times since she had left Tam. Mrs Greaves had reassured her. "The girls are fine. Tam was first up to the top of the climbing wall this afternoon. She's really taken to it. Such a lovely girl, I'll tell her you called."

"No, no, please don't. She'll just think I'm checking up on her." Which I am, thought Mags. "I'm glad she's okay. See you tomorrow."

Just as Mrs Greaves, Bradley, and Tam had predicted, the weekend passed without a hitch. Tam was a ball of energy when Mags arrived.

"It was amazing, Mum. I found a secret passage in the house, and a girl from Cambridge ate a worm for a dare, and we went to sleep after midnight last night, and I learned how to roll over in the canoe, and it was amazing, and cool."

Mrs Greaves herded the girls towards the door, Mags following.

"Can I borrow you for two minutes, Mrs Barkworth?"

The girls were already loading their cases into the car. "Get belted in," called Mags.

Mrs Greaves led her into a small office. Mags paled. "Is Tam okay? What happened?"

The Guide leader shook her head. "Nothing to worry about. It's just... well, it's better if I show you."

Mrs Greaves took a phone out of her pocket and thumbed the screen, flicking through photographs. "You saw the whiteboard outside? It's where we write each day's activities. When I came down first thing yesterday morning, someone had rubbed everything out."

"What? You think Tam might have... no, I'm sure she would never do anything like that. She's not that kind of girl."

"I know." Mrs Greaves stopped what she was doing and handed the phone to Mags. "I found this on the board."

It was another picture. Mags knew immediately it was Tam's work. The similarities were too distinct to be a coincidence. Again, it was a picture of a house, seen from a low vantage point. This time, there was a fence between the artist and the building, and much of the detail could be seen through gaps in the wooden panels. The house beyond was smaller than the first one, brick built rather than clapboard. Mags could see a yard with a swing, a plastic ride-on tractor and a few discarded toys. There was a large window to the left. In the room beyond, pans hung from hooks. There was a woman inside, facing away, a long plaited ponytail reaching down to the small of her back.

"I wasn't sure what to do," said Mrs Greaves. "I was amazed and annoyed at the same time. Whoever had done it had come down during the night, and even though it's a fantastic picture, we lost our whole schedule for the day. It took half an hour to do it again. I took a photograph, then wiped the board clean. I don't know if I did the right thing. I felt bad doing it. Such talent. I was angry, though. I'm sorry."

"No, no," Mags said. "I understand. How did you know it was Tam? Did she say something?"

"No. But she had blue marker pen all over her fingers when she came down to breakfast. When I asked about it, she was surprised. I know when a girl is fibbing, and Tam was telling the truth. Has she ever walked in her sleep before?"

"No." Mags didn't know what to say. She gave the phone back. "Could you send me a copy, please?"

Her phone pinged when Mrs Greaves sent it across.

"I'm sorry she ruined your schedule," said Mags.

"I don't think she even knew she'd done it. We often have a sleepwalker, or a wet bed. It can be a reaction to being away from home for the first time. We don't draw attention to it."

"Thank you. I appreciate it."

Mags put her phone in her bag and walked out to the car.

When Bradley called the following night, Mags considered not telling him about the picture. After reminding herself to notice when she was being irrational, she changed her mind. Bradley deserved to hear about it. Ria had pointed out he had lost a daughter too. Of course he wanted to soak up every bit of information about Tam, especially when he was away so much.

"Well, there was one thing," she began.

"What thing?"

She told him about the whiteboard. While she talked, she emailed the photograph to him. Seconds into her story, something happened that didn't help her paranoia one bit.

"Honey?"

"Yes?"

She heard a muted click, and a change to the quality of the line. "Sorry," he said, "just closing my office door. I couldn't hear you. Tell me again. From the beginning. You picked Tam up, and the Guide leader took you aside, right?"

Mags hesitated. "Are you recording this?" Even as she spoke, she wished she hadn't. How was he supposed to respond? If he wasn't recording the call, he would worry about her mental state, and if he was, well... she didn't want to think about the implications.

"Honey, are you okay? You've been so much better recently, but remember what Ria said. If you're getting too anxious, you need to consider going back onto some form of medication."

Mags rubbed her forehead. She should have kept her mouth shut. "No, no, I'm fine. I heard a click. That's all." It sounded pathetic when she said it out loud. "I think I'll have an early night. I'm tired. "

"Good idea, honey. Look after yourself. You and Tam

are the most important people in my life. Tell me about the picture, then maybe you should go to bed."

Mags told him. It was only later, as she turned out her bedside lamp, that she wondered—if Bradley was so concerned for her well-being—why he'd insisted on hearing about the new picture before letting her go to sleep.

CHAPTER NINE

Bradley came home buoyant—a possible breakthrough at work, apparently—and went on a charm offensive. Mags had been dreading the moment he brought up her paranoid phone call, but, when he did, he surprised her.

"Mags, let's talk," he said, pouring her a glass of Valpolicella.

Tam had already eaten, been read to and was fast asleep. Bradley had cooked his roast beef sandwich, a dish which had once sounded boring to Mags, until she tried Bradley's version. It took an afternoon to prepare. Beef knuckle slow roasted and left to rest. Char-grilled buns from the Jewish bakery on the next street. Homemade mayonnaise and barbecue sauce. "There are roast beef sandwiches, and there are Boston roast beef sandwiches."

And now he wanted to talk.

"Okay," she said, sitting up, frowning despite herself. He smoothed away the frown lines on her forehead, and she smiled. He'd done the same on their first date, and it had been the moment she fell for him.

"That phone call," he said.

"Bradley," she began, remembering her paranoia, but he held up a hand.

"No, no, you were right."

She raised her eyebrows.

"Not about me recording the call," he said. He took her hand. "But there's something we need to discuss. Well, something I want to say. I've been thinking about this a lot on this trip, and I've let you down. For years. I've never talked to you properly about... I've never talked to you about..."

Mags squeezed his fingers. She didn't dare say anything. Was he crying?

"Mags, I need to say this all at once."

Mags nodded. Bradley said nothing for ten seconds, as he marshalled his thoughts. He swallowed. She'd rarely seen him so uncomfortable. Bradley was always in complete control. If the adage was true—that a tidy desk meant a tidy mind—Bradley's mind had everything arranged *just so*, each piece of information placed where it needed to be. She watched him struggle to begin and was surprised by her own reaction. Part of her wanted to reach out to him, comfort him. Another part watched almost coldly, unconvinced by his glistening eyes and ragged breathing.

"Clara was born first," he said. Mags kept her eyes on her husband, but his gaze dropped to the table between them. In the eleven years since the birth, they had never talked about what had happened. Not once. At first, she had been too ill, then they had fallen into a pattern of avoiding the topic, scared of its effect on her mental health. On the few occasions they'd come close to a proper discussion, they'd backed away. She dug her fingernails into her palms and let him talk.

"Their heart rates were monitored, so we were told she

was in danger. The doctors tried everything, Mags, every-thing they could to keep her alive, but her heart failed. She was—"

He swallowed again, then lifted his eyes. He was crying. Even at the funeral, his eyes had been dry.

"She was beautiful, Mags. She looked like Tam, but there was something different about her. You could see she was her own person. She would have grown up into a different little girl, a friend and a sister for Tam. But I had no time to grieve. Not then. There was Tam, and you, to think about. Tam was strong when she was born. Healthy, breathing, crying. Perfect. I held her for a few seconds, but then they rushed around you and I knew something else was wrong."

Mags had no memory of the eighteen hours of her life that followed. Later, she was told she had bled heavily during the C-section. As soon as they had lifted the babies out of her womb, the surgical team diagnosed uterine atony. Her uterus didn't shrink back to normal size after the birth and she haemorrhaged. Bradley told her the surgeons lifted her uterus out of her body, wrapping it in sterile bandages to encourage it to return to its normal size. They did this three times before replacing it, and she spent nine hours in surgery as they kept her from bleeding out.

When she had woken up, she was a mother. And she had lost a child.

"Mags, I know you wanted to say goodbye to her."

Mags couldn't speak. She had never seen Clara. Never held her. Never said goodbye. There were special words for children whose parents were dead, or adults whose spouse had died, but there was no word for a parent whose child had died.

"We haven't spoken about it since," said Bradley, his

voice husky. "I always thought we would talk about it, but weeks passed before you were out of physical danger, and your mental health took a turn for the worse. I tried to be there for you, but it wasn't me you wanted. For months, you could barely stand for me to touch you. I did my best to stay supportive and to give you space when you needed it. You were bonding with Tam, finding your own way through, your own way to heal."

A tear rolled down Mags' face and over her top lip. She reached out and took Bradley's hand. He looked at her as he continued talking.

"It was the right thing to do, but it meant we never spoke properly about what happened. Post natal depression was only natural after what you'd been through. Maybe I should have been braver, maybe we should have talked early on. But I believed it might push you into a breakdown."

Bradley's voice dropped to a whisper, and he looked away again.

"I know you blame me for what happened after the birth, Mags." She tried to speak, but he shook his head. "That's fair, I guess, because I was the one who decided. And it was a decision I based on my own beliefs, mostly. We'd only spoken about it once. I doubt you remember."

Mags tilted her head forward. "I remember." Of course she did. It was one of those earnest conversations young couples have when their relationship moves towards a commitment. Children, marriage, finances, career aspirations, which country to live in. They had talked about all of this, long into the night, usually in bed. And, one night, they had discussed organ donation, both agreeing it was a moral imperative. If their death led to someone else having even a few more years of life, why wouldn't they want that to happen? Mags remembered how glib, how easy that conversation had been. She imagined herself going to sleep that night with a warm glow produced by her selfless moral stance. It didn't seem so glib when they weren't talking about their own deaths but that of their daughter. Not glib at all.

"You were still in surgery," said Bradley. "I was waiting for news. When a surgeon appeared, I jumped up, assuming she had an update about you. But she wanted to talk about Clara. Mags, we hadn't filled in any forms, and she wanted to ask about organ donation. There was a baby in Cambridge with kidney failure. Clara had gone, but she could help him live. I signed the form, Mags. I signed the form to save that little boy's life, and I said they could take her other organs to use for transplants, or research. They flew her body to Cambridge. The surgeon told me they would remove any viable organs. I knew that what was left would not be our daughter. I didn't want you to see that. When I tried to tell you, I got it all wrong."

That wasn't a conversation she would ever forget. Bradley had told her what happened to Clara as she held Tam for the first time. He must have hoped that, with new life in her arms, she might cope better with the loss; even— at some level—be glad Clara's death hadn't been for nothing. But, seconds after he had finished speaking, Mags remembered the hospital room becoming darker. Then her field of vision was shrinking, and her body shook uncontrollably. Before she lost consciousness, she heard an alarm going off, and was aware of Bradley lifting Tam away from her.

Bradley looked at her now, his blue eyes searching her face for clues to how she might react.

"Forgive me," he whispered.

She remembered something Ria had said during one of her sessions. Mags had complained she had never seen

Bradley grieve, not really. Ria, always ready to state the obvious, had pointed out that everybody grieves differently. Bradley had carried this horrible burden of guilt all these years. No wonder there was a distance between them, widening as the lack of communication kept them from healing this old wound.

She stood up and reached for him across the table, knocking her wine glass over as she did so. Then his arms were around her and she was pushing her face into his as if their flesh might merge. "There's nothing to forgive," she said. "Nothing. You did the right thing. I'm sorry we've never talked about it. I'm so glad you've done it now. Thank you. I love you."

They didn't make it upstairs. They didn't even make it out of the kitchen. They tore each other's clothes off like teenagers, and she didn't think about how uncomfortable she was, her head on the hard kitchen tiles; she only knew she never wanted to let him go.

They lay together afterwards, trembling. The only sound was the drip of red wine as it puddled on the floor beside them like blood.

CHAPTER TEN

I don't like the blood. There's too much of it. I'm getting better at judging the pressure I need, but it's only ever completely bloodless with those much weaker than I am. With the strong ones, there's always blood.

The father is strong. I thought he would be, which is why I visit him first. He struggles for a long time. If he hadn't been sleeping in the basement, the others would have heard him. It's strange. He fights for his life as if it is something he wants, something worth fighting for. I know the truth. I know he sleeps in a different bed to his wife because I've been watching them. She cries in the kitchen when he's not there, and I've seen him looking blankly at the TV with a glass of bourbon in his hand.

The fight goes out of him all at once. It's as if he realises I'm helping, that I'm not there to hurt anyone. This is always the point at which I am envious. Just a little. He is between life and death, between wakefulness and sleep. He stands on the threshold, and what he sees, I cannot see. Not yet. Not until my work is done, and I am allowed to rest.

I go upstairs, not worrying much about the small amount

of noise I make. Children sleep deeply, and if the woman wakes up, she will think it's her husband. She sits up in bed as I walk in, but she's not really awake yet, and in three quick strides I am across the room, on the bed, and I have her. The dim night-light shows her my face. There is a moment of confusion and fear as I wrap the device around her neck, before she relaxes. Everything is easier with her, and there is no blood. The last thing she does before the light leaves her eyes is to turn towards the door, towards the rooms at the far end of the house where her children are sleeping. I wish I could make her understand; I wish I had time to explain.

I always struggle with conversation. When I was a child, the doctors said my problems sleeping made it difficult for me to separate real life and fantasy. When I spoke to people, they sometimes looked at me as if I were crazy. When drugs didn't make me better, I learned to be more careful with the way I spoke, using words and phrases my doctors liked to hear, never what I was thinking. Now I speak just often enough to be seen as quiet, but not strange. Along with my average looks, it helps make me forgettable. And being forgettable means I can continue with my work. Sometimes I want to scream at people to look at me, to notice that an angel walks among them, a deliverer. But they won't understand. They'll lock me up. I can't let anyone stop me fulfilling my purpose.

I lay the woman's head on her pillow. Wherever she is now, I hope she can see that what I bring her family is a rare gift. If she understands that, she will be happy that I am going to her children now. More than happy. She will be joyous.

CHAPTER ELEVEN

Next morning, Mags was halfway to the station when she realised she'd left her phone. She checked her bag three times, indulged in some imaginative swearing, then turned back for home.

She spotted the phone on the kitchen table as she rounded the corner of the house. Mags wasn't forgetful. There had been a spell of absent-mindedness in the months after childbirth, but by the time Tam was at kindergarten she was back to being efficient and organised. Two drawers for stationery, a cloth bag on a hook hanging from the filing cabinet with two reams of printer paper in it, a cupboard by the door full of labelled keys, and a family calendar with colour-coded stickers showing who was doing what, when, and with whom.

And now she was leaving the house without her phone. She guessed what Ria would say. There was something in her subconscious yet to be resolved, something she needed to deal with. She ran through a mental checklist: low self-esteem, overprotective of daughter, unfounded lack of trust in husband. Nothing new. Although, she conceded, she may have made some headway with her trust issue. Mags remembered Bradley's hands pushing her dress over her hips on the kitchen floor, and she smiled.

She left her key in the door as she stepped across the kitchen and put a hand on her phone. A quick text to Kit telling him she'd be late, and she was ready to leave. As she crossed the kitchen, she heard Bradley's voice.

Mags stood still, listening. He was on the phone in his office. Without thinking, she slipped out of her shoes and padded into the hall. The basement stairs had a door at the top. It was half-open, but the door at the bottom of the stairs was shut. She didn't dare get any closer, because the basement stairs were creaky.

"—and there's no comparison with any previous examples. Yes, I've checked. Of course I kept them. All of them. I assume you checked them yourself? Yes. Yes. Completely different. I'm looking at it now. And you saw the other one? Remarkable, aren't they? What about the other subjects? Any similar findings? No. True. But you'd expect something, surely? Fifty-six subjects in all. Yes, she has routine blood tests. There's one coming up. Maybe it's hormonal. Have you got any closer to identifying which of the subjects... I know, I know. Well, keep me appraised of —"

Without even being aware she was doing it, Mags had leaned too far, trying to catch every word. As she overbalanced, she had no choice, bringing her foot down on the top step. Bradley wasn't speaking at that moment, and the groan of old wood seemed twice as loud in the silence. She held her breath.

"Hold on a second, will you?"

A creak of leather: Bradley getting out of his chair. Mags moved, backed up, turned the corner and slid across the tiled hallway, her stockinged feet barely leaving the surface, like a skater.

She skidded into the kitchen, scooped up her shoes, and grabbed her bag. For half a second, she considered bolting for the door, then she changed her mind and scooted behind the fridge. As Bradley's footsteps reached the top of the stairs, she crouched.

For a moment, she thought how ridiculous her behaviour was. She was hiding behind the fridge in her own house, so that her husband wouldn't find her. What was she doing? Mags got ready to stand up, make a joke of it. But, even as she told herself she would do it, she did the opposite. She didn't move, focusing on keeping her breathing quiet.

"Mags?" Footsteps at the far end of the hall, then nothing. She could picture him standing in the doorway of their open-plan living room. He came towards the kitchen.

Bradley stopped in the doorway and, for a few seconds, there was silence. Mags didn't move. She looked at her knees, pulled up to her chest, and noticed the bottom of her sunflower-yellow dress sticking out beyond the edge of the fridge.

Had he seen it? She bunched her fingers in the material and pulled it back out of view. Bradley's footsteps came towards her hiding place. She thought about what she would say when his face appeared around the side of the fridge. "Did you see a mouse? I was just checking." No. "Gosh, isn't it hot? But it's lovely and cool if you press your back against the fridge. You should try it sometime." Oh shit. She would sound like a mad woman.

The footsteps stopped. She closed her eyes and waited. Then the fridge door opened, and Bradley pulled out a milk carton.

He hadn't seen her. She was safe. What a strange word to use.

Mags listened to Bradley drinking milk straight from the carton and fought the urge to tut. She hated it when he did that. He belched, replaced the carton, closed the fridge and walked out of the room. A few seconds later, a door clicked shut, and the stairs creaked as he descended.

She didn't put her shoes back on until she was outside. Halfway down the path something nagged at her, something she'd seen. Or—rather—something she hadn't seen. She turned back a second time and looked in through the glass at the kitchen.

The picture on the fridge had gone.

CHAPTER TWELVE

K it and his husband David lived in a terraced house two minutes walk from Camden Lock. David, an accountant who worked in the finance department of a blue-chip company, had always been careful with his money, and had spotted an investment opportunity twenty years ago. He had bought the terraced house at auction, fifteen years before he met Kit, and had watched the value skyrocket in the meantime. He was ten years older than Kit, planned to retire early in another five years, sell up and move out of the city. Mags couldn't imagine Kit adapting easily to the country life. He loved being within two hundred yards of bars that served decent champagne by the glass.

"What's the latest?" Mags asked, as Kit ground the coffee beans.

Kit worked as a style consultant for a TV production company. He had spent much of his childhood devising a variety of outfits for Mags' discarded dolls. Now he did the same for real people. Some of whom were famous, which made the gossip irresistible.

Kit set down a glass of hot coffee in front of her. A cloud of steam hissed up from the machine and he twirled a white jug underneath the metal spout. He placed it next to the coffee.

"Soya?" guessed Mags. "Wheat?" The last time she had checked Kit's fridge, it had contained three bottles of champagne, two bottles of vodka, three packets of pre-packed salad and a whole poached salmon. Neither Kit nor David did dairy.

"Hemp," said Kit, pouring it into her glass, the dark and light liquids mixing hypnotically. He noted the sceptical expression. "Try it. It might surprise you."

Mags tried it. It didn't surprise her. It was bloody awful. "Lovely."

Kit laughed. "Fussy cow." He opened a pack of unsalted nuts and poured them into a bowl, shaking them in front of her as he sat down. "Not much to report. Justin hasn't learned his lesson after the paps caught him at the lap dancing club. He's got a taste for it, poor lamb."

"What?" Justin was one of the best known talk-show hosts on British TV. "Why? He could have any woman he wanted. Why go to one of those places?"

"Good God, Sis, you don't understand men at all, do you? It's a wonder you've kept hold of big bad Bradley for so long. Justin loves the illicit thrill of it all. He's doing something naughty, and he might get caught."

Mags shook her head. "Men are weird," she said. Then she thought of the way she had crouched behind the fridge in her kitchen. She had no right to call anybody weird. Remembering the fridge made her think of her picture. What had Bradley been doing with it? Was he talking about it on the phone? Who had he been talking to? Or was she just jumping to conclusions? Ria would say she was self-sabotaging, looking for behaviour that might fuel her lack of trust in her husband.

"Mags?" Kit had asked her something.

"I'm sorry, I sort of drifted off there, didn't I? What did you say?"

Kit brought his hand up to his quiffed hair, patting it. "There's something bothering you, Sis. Don't pretend there isn't. Out with it."

Mags told him everything, even the stuff that made her sound paranoid. She had always confided in Kit. That was what twins did. When, at fifteen, he had come out to their parents, it was Mags who had spent months mediating between Kit and their father, who had found it hard to take. Frank Thompson had been an old-fashioned man; it had been difficult for him to accept his son was gay. Their mum was fine about it, but she had always taken Dad's side in an argument, and it proved too hard a habit to break. After the most awkward Christmas of their lives, their dad apologised, and things had returned to something approaching normal. Kit had never forgotten the way Mags had stood up for him.

When cancer claimed Mum, and Dad followed within six months after a series of strokes, it had been Kit who had taken charge, Kit who had been the strong one.

While she was talking, her brother made himself another coffee, and brewed a pot of tea for Mags. He knew one coffee was her limit, that any more might contribute to her anxiety. It had been years since her last full panic attack, but she had no wish to risk another.

"Well, I don't want to be the one to tell you you're being delusional, but you're being delusional."

"No, go on, Kit. Say what you really think. I can take it, don't hold back."

"Well, I know you still struggle with trusting him, but

he's never given you any reason not to. I know you love him, and I know how you struggle with these weird feelings, but I can't tell you they are justified when I don't believe it. If he ever does anything iffy, I'll be the first to tell you. But what you've just told me doesn't mean a thing. I don't know why you would think he was talking about Tam on the phone. He works in a genetic research laboratory in America, Mags. They have studies there, they do experiments. They cut up pigs and torture chickens."

Mags winced and laughed. Kit joined her. "Well, whatever," he said. "I don't know what they do. I pick out the right shirts for overpaid celebrities who shag call girls in their dressing rooms. What do I know?"

Mags loved her brother's directness, even when he was puncturing her delusions.

"All right, all right," she said, "but why did he take the picture?"

"Yes, that's a very damning piece of evidence, Sis. What could a father possibly want with an incredible picture drawn by his daughter? You don't suppose—as unlikely as this sounds—that he wanted to have a good look at it? No. I'm sure you're right. He's scraping it for samples to send to a laboratory as we speak."

"I heard him say *I'm looking at it right now*. He was talking about the picture, I know he was."

"Well, yes, it's possible. Or... " when Kit was in full sarcastic flow, it was pointless trying to stop him, "perhaps, just perhaps, and—try to suspend your disbelief, because this is a crazy suggestion—maybe he was talking about a spreadsheet, or an email, or, say, an invoice, something equally unlikely. It's just possible, isn't it, that the picture had fallen off the fridge and he had put it on the counter. Did you look?"

Mags thought back to the kitchen. "No," she admitted, "I didn't."

"Right. Good. Now, I don't want you to take this the wrong way, but shut up, crazy woman. Can we move on to a less controversial topic? You said my favourite niece—"

"—your only niece—"

"—my favourite niece has drawn another picture. Can I see it?"

Kit had already admired Tam's first picture when he'd seen it on their fridge.

Mags found the photo of the picture from Norfolk and slid her phone across to Kit. He used his fingers to zoom in on the details.

"This is really excellent work," he said. "As good as the first. How about entering some competitions? She's amazing. This could be her thing. An artist in the family. I like that."

"I told you she doesn't enjoy it. She doesn't know I've seen this picture, and—according to her Guide leader—she has no memory of drawing it, just like the first one. I'm worried about her, Kit."

"You worry about everyone."

"True, but this is not like Tam. It's strange."

"Eleven-year-old girls *are* strange. Now, how about skipping the tea and having a glass of bubbly instead? It's lunchtime. I can make you a salad."

"What are we celebrating? Not that you need an excuse to pop a champagne cork."

"Justin's got a spot on the Tonight Show. Which means I get a week in New York." He poured two glasses. "I'm taking David with me."

"I'm jealous. When?"

"Fly out Tuesday, back the following Monday."

"Promise to call me with any juicy gossip?"

Kit clinked his glass against his twin's. "Anything to stop you drifting back to your old, paranoid ways, Mags. You have a beautiful, talented daughter and the gorgeous American hunk is crazy about you. Lucky sod."

Mags smiled. "All right, all right, I get the message."

A glass of champagne before lunch made her light-headed and optimistic. She should stop trying to catch Bradley out. His worst crime was drinking milk straight from the carton. Whatever was happening with Tam might be odd, but worrying wouldn't help anyone. Kit was right. She should be excited about her daughter's talent.

She said yes to a second glass.

Just before leaving, Mags kissed her brother's cheek, and hugged him.

"What's that for?"

"Things always seem better when I talk to you, Kit. Thanks."

He bowed, and Mags laughed, not suspecting that the next time they talked, the conversation would end with her feeling worse than she had for years.

CHAPTER THIRTEEN

F or the first time, I don't watch the chosen for days. That's always been the way I've worked before. Let myself be drawn to a place, watch it for a day or two, make sure I'm right. Make sure they need me.

Not this time. This time, I know right away. There's a kind of energy running through me, a confidence. I never felt anything like it before. I'm untouchable.

We're close to the airport when I spot the place and get off the bus. I guess some of the workers who get off with me are going there. I walk with them for a while, then stop at a newspaper stand. When they turn the corner, I back up and head for the place I saw.

When I get there, I see who I am here for. Two of them yelling, slapping each other, not caring who hears them fight. As I walk past, head down, baseball cap pulled low, the man shouts one last insult and steps in front of me. I bring my hand to my ear as if I have a phone in it. I needn't have worried, he's not looking. He's in a uniform. Airport security guard. She watches him go from the doorway. No goodbye.

No see ya later. Just a blank stare. She lights a cigarette and goes back inside. I keep walking.

I find a busy breakfast place half a mile away. Then I ride a bus into the city and go to places where there are lots of people. Easier to be forgotten in a crowd. I eat a hot dog for lunch. Late afternoon, I join the workers heading back to the outskirts, get out near the airport and find my way back, through the trees this time.

I settle down as it gets dark. I wait.

There is no need to be scared, I see that now. My purpose is becoming clearer, that's all. I'm being called. The universe moves in mysterious ways. Mother used to say that about God. Maybe she was right. Just because she was wrong about everything else, doesn't mean she was wrong about that. A broken clock is right twice a day, isn't it? Although I don't believe in the god she prayed to.

When it happens, when the universe shows me the way, it's like a flashlight giving me just enough to go on. I can see far enough ahead to know I'm on the right track. But this time it's like the light is shining at me, and it's blinding. I freeze, and my mind tunes out from everything around me. I'm here, but I'm not here. If someone talks to me I won't be able to answer. It's like I'm paralysed.

No one looks over to where I'm laying in the long grass. No one sees me. But for a few minutes, I'm dreaming with my eyes open. I don't fight it. I let it happen. And this time, I see things; I hear things. The signal is strong. It's like I'm being called home, but it's no home I ever knew.

I have to follow that call. First, though, I have to do what I came here to do.

When it's dark, I get up. I have to be real quiet, and careful, because this won't be easy. This is no house on its own. There are people just yards away. I will have to be quick, and

I must be quiet. But I will not desert the chosen. They need me.

I still don't know how this will play out. Two people in such a small space. If I bring my gift to one, the other will wake up for sure. What do I do then?

I'm thinking about this, when the door opens, and the man who was wearing the security guard uniform steps out. I'm standing fifteen, maybe twenty yards away from him, but it's dark, and there are trees behind me. He staggers a little, cups his hand and lights a joint. I guess he won't see me, anyway. He is pretty drunk. Perfect. Now I know what I have to do.

He paces from one end of his tiny yard to the other. The boundary of his property is marked by a trash can at one end and a basketball hoop at the other. When he is standing by the hoop with his back to me, I walk out of the shadows. I don't hurry. I don't have to. He doesn't see me or hear me, and I take the device from my pocket when I'm close.

He's taller than me, so I have to stretch a little to loop the wire round his neck. I wait until he is inhaling, the tip of his joint glowing red in the darkness. It's all done in one motion. Practice makes perfect. I pull the wire as tightly as I can, yanking him backwards and sideways as I do it. He trips over my outstretched leg and falls on his side. I push him onto his front as I strain at the wire. I get the pressure just right. He can't breathe, and my knees pin his arms to the ground. No blood at all this time, just thrashing, then twitching, then nothing.

The next few minutes, everything goes right. I unwrap the wire, walk to the door and open it. I stand still for one, maybe two seconds. The only sound is snoring. I follow the sound to its source, loop the wire around her neck and pull. The snores stop. She opens her eyes and sees me, and I notice *that look of recognition again. Some folk know I'm here to help them. She is one of the lucky ones. She goes quickly, and quietly, and I thumb her eyelids shut so she can sleep.*

Outside, nothing has changed, nothing has moved. I drag him back to the door, up the three steps and inside. I'm sweating, but I'm stronger than I look. A few minutes later, and they sleep together. I put his hand in hers. The love they never found for each other in life is theirs now.

I am humbled by this thought.

I remember the call, and I know I have to keep moving. I'm being guided. I have to go further than I ever thought I would go, but that's fine. Everything is fine. I will go wherever I need to go, and I will bring peace to those who need it.

CHAPTER FOURTEEN

Mags woke up from the dream crying. As always. She slid out of bed. Bradley was back in Boston. He usually sat with her after the dream, held her, stroked her hair. He did everything anyone might expect of a loving, concerned husband. But Mags couldn't bring herself to look in his eyes when she was at her most vulnerable. When the grief was fresh again. Because she never believed he felt the same way. And she hated herself for thinking that.

She crept down to the kitchen and made herself a cup of chamomile tea. She hated the taste, but it was four-thirty in the morning, and if she hoped to get any more sleep, it might help.

Mags let the tears run their course. By the time she had finished the tea, it was over. Her shoulders had stopped shaking, her eyes were dry, and sore. She stared at the table.

Ria's professional advice was to allow thoughts to come after the dream. Let them come, let her mind and body react, and see what she can learn from that experience.

All very well for Ria to say. No one who had lived

through it, no one who knew how raw the dream could be, would be so blasé in their recommendations.

Mags held her hands in front of her face. They were trembling. She knew she was being unfair to Ria. Ignoring her fears wasn't the answer. But, after more than a decade, Mags had hoped the worst memories might have faded. They had not. They came less frequently, true, but they were as hard to deal with as they had ever been. At least, with the memories, she had techniques to cope with them. Not so with the dream. The dream brought her back to the last place she wanted to be, the source of her greatest happiness, and her worst despair.

It always started the same way.

A circle of light above her, moving downwards. The bustle and hum of doctors and nurses doing their jobs. Then the first note of concern, a whispered conference to one side.

She recognised one voice. Bradley was talking to the surgeon, his voice hushed and tense. They'd been married for just over a year, celebrating their anniversary with a salad and a shared bottle of elderflower pressé, which she couldn't get enough of during her pregnancy. Being a twin herself, it shouldn't have come as a surprise to find two heartbeats picked up during the first scan, but—somehow— she had convinced herself there was only one baby nestled in her expanding abdomen.

Then Bradley was at her side. This part of the dream was always clear. Maybe because it was the last moment of her life untouched by the joy and tragedy that followed. Also, if she was being honest with herself, the last moment she trusted her husband. That was her problem, not his, but it didn't make it any less true.

He pulled the surgical mask down so she could see his face.

"What's the matter?" She wasn't panicking, but she knew something wasn't right. "How are the girls? Are they both okay?"

Tamara and Clara. Bradley said the names were too similar sounding, but Mags had already decided to call Tamara Tam.

Bradley didn't answer the question. Funny how these tiny evasions stayed with her, word for word. "Don't worry, Mags," he said, his cool fingers stroking her forehead, pushing her hair to one side before kissing her. "There are a few complications, and we need to give you a general anaesthetic."

He used the word we. Mags wondered what the obstetrician and team thought about that. Bradley was a genetic researcher, not a medical doctor, but his manner suggested he was running the show.

"No," she said grabbing his hand as he turned away. "I don't want to do that. I want to be awake. What's going on? What's wrong with my babies?"

Bradley nodded, not at her, but to someone behind her. She turned. A nurse was replacing the drip leading into the tube on her wrist. She turned back to Bradley. "I said no. I don't want to. Please..."

There were no memories after that. No memories of the operation, of the birth of her daughters. No memory of the silence from Clara, the attempts by the team to start her heart, or make her breathe. One of the children that had grown in her womb for nine months, nestled against her sister like a jigsaw piece, was gone before she could say goodbye. Gone as if she had never been.

The dream always ended the same way, with her watching the light move on the hospital ceiling. Not a surgical lamp this time, but a shadowed haze of natural light, sun streaming into the room, broken up by the branches of an elm outside the window. Bradley, to her right, asleep in a chair. Also to her right, close to her face, a hospital cot, and the snuffling, squeaking breaths of her new daughter. A surge of joy, then a realisation. No second cot. Pushing herself up on one elbow, wincing at an ache in her stomach. No other cot anywhere in the room. Glancing down at the perfect, tiny, impossible features of Tam as she slept. Then turning to see Bradley looking back at her, his eyes open, saying nothing. Not yet. Getting ready to choose his words.

That was when Mags woke up, every time. The moment before Bradley could tell her that Clara had died.

Mags gave up on any hope of getting back to sleep, turning on the TV and watching a show about Londoners selling overvalued properties so they could move out of the country, buy something palatial, and have enough left over to keep a flat in the city. Even in her tired daze, Mags recognised she shared their privileged position. Bradley's career had taken off in the years since they met. His father had made him a full partner in the research company after Tam's birth, and his salary meant Mags hadn't had to think much about money ever since. She didn't much enjoy being a "kept woman", but it had made sense for her to stay at home with Tam. The year of maternity leave had stretched to two, then three, then four. Mags promised herself she would go back to work when Tam started preschool, then decided it would be better when she was at school full-time. She postponed again to make sure Tam settled in okay. When she stopped talking about work, her friends and family stopped asking. Bradley insisted he would support her whatever she decided. Typical Bradley. Behaving in exactly the way a supportive partner should. Caring. Understanding. Bastard. Mags giggled at her own stream of consciousness. Maybe she was turning a corner, being able to see her problems as amusing.

As the TV couple debated whether they should keep horses in the stables of their new country pile, Mags flicked the remote off. It was six-twenty. If she got Tam up now, they would have time for breakfast at the café on the corner, a semi-regular treat when her dad was away.

Upstairs, she tapped on Tam's door. There was no response.

"Tam?"

She tapped again, then pushed the door open. The bed was empty. A momentary lurch of panic, then she pushed her head into the room and saw her daughter sitting at the desk, a pencil in her hand, drawing.

"Good morning, honey. You're up early. Are you sleeping okay? I thought we might—"

Mags stopped talking. Tam hadn't responded to her voice. She stepped into the room.

Tam wasn't looking at the piece of paper on the desk. She was looking up towards her bookshelves. When Mags got closer, she saw Tam's eyes moving left to right, up and down.

"What's the matter, sweetheart?"

Mags looked at a piece of paper. Although Tam was looking away, her hand was moving at speed, and the picture that was emerging was rich in detail.

The picture showed a caravan. A static caravan, one of many in a park. It was night-time, moonlit, the shadows deep and mysterious. The other caravans were vague rectangles, but the closest was as clear as a photograph.

Three steps led to a flimsy, half-open door. There was a long window to the left of the door. Through slatted blinds, she could see two figures. There was a palpable energy about them. Mags could see they were arguing, the smaller figure on the right holding its arms up towards the larger figure as if about to attack. The larger figure stood with arms crossed, but there was something about the tilt of the head suggesting anger.

Nothing about the picture gave away its location. Mags had spent many childhood holidays in caravan parks, but if Tam had ever seen one, it must have been on TV.

Tam wasn't seeing her bedroom at all. Mags watched her daughter draw with a mixture of astonishment and worry. About half a minute after she had walked into the room, Tam dropped the pencil, her head sank to her chest, and her eyes closed. Mags waited a few more seconds, then placed her hand on Tam's shoulder.

The response was immediate. Tam jerked backwards and looked up at her mother. For a sickening moment, Mags saw no recognition there. It was the blank stare of a stranger. Worse; there was something cold and dead about the look Tam gave her. Then it passed, and Tam was back.

"Mum?" Tam rubbed her eyes.

"Honey, it's okay. I'm here."

When Tam saw the picture on her desk, she pushed her chair back in shock. "Oh no. I was asleep in bed, Mum. I don't even remember getting up. What's happening? Am I going mad?"

Tam extended her arms. Mags hugged her. When Tam's grip became tighter, Mags realised she was crying. She cupped the back of Tam's head in her palm, just as she had when she was a baby, and murmured the usual platitudes.

After a while, Tam's sobs stopped, and she pulled a tissue from the box on her desk, blowing her nose.

Mags knelt down beside her. "Remember what Dad told you," she said. She wasn't convinced by Bradley's story about artistic talent bypassing the conscious mind, but her daughter was distressed. "I know it's strange, but it doesn't mean you're mad. You have a talent, and it's showing itself."

Distraction was still a viable option when confronted with an upset eleven-year-old. Mags kissed her on the cheek. "How about French toast at Benny's?"

Tam swallowed. She forced a grin onto her pale features. "Race you!"

Mags laughed. "No cheating," she called as Tam headed for the bathroom. "I'll sniff your armpits to make sure you washed them." She folded the picture in half, then half again, before tucking it into the pocket of her dressing gown. When she caught up with a triumphant Tam in the kitchen, she had almost forgotten about it. When Bradley called that evening, she didn't mention it. It wasn't until the phone rang three days later at 2am that she remembered it. After that, she could think about nothing else.

CHAPTER FIFTEEN

"Kit. Do you know what time it is? Are you okay? Is David all right? What's happened?"

There was a slight delay on the line, and they talked over each other at first. Kit reassured her.

"We're fine, we're both fine. I was so excited, I forgot about the time difference. It's the middle of the night for you, isn't it? I'm sorry, Mags. I just picked up the phone as soon as I saw it."

"Hang on a sec will you?" Mags turned on the lamp and picked up a pillow from the floor, sitting up against the headboard. "Okay. I'm awake now. What you mean? What did you see?"

"The picture on the fridge. I saw it on TV."

Mags pinched the top of her nose between thumb and forefinger and sighed. "What are you talking about? I don't understand."

"The amazing pictures Tam drew. You said you didn't know where the houses in the pictures were. It was nowhere you, or Tam, had ever been."

"Right." Mags remembered the new picture Tam had

drawn. She got out of bed and went to the door where her dressing gown was hanging. She plucked out the piece of paper as Kit was speaking.

"Well, I was just watching TV in the motel when I saw it. The one on the fridge. It's the same house, Mags. I took a picture of the TV. I'll send it to you."

"My mobile is downstairs. Wait a minute, I'll get it."

"No, go back to sleep. It can wait until morning."

Mags was halfway down the stairs. "I'm awake now, Kit. Stop apologising."

Mags didn't like mobile phones in the bedroom. Bradley's father often texted five times a night from Boston, and Bradley would answer if his phone was on the bedside table.

Her phone was charging on the counter. There was one message. She clicked on it.

"Well?" said Kit. "Tell me I'm not going mad."

Mags looked at the photograph. It wasn't great. The angle was different, and the colours were a distraction, since Tam's drawing had been in charcoal. But there was no doubt Mags was looking at the house from Tam's first picture.

She was about to ask where the house was when she noticed the caption on the bottom of the screen and squinted to read it. Her mouth went dry. She sat down hard on the bottom step, worried that she was about to fall. Kit was still talking.

"It's at a place in Georgia. A news item was playing when I turned on the TV. What are the odds? It's incredible, isn't it? I couldn't believe what I was seeing. Where do you think Tam saw it? On TV? I haven't seen anything about this at home. Have you?"

Mags was still looking at the caption. *Four found dead at scene.*

"Dead? Who's dead? What happened there?" she croaked. Kit wasn't listening.

"Not now, David, I'm talking to Mags. I said no. What's wrong with you? You're like a dog on heat."

"Kit. Who was found dead?" Mags went cold. She sat down at the kitchen table, her mobile phone in one hand, the house phone pressed against her ear.

"Oh, it's a serial killer, I think." Kit sounded as casual as if they were discussing a soap opera storyline. "That must be why Tam saw it. Must have been on the news, or maybe the internet? Just google the bedroom murders." She heard giggling, and a hissed, *"David,"* followed by a muffled reply. "I have to go," said Kit. "See you when I get back. Love ya!" The line went dead.

Mags fetched her laptop from the front room, taking it upstairs. In the bedroom, she opened it and typed *bedroom murders.*

It was there. The first story was from a local news site in Statesboro, Georgia. *Bedroom Killer Strikes A Fifth Time. Couple Murdered Yards From Their Neighbors.* Mags clicked through and scanned the article.

It was text only, so she went back to the search results, and clicked on images. Seconds later, she brought both her hands up to her mouth, and stared at the screen in horror.

She recognised two of the five crime scenes that populated her screen. One of them was on her mobile phone. The other was on the fridge.

After dropping Tam at school next morning, Mags came straight home and went up to her daughter's bedroom. She remembered hiding things from her own parents, although she had been older—fourteen or fifteen—and she was only concealing cigarettes, a photo of a penis Sarah Gordon had given her, and a packet of condoms she had bought as a dare.

This was different. Tam was mature for her age. And there had been no internet when Mags was a teenager.

She booted up the laptop they had given Tam on her eleventh birthday. There had been a discussion when it was handed over, during which certain rules were laid down about its use. Neither she nor Bradley had wanted Tam to be left behind by her schoolmates—many already had mobile phones—but they were cognisant of the dangers of the internet. Most of the supposed problems, Bradley argued, were exaggerated by journalists needing to fill magazine and newspaper pages with inflammatory material aimed at parents. But the lack of censorship online meant the burden of protecting their daughter from violent, or sexual, material fell to them. Mags was more worried about social media, with bullies able to hide behind an anonymous username. Tam had agreed to only use the laptop downstairs at the kitchen table. Within a few months, they allowed her to keep it in her room, reserving the right to knock and enter her bedroom at any time. If they found she had abused the agreement, they would confiscate the laptop.

Tam had been as good as her word. She always checked with them if any website she discovered worried her, and she didn't show the slightest interest in social media. She had no email address, which meant the newsletters she received from the PG Wodehouse appreciation society came to Mags. Tam used the laptop for homework and for games, but there were few of the latter, as she was happier on her beanbag with a book.

Mags went straight to the internet history. It went back to Tam's birthday, and it was all innocent. Well, not entirely. Mags stifled a giggle when she saw the Google search of six weeks earlier for *do boys' willies really get all stiff?* Mags was proud to note the correct use of an apostrophe. Tam had not found a satisfactory answer online, because Mags remembered her asking the question around that time. Tam had shaken her head in disbelief at her mother's confirmation.

"Seems a bally inconvenient way of going about things."

Mags had shrugged. It was hard to disagree.

It took Mags an hour to check any websites that looked unusual, but there was nothing to find.

She searched the bedroom next. Every time she felt bad about what she was doing, she thought of the pictures, and got back to work with renewed determination. There was no hidden mobile phone, no secret diary. Not even a packet of condoms. Mags closed Tam's bedroom door and went downstairs with a mixture of relief and confusion.

When she picked Tam up from school, Mags took her for a hot chocolate at Benny's. The Italian café was a family favourite, and Tam's drink was always overflowing with cream and marshmallows. She took a sip and smiled at Mags, a frothy white moustache on her upper lip.

They talked about school for a while. Tam was learning to play the ukulele, and it had sparked an interest in music. She was mentioning the names of singers and bands Mags had never heard of.

This is how it begins, thought Mags. *First, music I don't know, then new slang I can't follow. She's growing up.*

Mags thought back to the secret language she and Kit had used as children. To outsiders, it sometimes looked as if they could understand each other with no words at all. In fact, since birth, they had developed a series of short-hand looks, signs and sounds that could communicate an array of complex messages. It had changed when they'd hit puberty. For about eighteen months, their unspoken language had become heightened. As they'd grown up, it had faded, but sometimes they had known things they shouldn't have been able to know. One night, at three-thirty-eight in the morning, fourteen-year-old Mags had woken up, crept downstairs and stood in front of the phone, her hand on the receiver. Without considering what she was doing, or why, she lifted the phone to her ear at the exact second Kit called. He was at a friend's and had fallen asleep there. He needed someone to let him back into the house. Ten minutes later, when Mags unlocked the backdoor, he gave her a kiss on the cheek, and they went back to bed. Neither of them ever mentioned the impossible nature of what had occurred. It was natural to them.

Mags realised Tam had asked her a question, and she tried to review what she had been talking about. Nope. No idea.

"Cool," she said.

Tam laughed. "You think he's cool? I agree."

With no idea who she had just praised, Mags changed the subject, trying to be as casual as possible.

"Oh, by the way, I saw a photograph of a house just like the one you drew - the one on the fridge."

Tam stiffened and took another mouthful of hot chocolate. Mags ploughed on as if she hadn't noticed her daughter's wariness.

"Uncle Kit's working in America. He saw it, took a photo."

Mags took her phone out of her pocket and found what she was looking for. She had cropped the headline out of the picture. She held it out.

"'Terrible photo," said Tam. She looked at the phone for a few seconds, then handed it back. "Yes, it looks the same. That's weird, isn't it?"

Mags maintained her casual manner, determined not to worry her. "I suppose," she said. "At least we know it's an actual place."

"Is it in Boston?"

Tam had visited her grandparents in Boston the previous summer, the only time she had been to America. It was only the third time she had met Bradley's parents.

"No, honey, it's not. It's much further south."

"So where did I see it?"

Damn. That was the question Mags had hoped Tam might answer.

"I don't know. At school, maybe? Have you been learning about America?"

Tam shook her head.

"Something on TV, maybe? What are you watching at the moment?"

"Jeeves and Wooster." No surprise there. Would the Wodehouse obsession fade now that Tam was getting into music and watching YouTube videos? Mags felt a pang of sadness at the thought.

"What about the YouTubers? Any of them American?"

Tam smirked when Mags said *YouTubers*. "Yes, a couple. But their videos are inside, usually in their bedrooms." She picked up the long teaspoon and fished the last of the marshmallows out of the bottom of the cup. "Am I weird, Mum? I don't want to be weird. And I don't want to do those stupid pictures."

"You're not weird, Tam. I'm guessing you saw a photo of that house somewhere. It might have been in the background of one of your YouTube videos, or in a book. Who knows? The fact that you don't remember where you saw it ties in with Dad's theory."

"It does?"

"Yes. Dad says the human brain never forgets anything. If you see something once, it's in your memory forever. But if it's not important, it gets filed in some dusty corner."

"But my subconscious can find it there." So Tam was listening when Bradley talked science.

"Exactly. You might have seen that house once, for a split second. When you draw, your conscious mind isn't doing it. It's your subconscious."

"Mm." Tam stirred the bottom of her empty cup. "Sounds plenty weird to me."

Mags silently agreed. Even as she had explained her theory to Tam, it had sounded shaky. She took a breath, trying to keep her tone as casual as possible.

"Tam? Ever heard of the Bedroom Killer?"

She watched Tam for her reaction. Nothing. Not a flicker of recognition. "Is it a movie?"

"No. Never mind. Come on, I'll watch a *Jeeves* episode with you."

Hours later, with Tam asleep, Mags put her hand in her dressing gown pocket, and brought out the latest drawing. She unfolded it on the coffee table.

The detail was remarkable. Just like the first two pictures, this was a real place. The theory that they were copied from a photograph was compelling. Perhaps her bullshit theory was right. Tam might have seen something on the internet, in the sidebar on YouTube, perhaps. An image that her conscious mind had absorbed, then reproduced later.

In which case, this third image must be somewhere online. It wasn't the scene of one of the *Bedroom Killer's* murders, so she must have seen it somewhere else.

She opened the laptop. There was a new email. She had put a google alert on the words *Bedroom Killer,* and *bedroom murders.* There had been thirty-seven new results since that afternoon. She clicked on the top one.

BEDROOM KILLER'S BODY COUNT REACHES DOUBLE FIGURES.

The Bedroom Killer had struck again. The article detailed his modus operandi with lascivious attention to detail. He had garrotted his victims before arranging their corpses in bed as if they were sleeping.

There was a picture. A trailer park in Georgia. Not a caravan park in England.

She dragged her eyes away from the screen to confirm what she already knew. The picture Tam had drawn was of the trailer where Bill Crawston and Jeanette Franchi had been murdered, their bodies found tucked up in bed.

Her daughter was drawing detailed pictures of murder scenes.

CHAPTER SIXTEEN

M ags made a pot of tea and sat in the glass box at the back of her house, looking out into the garden.

The laptop was open on the kitchen table next to her, but she was sick of looking at it. Sick of trying to work out what was going on. For two days now, her anxiety had coiled around the top of her spine, preparing itself to squeeze into her mind and whisper its poison. If she let it have its way, she wouldn't be able to help Tam. She wouldn't be able to do anything except crawl to the settee and wait it out. That wasn't going to happen.

She pulled a chair up to the corner cabinet, stretching up to the top shelf and retrieving a blister-strip of pills. There were nine antidepressants left. Three days' worth. Her thumbnail punctured the foil. Five years of these pills, then another three trying to get off them. Ria's talking therapy had paid off, leaving Mags drug-free with a variety of techniques to deal with her anxiety.

It was only when her left calf cramped that Mags realised she was still standing on the chair. She put the pills back and closed the cupboard door. No. She could get through this without them. Tam needed her. She could do it.

The US road map was in a kitchen drawer. Mags remembered the nights she and Bradley had spent planning a route up the west coast, from San Diego to Vancouver Island. When Mags had fallen pregnant, they'd postponed it until the twins would be old enough to come. Then Clara had died. The highlighted route on the map was all that remained of the planned trip. Mags drew circles around locations of murders attributed to the Bedroom Killer. There were five in all. The last three were all within a hundred and fifty miles of each other.

Mags went upstairs and pulled a suitcase out from under the bed, brushing a cloud of dust from the top.

Tam had shown no sign of recognition at all when she'd mentioned the Bedroom Killer. No sign at all.

If she was going to find out why her daughter had an unconscious obsession with a serial killer, she would start by seeing the murder scenes for herself.

"Of course we'll have her. She's our favourite niece. Right, David?" David looked up from the metal figurine he was painting. Forced to guess, Mags had called it a troll, but David had snorted in mock-outrage, and insisted it was obvious the tiny monster was an orc. He had given this orc a brown jacket, black trousers, a white face with yellow eyes, and bright red horns. This was David's way of relaxing. He put the brush down and grinned.

"I'll be honest with you, Mags. I always thought I hated kids. Two reasons why I changed my mind. The first was your twin brother."

Kit smirked.

"He has decided to behave like a fifteen-year-old for the rest of his life. What might have been irritating in some, is strangely endearing in him."

Kit acknowledged the compliment by blowing a kiss.

"And then there's Tam. How on earth an American contributed anything towards a kid capable of speaking like Bertie Wooster is anybody's guess. I imagine she must have got ninety-eight percent of your DNA."

"Oh no," contradicted Kit. "Tam is far too good-looking for that. She got plenty of those gorgeous Yank genes."

"Whatever. She's a pleasure to be around, and we'd be delighted to have her as a house guest for as long as you'd like."

Mags forced a smile. "Thank you. It's only five days. I really appreciate it. I'll bring her over after school."

At the door, Kit caught up with her and watched her put her shoes on. He folded his arms.

"What?" she said.

"You're flying to Boston to surprise Bradley," he said.

"That's right."

"You. Margaret Eileen Thompson."

"Barkworth."

"Don't change the subject. You've never been sponta-neous in your life."

"Yes I have."

"Name one occasion. Ever."

She knew this was an argument she couldn't win.

"I'll be late picking up Tam."

"Ha!" Kit was triumphant. "It's not even Bradley's birth-day. Or your anniversary. Now stop bullshitting and tell me what's going on."

She avoided looking at him, but Kit put a hand on her

arm. The facade she'd kept in place since she'd arrived crumbled.

"Twin power!" crowed Kit, then stopped. "Shit. What's wrong, Mags. He's not cheating on you, is he?"

"No, he bloody isn't. It's... it's nothing."

"It's not bloody nothing, Sis. Come on. No secrets."

There had never been secrets between them. The idea seemed ridiculous. But Mags knew she couldn't share this. She didn't even know what *this* was, yet. She only knew she had to get out there, see it for herself, try to find out what the hell was going on. Was some murderous sicko posting pics of his victim's homes? *Had* Tam found some horrible dark web page? That was hard to believe, but it was even less conceivable that Tam would lie to her face. So what did that leave?

She shook her head. "No secrets, Kit. But you will have to trust me. I'm not ready to talk about this yet. Give me these few days. We'll talk when I get back."

Kit hid the look of betrayal as fast as it appeared, but Mags saw it. It was the first time she had held something back from her twin brother, ever.

He hugged her. "Be careful."

"I will."

"And Sis?"

She looked back at him as she opened the door.

"Give Bradley one from me, will you?"

———

She called Bradley from the airport.

"Atlanta? What the hell's in Atlanta? And why don't you wait until we can go together?"

Ticket bought, checked in, and sitting in the departure

lounge, Mags felt as if Bradley was speaking to her from a million miles away. She sipped an orange juice.

The flight would see her in Atlanta by five in the evening, local time.

"Bradley, we never go anywhere together. Without Tam, I mean. And I never, ever, go anywhere on my own. I'm coming to see my husband, okay? When I was browsing flights, I saw a great deal for Atlanta. I loved *Gone With The Wind* when I was growing up."

"You never mentioned it." He sounded pissed off. The moment of reconciliation and passion on the kitchen floor seemed like years ago.

"I don't tell you everything, you know." Like the fact that our daughter is drawing pictures of murder scenes in America.

"Yeah. So it would seem. Look, Mags, it's not that I don't want you to come."

"Are you sure? Because that's how it sounds."

His voice became softer. Mags had the unsettling thought that Bradley was playing a part, that he was uninvolved with what he was saying. He knew what a loving husband who was working hard would say, and he knew the tone of voice he should adopt to say it.

"Hey, I'm sorry, Mags, I'm sorry. You took me by surprise, is all. It's so unlike you."

Mags couldn't argue that point.

"The research project we're involved with at the moment - it's at a critical stage. I'm working fourteen-hour days, honey. It's just bad timing, plain and simple."

"Yes, that's the problem with acting on an impulse, I guess. But I'll take what I can get of your time. Your mother can show me around Boston while you and Todd change the world in your lab."

"Yeah, well, maybe."

"Anyway, I'll be a few days in Atlanta before coming up to you. Hey, if it's such a bad idea, I could always fly straight home."

His hesitation was tiny, but it was there. "No. No. I'd love to see you. Can't wait. Call me from your hotel."

"I will. The flight's boarding. Got to go."

Bradley had recovered his poise. "I was wrong. It's good. I'm glad you're doing this. I thought we were past surprising each other. It's good we still can, right?"

Mags thought of all the lies she'd just fed him.

"I'll call you when I arrive."

CHAPTER SEVENTEEN

Atlanta welcomed her with a tropical-style thunderstorm during the ride from the airport to the hotel. Even the short walk from the terminal building to the taxi rank had made Mags sweat. From the cool of the cab, she watched great sheets of water pound the wide streets, obscuring her view. Where the water hit the hot blacktop, clouds of steam rose. It all added to the dream-like state of mind brought on by long haul travel. She was glad of this as she stared through the rain-spattered glass. Going over and over the few facts she knew about Tam's drawings wasn't getting her any closer to finding out what was really happening.

The first ten minutes of the drive could have been on the outskirts of any American city, but when they reached downtown Atlanta, the Diet Coke billboards gave way to trees. Gleaming skyscrapers flashed behind dripping branches. Mags could have sworn she caught sight of a mediaeval-looking church through the rain.

She paid the driver when they arrived at the hotel. A doorman trotted down the steps from the big glass and chrome doors and held an umbrella over her as a concierge lifted her luggage from the cab. In the lobby, she checked in and followed the concierge up to her room.

Sitting on the edge of the bed, Mags fought the temptation to fall backwards and doze on the clean sheets. Instead, she picked up the phone. It was a short call. Bradley was at work, and she was tired. She wanted to call Tam, but it was far too late in London.

The room was generously proportioned, with two enormous beds. She had forgotten that American hotels often had two double beds in them. She wondered why? Perhaps Americans were more adventurous than she gave them credit for. Perhaps it was the opposite. Behind closed doors, did couples demand one enormous bed each? She didn't know.

She stared at the city through the picture window. The rain had eased, leaving silver streaks on the glass. The trailer park Tam had drawn was near the city limits. Her thoughts kept returning to the picture, like a child picking at a scab.

It was too early to sleep. She needed to keep herself awake until at least nine or ten o'clock local time, or she would wake up in the middle of the night. But she couldn't face going outside, having to make conversation. Not yet.

Mags scrolled through the menu on the huge flat-screen TV hanging on the wall, selecting a loud, violent movie she would never normally watch. She pulled an old-fashioned, high-backed wooden chair from the desk in the corner and positioned it in front of the screen, rather than sitting on the bed. Two hours later, she was still awake, but she was struggling. All she could understand about the movie was that it involved giant robots speaking in voices so deep that her earrings rattled on the desk. She stood up and paced for a few minutes, then ordered room service. Twenty minutes later, a seafood salad and a large glass of bourbon arrived. She ate the salad, ordered a wake up call for 7am, showered, crawled into bed and swallowed a sleeping pill with the bourbon.

"What the hell am I doing here?" she said out loud.

———

"You a reporter?"

A rosary hung from the rear view mirror. Most cab drivers with religious accoutrements in their vehicles drove with a disregard for traffic laws and speed restrictions that suggested reliance on supernatural help. Ahmed—as his ID card revealed him to be—drove with the exaggerated caution of an octogenarian retaking his driving test.

"Yes," Mags answered, surprising herself. She didn't have a better explanation for why she was heading to the scene of a recent murder. "That's right. A reporter."

Ahmed coughed in a way that suggested disapproval. "The Brits care about what's happening in Atlanta?"

"Oh, well, I'm not a normal reporter. I don't work for a newspaper. I mean, I do sometimes." Mags remembered how hard it was to prevent a small white lie turning into a complicated mess. "I write for a psychology magazine. That's what I'm working on now. A feature about the psychology of a killer."

This seemed to mollify Ahmed. "Oh," he was nodding now "that's interesting. We have to understand how these people think, if we going to stop this kind of thing happening."

"Yes, that's right." The city centre had given way to suburban neighbourhoods, and these were thinning out. They were close to the airport. The wet streets had steamed dry, and—according to the weather report that morning—temperatures would peak at thirty-one degrees. She had picked out her lightest blouse and a pair of linen trousers.

"You see, most of the newspaper reports, they say he's a monster," said Ahmed. "But that's wrong, I think. Once you call someone evil, or say they are a monster, you are not learning what made them that way. Nothing comes from nothing, right? We have to at least try to understand what kind of hell someone has gone through to turn them into a murderer." He touched the crucifix on the rosary. "And we have to forgive them."

He brought the cab to a halt. "The trailer park is just around the corner. I don't want to drop you right outside. Folks are still hurting, and they've had to deal with a lot of rubberneckers. They are not very neighbourly towards strangers at the moment, ma'am, if you get my drift. You want my advice?"

"Yes. Please."

"If anyone asks you, don't tell them what you told me. They just lost someone, murdered right next door to them. These folk won't want to hear how a horrible childhood made him a killer. They want him dead."

Mags paid him and got out. "Thank you," she called as Ahmed drove away, his hand waving from the window.

She followed his directions. This part of the city was rundown, some shops boarded up, others selling cheap brands. When she rounded the corner, she stopped. The trailer park began when the line of shops ended, about thirty yards further on her left. A knot of people stood near the bright yellow police tape. She took a few deep breaths, composed herself, and walked on.

As she got closer to the police tape, a bead of sweat trickled between her shoulder blades and into the small of her back. It wasn't just the humidity. She had never been much of a liar and keeping up the pretence of being a reporter for two minutes on a cab ride was different thing to maintaining it for people whose neighbours had been murdered.

Ten yards away, a burly cop, his arms crossed, was protecting the perimeter of the crime scene.

She couldn't do this. What was she going to say? "Hello, someone might be showing photographs of the murder scenes to my eleven-year-old daughter in North London. Afterwards, she goes into a trance and produces a brilliant drawing of the scene, using an artistic talent she never displayed before."

They'd lock her up. In a cell, or—more likely—a psychiatric institution.

Mags walked away, then stopped again. This was ridiculous. She had travelled thousands of miles to see this for herself. She could hardly walk away now.

When she turned back, the cop, middle-aged, his collar tight and stained with sweat, was looking at her. She swallowed and walked towards him. She tried for a facial expression that suggested professionalism combined with an attitude of been-there, done-that, nothing-new-to-see-here.

It didn't have the intended effect. Quite the opposite. When she was within a few feet of the cop, he frowned, rested the heel of his palm on the butt of his gun, and held his other hand up to stop her.

"That's far enough, Ma'am."

Mags swallowed again. Her throat had dried up. "Excuse me, officer. I can walk here, can't I?"

The cop looked at her with distaste. "You're not from this part of town, ma'am, with that accent, I'm guessing not even this country. So what brings you to our charming neighbourhood this morning? Visiting a friend?"

"No, not exactly. I'm, er, I'm—"

"Yeah. I know what you're doing." The cop spat on the ground. "Murder junkies. I've seen plenty in my time. You're my first Brit, though. Don't get me wrong. That doesn't improve my opinion of you. You're still a sicko. Now turn around and go back where you came from."

This wasn't going well at all. "No, that's not it at all. I'm... I'm a reporter, researching a piece on serial killers. I'm, I'm looking into the psychology common to, you know, the background, um, the reasons someone might, that is, well, you know..."

Under the cop's glare, her story sounded ludicrous to her own ears, and she shut her mouth just to stop herself digging a deeper hole.

"Yeah. And I'm the Queen of England. Now, go back to your nice hotel before I get mad."

Mags, flustered, backed away a couple of steps. "It's not what you think, officer. I'm not the kind of person who gets off on murders. I promise you." The cop's expression didn't change. Mags fished her phone out of her handbag, stepped to one side and, pretending she was making a call, took a photograph. At the sound of the shutter, the cop looked first at the phone, then at her. She was such an idiot. Didn't even put her phone on silent.

"Scram," growled the cop. Mags made a noise like a distressed small animal and scurried away.

As she turned the corner, she looked back at the trailer park. The cop had stepped a few paces forward onto the sidewalk, his hands on his hips, and was staring in her direction. With a burst of speed, she made it round the corner and out of view. Tears blurred her vision, but she shook her head and blinked them away. She hadn't planned any further than this moment and didn't have the first idea of what came next.

Mags just wanted to get back to the hotel, have a shower, and decide what to do next. There was no taxi stand in sight, and she hadn't seen a passing cab since arriving. Her phone had no 3G signal. She scanned the street for somewhere she could go to ask for the number of a taxi company. When a passing car slowed down, she picked a direction and started walking as if she were late for a meeting.

"Hey, lady, wait up."

Mags looked round. The estate car—station wagon, she reminded herself—had turned and was driving alongside her. The window was down, and a man wearing a pale cream hat leaned across the passenger seat, sunglasses perched halfway down the bridge of his nose.

"Me?" She pointed to herself, stupidly, as there was no one else on the sidewalk. She recognised him now. He had been at the trailer park, hanging back a little, writing in a notebook.

"I heard that cop give you the brush off. He pretty much gave me the same treatment, but I'm a little long in the tooth to get upset by it. We're in the same game." She stared in confusion. "Reporters," he said. "Wanna compare notes over a cold drink?"

As the parent of an eleven-year-old, Mags had often spoken to Tam about stranger danger. She took a step forward and stopped. What kind of idiot gets into a car with someone she met at the scene of a double murder?

The man in the car chuckled goodnaturedly. He looked like he was in his early fifties. Slightly overweight, and she suspected the hat hid incipient baldness. He opened the glove box of the car and pulled out a laminated ID card, holding it up to the open window. "Here you go. Don't blame you for being suspicious."

Mags stepped up to the curb and took the proffered card. In the photograph, he wasn't wearing his hat. Mags noted she was right, his hair was thin and patchy. Patrice Martino, member of News Guild-CWA. For all she knew, he could have printed it at home, but it looked official enough, and she was all out of better ideas.

"I'm Mags. Mags Barkworth." He didn't ask for her credentials, and she didn't offer them. He leaned over and opened the door.

"Jump in," he said. "I know a place where they do great iced tea. You Brits are big on tea, right? You'll love this."

It probably wouldn't be appropriate to correct him and tell him tea should only be consumed hot. Mags slid onto the seat, closed the door, and—as the window slid back up—enjoyed the cold blast from the air conditioning.

It wasn't a café he drove to, but a bar. Giovanni's, only a few blocks away from the trailer park, might as well have been in a different city. It was one of a cluster of smart restaurants and bars, and the tables outside were already busy at mid-morning. Martino led her through to a booth inside. It was dark and cool. She accepted the iced tea, and had to admit, despite her prejudices, that it wasn't a bad drink on a humid morning.

"I find places like this in every city I visit," said Martino. "You go back far enough in my family, it's all Italian stock. Like most Americans, I like to maintain some kind of connection with the old country, even if it's just a habit of eating too much pizza." He patted his stomach, smiling.

Mags sensed the conversation was about to move on to the reason she was here. She spoke first. "So you're a journalist, too. Who do you write for? And what are you working on, Mr Martino?"

"Call me Patrice." He sipped his drink, then took his hat off and put it on the bench next to him. Perhaps he wore the hat for the shade it provided, rather than vanity. He made no attempt to rearrange the wispy tufts of hair that remained around his temples. "Served my apprenticeship with the New York Times. Been freelance for fifteen years now. Sometimes I find my own stories, sometimes the feature editor of one of the nationals throws me a bone."

"And which one is this?"

"This is a little of both, Mrs Barkworth."

She considered asking him to call her Mags, but decided against it. Better to keep this on a more formal footing.

Patrice paused, as if waiting for permission to use her first name. When it was unforthcoming, and the silence was about to become awkward, he spoke again.

"Serial killers are always good subjects for a feature," he said. "And this ain't my first rodeo. It's a fascinating story, and I wanna be there when it ends, which won't be long now."

Mags looked at him in surprise. "You think it will end soon? Why?"

Patrice didn't answer. He unzipped his messenger bag, took out his notebook and a pen, opened it and wrote Mrs Margaret Barkworth at the top of the blank page.

"What are you doing?" said Mags.

He put down his pen. "So far, you've asked all the questions, Mrs Barkworth. Okay, that's fine. You're a reporter. But it's tit-for-tat. You need to answer some of mine. Who do you write for? Why cross the pond for this story? What's your angle?"

He picked up the pen again. It was uncomfortable,

lying to this man. She took another sip of her drink to give her more time.

"I'm freelance too," she said. "I'm looking at the psychology of killers, and this case is interesting. The whole bedroom thing, the way he arranges them. It must stem from something in his background. Some trauma or other."

"Sure. Makes sense." He wrote nothing down, though. He looked at her face for five, six seconds. She watched him come to a decision.

"Mrs Barkworth," he said, "we're writing different stories, for different markets, in different countries. How long are you here for?"

"Two, maybe three days."

"Okay. I'm driving to Hinesville today."

Mags looked blankly at him. She recognised the name, but jet lag was preventing her from making a connection. Then she had it. The picture on the fridge. "The murder scene?"

"Right. It's been three weeks since the killings in Macon, two months since Hinesville. Long enough for the circus to have moved on. I think I can get us into the house."

"How?"

"I've been doing this a long, long time, Mrs Barkworth. I have my methods. Wanna tag along?"

She hesitated.

"Check me out," he said.

"I beg your pardon?"

"Check me out. Google me. I want you to know I am who I say I am. Google me. I insist."

"My phone isn't connecting," she said.

He slid his phone across the table. "Use mine." He clicked it on. The home screen was a photograph of a pretty girl in her mid-teens.

"Your daughter?"

"Yeah. Hannah. Takes after her mother for looks. More like me in personality. Thank God."

Mags looked up at that.

"Divorced," he said.

She didn't comment, just typed Patrice Martino into the search box. A few seconds scanning the results confirmed his identity.

"Shortlisted for the Pulitzer Prize?"

He shrugged. "It was a helluva long shortlist." Mags decided she liked him.

"You didn't answer my question," she said, handing the phone back.

"Which one?"

"You said you wanted to be there when it ends. I asked you why you think it's ending."

"Fair question, Mrs Barkworth. I've written features on two serial killers, which meant researching dozens more. None of them had much in common apart from extreme violence and being fucking crazy. Sorry. I'm sure you have a better psychological word for it."

Was he teasing her?

"Anyhow, in every serial killer case, there's an acceleration along the timeline."

"What do you mean?"

"Look at this guy, for instance. First killing? Nearly a year and a half ago in the Everglades. Since then, he's always headed north, and he's got a taste for it. Second murder, six months after the first, just south of Lake Placid. Then he heads up to Ocala, but he only waits three months this time. Eight weeks later, he garrottes the couple in Hinesville. After that, he only waits five weeks before killing a family in Macon. The gap between Macon and

Atlanta? Eighteen *days*. He's gonna screw up, and he'll screw up soon, because whatever's driving him to kill isn't giving him enough time to plan properly anymore."

"Any idea what *is* driving him, Mr Martino?"

"Patrice. Please. And no. That's more your department. What do you think?"

Mags took a long breath. "I think we can talk about it on the drive, Patrice. And you had better call me Mags. 'Mrs Barkworth' makes me sound like the headteacher of an all-girls boarding school."

He smiled at that. "It's a four-hour drive, Mags. You might wanna use the restroom before we leave."

CHAPTER EIGHTEEN

They stopped for lunch at a gas station. One-thirty. Half-six in the evening in London. While Patrice ordered, she went outside and called Kit.

"Mags? That you? Hope it's not too boring over there. You're missing all the fun. How was Margaret Mitchell?"

"Who?"

"Frankly, my dear, I don't give a damn."

Mags remembered the excuse she'd given for flying to Atlanta rather than straight to Boston. "Oh, I didn't hear you right. Not a great line. Yes, amazing. The houses are incredible. Like being in the movie. You all okay?"

"Everything is fine, Sis. Hang on, I'll fetch her." A few seconds later, there was a breathless giggle at the other end of the line.

"We're making pizza, Mum. It's brilliant. We made the bases first, and Uncle Kit had the video on YouTube where they show you how to spin it on your finger. Mine went in my hair, and Uncle Kit's went out of the window. It was top notch. We're going to watch TV when we eat the pizzas. I put pineapple and olives and mushrooms on mine. And three different cheeses. It smells amazing, Mum. I wish you were here. What's it like in America? Is Atlanta different to Boston? When are you seeing Dad? Rosa has got a puppy. She wants to bring it round to the house. Can she? Can we have a puppy?"

Tam was always like this when she spent any time with Kit. Mags rolled her eyes. "No, I don't think we can have a puppy. It wouldn't be much fun for it, where we live."

"We could always move out of London. Get a country pile. Then could we have a puppy?"

Mags laughed. "We're not planning on moving just yet, Tam. But Rosa can bring her puppy over and you can play with it."

Tam squealed. "Thanks, Mum. I have to go, my pizza's ready. Love you love you love you, come home soon, I miss you. Love you love you love you, bye, bye..."

Kit came back on the line.

"We're going to eat, Sis. Everything okay over there? Anything you want to share with your twin brother?"

Mags wished she had confided in him. She would rectify that when she got home. "I'm back on Sunday. Let's talk about it then."

"Sounds like a plan. Maybe we can discuss my impending separation at the same time. David is eating a pizza with anchovies and pineapple on it. Legal grounds for divorce, surely?"

"A criminal offence," confirmed Mags. "Enjoy your pizza. Thanks for looking after her. Love you."

"Love you too."

After lunch, they made good time, arriving in Hinesville mid-afternoon. It was only three weeks since the bedroom killer had visited this quiet town. Mags wondered how Patrice intended to get them into the house where it had happened. The address he tapped into the satnav led them to a small business park. Patrice stopped the car outside a real estate office.

"Better if you wait here," he said. "I'll be back in a few minutes."

Mags watched him through a large glass window. Patrice stood in the small reception area. As a young woman approached, he took off his hat. At first, the woman's arms were folded and she shook her head but, as she listened to him, her body language softened. After a couple of minutes, she put a hand on his arm as he dabbed at his eyes. She nodded, smiling, and he walked out to the car.

"Well?" she said, as he climbed back in.

"Joanna was very helpful."

The young woman appeared at the side of the building. She waved at Patrice and, getting into an open-topped Miata, drove off. They followed.

Seven minutes later, they drew up in front of a familiar house.

"Oh," said Mags, a weight dropping into her stomach. It was the house from the picture on the fridge. White clapboard, ivy, a tiled roof. She swallowed the bile that rose in her throat. "Surely it's not open to potential buyers yet?"

"We have around thirty minutes, Mrs Martino," said Patrice, the corner of his mouth curling into a smile.

"Mrs what?"

Martino walked around the outside of the car and offered her his hand. The estate agent—realtor, Mags reminded herself—waited at the screen door.

"I told Joanna this was my second marriage," he said. "She thinks my first wife died three years ago. You and I met while I was on a trip to London. This is your first time in Georgia. You want us to live in Britain, but I want us to stay here. When I saw this house on the news, I knew you'd love it. The problem is, we go back to London tomorrow. This is my last chance to persuade you."

"That story convinced her?"

Patrice's smile broadened. "I had a clincher. I said the real reason I want to stay is because I could continue to leave flowers on my first wife's grave in Atlanta. Even though her dying words were that I should try to love again, I still think leaving the country would be a betrayal. Joanna cried."

Mags eyed him. "Well. You're quite something."

"Thank you."

"It wasn't a compliment."

It was a beautiful home, but Mags couldn't think of it that way. Every room reminded her of what had happened. The kitchen where, just a few months before, a woman had prepared a final meal. The bathroom, with toothbrushes in a beaker. When they reached the bedrooms, Mags didn't want to see any more.

"Is it okay if I look outside?"

"Sure, honey." Mags suspected Patrice was enjoying this. "See you downstairs."

Outside, Mags breathed fresh air with gratitude. In the dirt at the edge of a well-maintained flower bed, a trowel lay abandoned. Her chest was tight, her breathing shallow. She took a few moments to take control, calm down, wait for the tingling in her fingers to stop.

She left the yard by a wooden gate and walked up the slope leading to a wooded area. From there, she turned and looked at the house. It wasn't quite the right view. She took the picture out of her bag, unfolded it, and compared it to what she could see. Ten paces back and she was among the trees. She stopped, looked at the picture, then up at the house. Almost right. She took a step to her right and crouched down. Better, but not perfect. Looking around to check she was unobserved, she lay flat on her front. That was it. What she was seeing now matched the picture. She stood up again. As she did so, there was movement in a window. She looked up and saw Patrice and Joanna looking at her. She folded the paper and stuffed it into her bag, brushed herself down, and went to the car.

The realtor gave her a questioning look when she emerged, but said nothing.

Patrice didn't speak until they had driven two blocks. "Any deep psychological insights?"

"A few." She yawned, feigning more tiredness than she felt. "How far away is the hotel?"

Patrice had offered to take her to Atlanta that night, but he'd admitted he was tired. He'd rather write up his notes and drive her back in the morning. She wondered what her husband would make of her spending the night in a hotel with another man. Well, not that she was spending it with Patrice, exactly. Even so.

She would have to call Bradley from the hotel and tell him about it. Yes, she'd definitely call him. Mags almost convinced herself that she meant it.

CHAPTER NINETEEN

Towards the end of her third glass of wine, Mags acknowledged to herself that she was flirting. Not much, but a little. And she was enjoying it. She would never be unfaithful to Bradley, but she had to admit she appreciated the attention Patrice was giving her. It had been a long time since she had been alone with a man other than her husband. She had forgotten how it felt.

Even when Bradley had first asked her out, it had seemed strange to her. Subsequently, everything had followed a predictable pattern, but none of it seemed normal somehow. They met at a party, Bradley took her number, and called three days later. They slept together the fourth time they met. She spent the night in his hotel room before he flew back to Boston. Emails and phone calls followed. He started to spend more time working in London and admitted much of that decision was down to her. The engagement, marriage, and pregnancy seemed inevitable, like she was on train she had boarded in her sleep. It hadn't seemed that way back then. Ria had once suggested Mags was projecting her subsequent bouts of anxiety and depression back through time to re-frame the beginning of her marriage.

And yet she was positive their courtship had never been as relaxed as this. Maybe it was because she was older, and married, and knew herself better. But it occurred to her that, had she been single, she would have gone to bed with the American journalist she had only met the previous morning.

"Wanna share? It must be something good."

Mags jumped, caught daydreaming. She blushed, despite herself. "I'm sorry?"

"Don't be." Patrice's expression was direct. For a second, she half-considered telling him, which deepened her blush. He smiled. "It looked like you were thinking about something that made you happy. You smiled. I was just being rudely curious, wondering what that might be."

Flustered, Mags finished the wine in her glass and stood up. "Oh, nothing, not really," she said.

"Another glass?" Patrice was draining his.

Mags shook her head. Now she was standing, she realised she was tipsy. "No, thanks. Not for me. You go ahead."

"Nah, I'm done too. But I insist you try the bourbon here. It's one of my favourites."

"All right," said Mags. "A small one, though."

She threaded her way through the tables to the restroom at the back. Looking in the mirror as she touched up her make-up, she frowned at herself. She was here to find out, if she could, what was going on with Tam. Now she was flirting with a stranger. Martino might be charming, and refreshingly direct, but she was married. She would fly up to Boston, spend a couple of nights with Bradley and his folks, then go home. If Patrice was right, the killer would be caught soon. When that happened, surely whatever Tam was going through would stop.

She nodded at her reflection. Yes. It would stop.

Mags turned the wrong way leaving the restroom and found herself in the bar area of the hotel. A sign on the wall pointed to the reception, so she came back into the restaurant through the other door. When she got close to the table, she saw that Patrice had a piece of paper in his hand. He was studying it, keeping it low to the table, and his eyes kept flicking up towards the door leading to the restrooms. She slowed, stepping to her right to get a better view of the table. The first thing she noticed was her handbag on the seat next to him. Then she saw what he was looking at. It was Tam's picture of the Hinesville house.

She walked up to the table.

Patrice looked up. "Shit."

"Shit indeed." Mags held out her hand. He re-folded the picture and gave it to her. She put in her bag and took her jacket from the back of the chair.

"Sit down, Mags."

"I don't think so, Mr Martino. I don't think we have anything more to say to each other."

She walked away, but he raised his voice.

"Mags."

She turned. He pointed at the glass of bourbon in front of her place. "Sit," he said. She didn't move. He looked up at her. "I've been straight with you from the moment we met, but I'm not sure you've said even a single word of truth since you first got in my car. Is your name even Mags Barkworth? Because I could find no writer of that name."

"Yes, it's my name. And, whatever you think of me, it gives you no excuse to go through my things."

"I apologise for that, Mags. Here's the thing. I like you. I knew you were spinning me a tall tale early on, but I didn't think you were doing it for the wrong reasons. Even though you were lying about something, I trusted you. I still do. You haven't told me why you're really here, but I'm guessing you have your reasons. I just wish you'd been able to tell me what they are. Please, sit down. This bourbon is not cheap."

The moment stretched out. Patrice did nothing to fill the silence. He put his hands on the table, looked at her and waited.

Mags sat down. "You're right," she said. "I'm not a reporter. I'm a mother, and I'm worried about my daughter."

"Now that is something I know about. Try me."

Mags looked him in the eye. If she still hoped to find out anything that might help her on this trip, Patrice would be the man to turn to. He was researching the murders, and he'd written about similar cases. Her instinct was to trust him. Then again, that same instinct told her to distrust her husband. God, she was tired.

"Fuck it," she said.

"Excuse me?"

Mags lift her glass and tried the bourbon. An ice cube touched her upper lip as the smooth fiery liquid dropped down her throat. "You heard me," she said. "I said fuck it. Wow. That is good bourbon."

"Yup."

"Okay, Patrice, I'll tell you why I'm here. But swear it's off the record."

She waited. Patrice nodded. "Whatever you tell me is between you and me, I promise. On my daughter's life."

She told him everything. Patrice was as good as his word, listening without judgement. He made notes, a mixture of shorthand and what looked like doodles, drawing arrows from one idea to another. His questions were pertinent, and useful. He asked about Tam's internet access at home, how much TV she watched, and how conversant she was with technology. He asked about her friends and her interests. When Mags told him about her love of PG Wodehouse, Martino smiled.

"Sounds like a great kid."

"Cheers. She is. I'm lucky. I mean, we are lucky." She felt herself blush again at the omission, but Patrice didn't seem to notice. He put his pen down and sat back. His bourbon was untouched. He took a sip.

"Okay, there is a simple explanation, but you won't like it."

Mags leaned forward. "What I like or don't like doesn't matter. I want to help her. You didn't see her face when she drew the picture. It was scary. Like she wasn't there."

"That's one part of the explanation. It is possible she is having absence seizures. Possible, but unlikely. Still, you should get her checked out."

"I've heard of those. Epilepsy, right?"

"Right. My daughter's best friend suffers from them. She was the only one in her year who didn't learn to drive, because she never knew when she might have a seizure."

"Well, that's one good thing about having a scientist husband. Right from the start, right from when Tam was born, especially since..." There was no need to tell Patrice about Clara. Mags had never spoken to anyone else about her other daughter apart from her family, and Ria. Too painful. Not relevant, either. "Tam has had blood tests four times a year since she was born. Bradley insists we all have a full medical twice a year. Something like this would be picked up."

"Maybe. I said it was unlikely. But it's not impossible. I still think you should look into it."

"I will. But Bradley is a genetic researcher at one of the top companies in Boston. If there was something wrong with Tam, he would have found it. What was the other part of your explanation?"

Patrice picked up his glass and finished his bourbon. "Look, Mags, every mother thinks they know their kid. And it sounds like you two are real close."

"We are."

"Try not to take this too hard. Girls are programmed to push themselves away from their parents in adolescence. Usually later in their teens, but girls mature faster. Has Tam reached puberty?"

Mags thought back to the day of the first picture, the mixture of pride, sadness, and worry when Tam had told her about her first period. "Yes," she confirmed

"Then I'm probably right."

"Right about what?"

"Mags, Tam may be more conversant with technology than you suspect. You and I remember a time when the only computers we saw were in movies. It's different for our kids. They've already forgotten more about technology than we will ever know. They're always a few steps ahead of us. No need to hide a secret diary under your mattress if you can use the latest software."

"But I checked her computer. I told you. She hadn't even cleared her internet history. There was nothing to see, Patrice."

Patrice sighed. It was the sigh of a man who wasn't enjoying himself.

"I'll wager a hundred bucks here and now that your daughter is using a different internet browser for what she really wants to look at. The one you checked is the one she's happy for you to see, which is why she hasn't cleared her history."

"No. No, she wouldn't do that. I'm not being naïve. I understand that mothers and daughters drift apart, particularly in the teenage years. But it hasn't happened yet, with Tam and me. We are, we are — "

"Tight? A team? Friends, as well as mother and daughter?" Patrice spread his arms out, palms open. "I'm sorry, Mags. I'm not making fun of you. I learned some of this the hard way. With Hannah it was drugs."

He looked away from her for a moment. Mags put her hand on his. "I'm so sorry, Patrice. That must have been awful. But, I promise you, I know Tam, I understand her."

Patrice's smile was weary. "She's a smart girl, right?"

"Yes. She is."

"Here's another guess, then. I bet there was something in her history that wasn't entirely innocent, but nothing to make you worry. Something to make you think she wasn't hiding anything. Am I right?"

Mags remembered Tam's search for erections. Shit. She noticed her hand was still resting on Martino's. She moved it.

Patrice saw her expression change. "If she knows how to install and hide another browser, I'll bet she can do it so you'll never find it. But at least there is an explanation. And I know this won't help much now, but when you've had some time, you'll know I'm right. It's not unusual for kids to get obsessed with violent crime. Some like to watch horror films before they're allowed to. Some read about murders. They might even collect knives, or other weapons. Ninety-nine times out of a hundred it means nothing. They're just exploring the worst of the adult world. If Tam is obsessing over a serial killer, at least she's chosen one on another continent. It's a safe way for her to look at the awful things one human being can do to another, the things her parents protect her from. And I'm guessing you're a protective parent."

Mags raised a hand to get the attention of a waiter. "Another two bourbons," she said. "Large ones, please."

"Dammit," said Patrice. "I hate to be the one to point this out, Mags. It's not easy to face. Your relationship with your daughter is changing, but you two sound as if you have a fantastic foundation. This is probably nothing to worry about. Nothing at all."

"I feel like a fool," said Mags, as the drinks arrived. "I flew halfway across the world so an Italian-American journalist could tell me my daughter is better at using the internet than I am."

"Sorry."

"Still doesn't explain the drawings," she said, taking a sip. Her eyes were heavy.

"No," agreed Patrice, "it doesn't. Your husband's explanation may well be the right one. Most of my breakthroughs— when I've been writing an investigative piece—come out of the blue. In the middle of the night, sometimes in the shower. The subconscious mind is still the great unknown as far as neuroscience is concerned."

Mags stood up. "Thank you for today. In fact, thank you for everything. I'm going to bed."

Patrice raised his glass. "I won't be far behind. Nine o'clock okay for breakfast? I'll drive you back to Atlanta."

Mags leaned down, her lips brushing his unshaven cheek. "You're a good man, Patrice Martino."

"Yeah. So my bartender tells me."

By the time she got back to her room, Mags was wiped out. She hadn't realised the effect of carrying this secret, not talking to anyone about it. Then coming out to America, putting the Atlantic Ocean between her and Tam.

It was just gone midnight when Mags got into bed. She plugged her phone in to charge.

She woke twice during the night, both times after the same nightmare.

She was standing in her kitchen at home, facing the fridge. Tam's first picture was on it. It looked so real the rest of the room seemed dreamlike. She took a step towards the fridge, and the kitchen blurred around her. The familiar room seemed pixelated, half-formed, like a photograph downloading in the early days of dial-up internet. But Tam's drawing was sharp, crisp, real. She took another step. The picture expanded to meet her. Another step, and her foot came down on dusty dry earth. She was back at the Hinesville house, but this time, the world was a charcoal picture. There were no colours, only gradations of black, grey, and white. The front door was open, and she walked towards it. As she stepped into the house, she wasn't in the kitchen, she was standing upstairs, outside the children's bedroom. The door was ajar. Just a few inches, but it was enough. The charcoal world darkened around her, and she heard a child struggling to breathe. She ran towards the door but it got no closer. The awful sounds from inside the bedroom got worse, and she ran faster and faster, her sides hurting with the effort, her lungs burning. All at once, the strangled gasps ceased. She burst through the door and woke up in the darkness of her hotel room.

The second time Mags woke up, it was 6:10. She got out of bed and opened the curtains, looking out over the unfamiliar town. After a shower, she packed a bag and pulled a chair over to the window. From there, she watched the sun rise over the town where a killer had murdered a family, then tucked them back into their beds as if they had drifted off in their sleep. And he was still out there, looking for his next victims.

CHAPTER TWENTY

Mags called Bradley from a diner a few miles off the I-16 on the outskirts of a small town called Dublin. The town names were a strange mixture of the familiar and the exotic. Dudley and Chester were neighbours with Yonkers and Tarrytown. The next big town was Warner Robins, which sounded like a movie studio or ice cream manufacturer.

While Patrice went inside to use the restroom, she paced up and down the small lot. Theirs was the only car parked in front, but Patrice said the place had an excellent reputation for all-day breakfasts. He had timed their arrival to coincide with the lunch crowd thinning out.

Bradley sounded distracted, irritable. "When are you getting here?"

"Seven-ish. You needn't pick me up from the airport. I'll get a cab."

"Honey, I can't spare you much time. I appreciate the romantic gesture, I really do. I know how hard it must have been for you to fly here on your own to see me, but one of our projects is at a critical stage. We're working all the hours we can. Have dinner with Mom. I'll get away as soon as I can, but I'll have to be up real early and into work again. I feel terrible about this, Mags, but there's nothing I can do. Dad and I need to be there. Let's talk about it tonight. I'm sorry, honey."

Her relief and guilt were evenly balanced. She could cut her Boston trip from three nights to one. She and Bradley's mother had little in common, so no one would put up much resistance if she went home early.

"It's okay, don't apologise. I can't expect you to drop everything just because I've been spontaneous for once in my life."

"I wish I could. But thank you for understanding. I love you."

A memory of their urgent, unplanned coupling on the kitchen floor came into Mags' mind. For a moment, it had been like the early days, giving herself up to her need for him. She didn't want the distance between them to creep back in, but it had been there for too long, like so much background noise.

Patrice was sitting at a table near the back, and the waitress was topping up his coffee cup. He waved her over.

"Connie here recommends the all-day farmer's slam."

The waitress, an older woman with a ready smile, nodded. "Best breakfast in Georgia."

"Sounds good. And a coffee with cream, please." Mags slid onto the bench opposite Patrice.

"Sure thing."

When the food arrived, it was as good as Connie had promised. Mags left the French toast and fried potatoes, but there was no way she could eat another thing. Patrice eyed her toast.

"May I?"

Mags laughed. "You're telling me you can eat more?"

"My doctor would tell me not to, my ex-wife would disapprove, but hell, yeah. When it tastes this good, it seems wrong not to."

He only managed one more piece and looked ruefully at what remained. "It's a crime. Still, I guess I should eat less, exercise more. I could stand to lose a few pounds."

"You wear it well." She said it without thinking and looked away. Patrice pretended not to notice. He put his coffee cup to one side. "Can I take another look at the pictures? If you'll let me photograph them, I can send them to a friend. She specialises in investigative pieces about technology, and she's written some exposés of criminals using the dark web. If anyone can help trace where Tam might have seen the crime scenes, it'll be her."

Mags watched as Patrice unfolded the pictures and spread them out on the table. "It's the angles that interest me," he said, squeezing the bridge of his nose. Mags had noticed him do this a few times when thinking. "The angles are strange. I checked the press images online last night, and none of them match Tam's pictures. That's why you lay down outside the house yesterday, right?"

"Yes."

"Interesting. The only possibility I can think of is that someone has accessed the police database. If the killer had the house under surveillance for a day or two, and the cops found evidence of that, they would have taken photographs from his hiding place. That's my best guess. May I share these photographs with my friend? No one else."

Mags agreed and watched him photograph the two pictures. She shared the Guide camp picture from her phone. As Patrice refolded the drawing of the Hinesville house, he frowned, took out his notebook, and wrote something down.

He looked at his watch. "What time is your flight?"

"Four-thirty."

"You'll be there a little early."

Patrice was quiet in the car, and his fingers regularly came up to the bridge of his nose. Mags glanced across a few times, wondering what he was thinking. Finally, he spoke.

"The date on the Hinesville picture. It's wrong."

"Wrong?" Mags opened her bag and took out the picture. She had written the date on the back. *Thursday, May 14th.* She opened the calendar on her phone. She had noted the day there. Not because of the picture, but because it was the day of her daughter's first period. "It's the right date," she said.

Patrice had driven up to the back of a truck doing about forty-five miles-per-hour. Instead of overtaking, he hung back, matching its speed, pinching the bridge of his nose harder. "It can't be."

"I just checked. It's right."

Patrice flicked the indicator, pulled over to the side and brought the car to a stop.

"If you're right, maybe it's time we went to the cops."

"Why? What's changed?"

Patrice answered with questions of his own. "The Atlanta picture. The trailer park. When did Tam draw it? What time?"

That was also easy to remember. It had been the day Mags was up early after her nightmare, the day she had walked in as Tam was drawing. "Friday," she said. "Friday before last."

"What time?"

"Early. About six-thirty. Why? What you mean, the date's wrong?"

Patrice took his hat off and put it on the dashboard. "Six-thirty your time. Atlanta is five hours behind. It was one-thirty here. Middle of the night."

Mags thought of the trailer park drawing, its suggestion of darkness.

"The bodies were found mid-morning." he said. "About ten hours after she drew it. And the Hinesville house—if your date is right—well..."

"What?"

"She drew that picture a day and a half before that family died."

"Before?" It sounded strange, as if it was a word she had never used. The air in the car was hot and dry. Mags licked her lips and stared at him.

"Mags, this is more serious than I thought. If your daughter has found somewhere online where this psycho is posting photographs before he commits the murders, we have to go to the cops."

A sensation of coldness radiated through Mags' body. It started in the centre of her chest, a kind of tight numbness. From there, it spread outwards. Her body belonged to someone else, the blood in her veins replaced by a freezing, viscous liquid, pumped relentlessly through her circulatory system. She looked at Patrice but didn't see him. She saw a stranger, in a hostile country thousands of miles from where she needed to be. What if Tam's mental state when she was drawing wasn't down to epilepsy, or some other illness? It had been as if Tam had been looking at something Mags couldn't see, drawing something she saw through someone else's eyes. A horrible, impossible idea began to take on definition, its terrifying implications crystallising even as Mags tried to reject it.

"Impossible. That's impossible."

"What is?" She must have spoken out loud. Patrice's voice was distant, and his side of the car seemed to recede as she looked at him.

"I need to make a call," she said.

It took almost a minute at the side of the freeway in Georgia, in the heat and the humidity, for Mags to regain enough control of her body to call Kit. Her hand shook so much as she tapped the screen, it took five attempts to press the right number. Everything she had learned from Ria, every breathing exercise, every technique, had deserted her now she needed them most. The only thing she could remember was to breathe deeply, but it was next to impossible. She tried. As her phone signal bounced off a satellite in orbit and found a tiny piece of metal, glass, and plastic in London, she forced air into her nostrils, held it, then released it raggedly through her mouth.

She pressed the phone hard against her head. There was a click. Laughter.

"Mags." Her brother's voice. Tam and David in the background, disputing how many houses Tam was allowed to put on Vine Street. They were playing Monopoly.

Tam was fine. They were all fine. Of course they were. It was a moment of madness on her part, nothing more. Her mental health had taken a knock because of the idea that had struck her in the car. The idea had threatened to overwhelm her, push everything else out of her mind. She wouldn't be any good to anyone if she let that happen. No good for Tam, Bradley, or herself.

She held the phone against her chest, and leaned forward, hunching, bending her legs, taking bigger lungfuls of oxygen. The tingling of her skin lessened, and she focused on regaining control.

A tiny muffled sound came from the phone. She held it back against her ear.

"Can you hear me, Mags? Terrible line. Maybe it's the weather." Mags looked up into a cloudless blue sky. "It's sunny here," she managed.

"Lucky you. We've had a thunderstorm this morning. Our trip to Hampton Court maze was a wash out. Which means Tam gets to thrash us both at Monopoly, so she's not too disappointed. Do you want to speak to her?"

Mags could hold it together with her twin, but she wasn't convinced she could stop the tears if she heard her daughter's voice. "No, don't drag her away from the game. I'll be flying to Boston in a few hours. I'll call later."

"Well, good to hear your voice, Sis. Everything here is— as your precocious daughter would say—tickety boo. Although I'm jealous of you getting all the good weather. Hold on a sec."

After a few seconds of silence, Kit spoke again. "Just wanted to go somewhere Tam couldn't hear me. She was weird about it. Don't know why. I think she should be proud, having such an amazing talent. But it seemed to upset her."

"What did?" The prickling sensation on her skin came back. "What upset her?"

"She's fine now. It was over an hour ago. We distracted her with some rampant capitalism in the form of a board game."

"Kit! What upset her?"

"All right, all right. It was the picture she drew this morning."

Mags teetered on the edge of losing control. She would

not let that happen. With a monumental effort of will, she forced all her attention on Kit and what she needed to say to him. "Listen Kit. Do something for me. It's important."

Kit, always the joker in the family, heard the change in his sister's voice. "Tell me."

Mags hissed out a breath through clenched teeth. "The picture. Take a photograph. Text it. Do it now. I'll call you back when I have it."

There was a pause, longer than she could attribute to the delay on an international call. Then Kit chuckled, the relief obvious in the sound.

"No need, Sis."

"What do you mean, no need? Kit, I am deadly fucking serious here. Send it to me."

Kit's tone was conciliatory. "No, no, don't get me wrong, I am taking you seriously, Sis. I promise you. It's just that I don't need to send it. Tam's picture—which is brilliant by the way, we might even get it framed—is of number two hundred and seventy-three, Aubrey Terrace."

Mags stopped breathing.

She knew that address.

It was in London. Camden Lock. Kit's address.

Tam had drawn Kit's house.

CHAPTER TWENTY-ONE

When Kit and Mags were ten years old, they had asked their parents for BMX bikes. They had seen kids their age at the park, and their jumps made it look like they were flying. It looked effortless, graceful, exciting. The twins nagged for months, and on Christmas Day, two easily identifiable shapes waited under sheets on either side of the tree.

On the days when the snow and ice didn't stop them, they took their new bikes to the patch of green space behind the school and practised. Neither of them mastered the tricks they'd seen the other kids perform, but talent wasn't necessary for Evel Knievel-style jumps. Or so they told themselves. They borrowed a wooden plank from Dad's shed and loaded a rucksack with old bricks. The first attempt was undramatic. The ramp was only two bricks high, and neither of them quite had the nerve to attack the jump at speed, instead freewheeling towards it. As they were packing up, Mags noticed a small group of other riders passing, sniggering.

The twins returned the next day with an extra plank.

They built one ramp five bricks high, left a gap of six feet, and placed the landing ramp there. They had constructed their jump at the bottom of a slope behind the terraced houses. Mags won the coin toss and pushed her bike to the top of the hill. When she turned round, her hands tight on the brakes, the slope seemed much steeper, the plank impossibly narrow. She had been about to give it up, when she noticed the same group of kids watching from the road.

"Evel Knievel," she whispered. She looked at the chasm between the two makeshift ramps. "Grand Canyon."

She released the brakes, and the bike began to move. Her momentum built quickly, and she focussed on the ramp. She would hit it dead centre. She knew her speed was sufficient to launch her impressively into the air. And she knew they had placed the ramps too far apart.

The bike dropped towards the far ramp. The front wheel hit it hard, and her right wrist snapped. Mags twisted as she fell, and her cheek scraped across the edge of the bricks, later blossoming into a purple, green, and black bruise that lasted a week. She landed on top of her right arm. A roar of noise was followed by silence, and she blacked out for a few seconds.

When Mags opened her eyes, Kit was bending over her, his face white. She tried to breathe, and couldn't. Kit was wheezing too, with that weird twin connection everyone but them made so much of. She panicked. She had never been winded before, and even the agony of her shattered arm wasn't as bad as the terror of not being able to suck enough air into her lungs.

Mags remembered that moment now. This panic attack approached with the inevitability of that badly placed ramp. Her anxiety always followed a pattern. She would worry about one thing, then remember something else she needed to take care of. Once two or three subjects were circling, her attention inevitably lurched back to the horror of Clara's death. The memory of this would bring the loss of her daughter to the front of her mind and her thoughts, no longer under her control, would gain critical mass. That was when the symptoms became physical. The clench and burn of being winded, unable to find sufficient air to sustain life. The hundreds of thoughts jabbing at her consciousness coagulated into a cloud of terror and misery; enveloping her, squeezing every happy thought out of her mind as easily as wringing soapy water out of a flannel.

Tam had drawn a picture of Kit and David's house. Her daughter was—somehow—connected to the mind of a killer. Whether this was true didn't matter because Mags was convinced it was, and that knowledge tipped her into a full-blown attack. Eleven years ago, she hadn't been able to help Clara. Mags had thought nothing could be worse than that feeling of helplessness, but she had been wrong. Her conviction that a murderer had travelled to London, and was planning to kill her daughter, combined with her being —at best—a twelve-hour journey away, smothered her, drove her to her knees.

The phone slipped from her fingers. Her vision darkened. Sounds receded like they did after a swim, ears clogged with water. She took tiny gasps of air, never getting enough.

This must not happen. She had to warn Kit, tell them all to get out of the house. Now. But the pressure and the urgency added fuel to her attack.

Mags fainted.

When she opened her eyes, she was still kneeling. Patrice had grabbed her shoulders. He was sitting beside her on the dirt edge of the highway, his arm around her, drawing her towards him to lean on his shoulder. She couldn't turn to look at him, could do nothing other than stare at the ground. A faded Hershey bar wrapper skittered a few inches every time a car passed. She gulped, taking tiny yelps of air like a dreaming dog.

She had to warn them, had to tell Patrice. When she tried to speak, the words wouldn't form. "I-I-I-"

Patrice rubbed her arm. "Panic attack?"

Mags nodded.

"My mother used to get them," said Patrice. "She was addicted to Valium. When she stopped taking them, she had panic attacks. I learned how to help her. I'm going to talk. Your job is to listen."

Mags shook her head. She had to tell him. Had to save her daughter, her brother and David. Had to find a way of getting the words out. Forgetting every coping mechanism she knew, she tried to impose control over what was happening. It didn't work. Her yelping breaths became more frequent, and more painful. The darkness threatened to return.

"I'm serious, Mags. I know something just happened that brought on an attack. Something you need to deal with. I understand." He squeezed her shoulder. "But, however hard it seems, you need to let go of that for now. I want you to pay attention to what I'm saying. We'll talk about every-thing else soon. First, we need to get you better, okay?"

Patrice's voice was calm and quiet. Mags latched onto it like a drowning woman grabbing a rope.

"Let me tell you about my favourite book. It might surprise you. Graham Greene. The End Of The Affair. I read it first in my late teens. I read every book he had writ-ten, and that was one of the few that didn't impress me. Years later, after my divorce—older, and maybe a tad wiser

—I picked it up again. That second read was a revelation, Mags. That's the thing about great novels, isn't it? It only takes two people to make it great: the writer and the reader. The writer has done their part, but we have to bring something to it too. It was a different book the second time. About a third of the way in, I slowed down, drinking in every word, every phrase. It's not a long book, and I didn't want it to finish. It's about a guy who has an affair with a friend's wife during the Blitz. When the story begins, the love affair is over, but he's never been able to get past it. He hires a private detective to find out why she left him. Like many Graham Greene stories, it involves God, and religion. I don't think God comes out of it too well. I'm not even sure love comes out of it too well. It's the kind of story that keeps you awake at night, asking questions. Does life have meaning, or is that a concept humans mistakenly apply in the hope that their existence has value? Does God exist? If he does, what kind of God? It didn't change my mind. I'm an atheist. But a much better writer than I'll ever be believed in God, and that made me less dismissive of those who make the same choice. It also taught me that love—whatever that is—is not always a force for good. It can be unhealthy. That makes it sound like a depressing read, but somehow it isn't. It's as bleak a book as Greene ever wrote, but I always come away from it uplifted. I couldn't tell you why, Mags. Maybe, by writing beautifully about darkness, he brought some light into it. I don't know."

Mags listened to him speak. Her breathing was returning to normal.

"I've never talked about that book to anybody. Too private. I should have talked about The Princess Bride instead. Now that's a story where the movie was as good as the book, probably because the same guy wrote it. Oh well, too late now. How ya feeling?"

The worst was over. Mags knew what she was supposed to do now. She was supposed to ease her thoughts away from what had brought on the attack and mindfully perform a simple task. If she had been at home, she would have mopped the floor or done the washing up. Find something to focus her attention on. The thoughts would come back—there was no stopping them—but she would be better prepared. The problem was, she had no time. She had to do something about Tam, and it had to be now. Even as she decided, darkness reappeared at the edges of her vision.

One step at a time.

"My phone."

Patrice handed it to her. She thumbed it on and went to *recent calls*. Only allowing herself to think one step ahead of what she was doing, she pressed call. The battery was at three percent. *Shit.*

Kit picked up after the first ring.

"Mags? Are you okay? We lost you."

One step at a time.

"Kit, you need to get out of the house. All of you. Do it now."

One advantage of being a twin was that there was no need to explain. Kit knew she meant it, and he knew it was urgent. "Okay, Mags. Where should we go?"

"It doesn't matter. I'm coming home. I'll call as soon as I land. Don't go back to the house. Do it now. Please."

"Okay, Mags. I'll call you back when we're out."

"Wait!"

"I'm still here."

"The picture. Which side of the house did Tam draw?"

The briefest of hesitations. "The front. Why?"

"Leave by the back door. Don't go round the front. Get a few streets away, then call a cab."

"You're scaring me."

"Good. Get out. Now." Mags ended the call.

One step at a time.

She turned to Patrice. "Airport," she said.

CHAPTER TWENTY-TWO

In the car, Mags breathed as if in labour, every breath hissing out. The dashboard clock ticked through the longest five minutes of her life. She called Kit back.

Her phone was dead.

"No... no." She waved it at Patrice. "Charger?"

"Different brand. It won't fit your phone. Wanna borrow mine?"

He handed it over. The only numbers Mags knew by heart were her home number, and the three numbers they'd had growing up. She couldn't call anyone.

"Shit, shit, shit." She breathed faster.

"Mags." That same calm tone. She turned, wide-eyed. "Don't know the number?" he said. She nodded miserably.

"Okay, that's something you can do nothing about. But I heard what you said on the phone. They are getting out of the house, right?"

"Yes. Yes."

"Okay. You did what you needed to do. Now take a few minutes, listen to me talk nonsense again, and let your breathing go back to normal. Got it?"

Ten minutes later, and after he'd thoroughly explained his issues with the Star Wars prequels, Mags' breathing no longer sounded like an asthmatic puppy. Patrice called the airport.

"What's the first flight to London leaving after,"—he checked the satnav—"six o'clock this evening? Thank you. Could you put me through to the ticket desk, please?" Long seconds passed, then "Hello? Can you tell me if there are any seats left on the eighteen fifty to London? Great. Hold on."

He looked across at Mags. Her breathing had steadied, but she was sweating and her skin looked pale and waxy. "I'll take it. Ticket in the name of Barkworth. If I pay now, can she pick it up at the desk? Thank you, you're very kind."

He gave his credit card number and ended the call. "I'll drop you at the terminal. Go straight to the Virgin Atlantic desk. There's a ticket waiting. You get in at six fifty-five."

Mags swallowed. "I'll pay you back. Give me your bank details. I'll pay you back, Patrice."

"We'll talk about it when you call me. You have my number and my email. Mags." She looked at him. "Do I need to take this to the cops? What's happened? Are you able to tell me?"

One step. One step at a time.

Mags tried to imagine she was describing a movie, not real life. It helped. She told Patrice about Tam's latest picture as if it were someone else's daughter, someone else's brother, and someone else's brother-in-law who were being stalked by a serial killer.

When she had finished, he was quiet for a long time, his fingers constantly on the bridge of his nose.

"This is fucked up. You know that, right?" He didn't wait

for her to answer. "You believe Tam has some kind of telepathic connection with this psycho, right?"

At the mention of her daughter's name, Mags felt the tears spill over her eyelashes. Patrice glanced at her, then back at the road.

"Keep breathing, Mags. I can't go to the cops with this. They'll laugh in my face."

"You don't believe me."

"That's not what I said. Everything I know, everything I've learned, every story I've researched and written, tells me that there's no way that a serial killer in America can communicate telepathically with an eleven-year-old girl in London."

"You don't believe me," she repeated.

"I'll level with you, Mags. I don't *want* to believe you. Partly because I'm a reporter, and everything is circumstantial. But mostly, I don't want to believe you because of what's happening in London. If it's true, your family is in terrible danger. And I don't want that to be true. Look, you said yourself that you struggled with your mental health. That you've had panic attacks before."

"So I'm crazy? Fine."

"Again, that's not what I said, Mags."

"You didn't have to."

They arrived at the airport in silence. Mags was out of the door and dragging her suitcase from the back seat before Patrice had taken his seatbelt off.

"Mags."

She turned and looked at him. Rumpled, hat in hand, his eyes trying to communicate something he couldn't put into words. Or maybe he was just relieved to see her go.

"Thank you, Patrice," she said. "Thank you for getting me here."

She was in the terminal building, heading for the check in, when she heard running footsteps behind her.

"Mags! Wait up."

She slowed, but didn't stop walking. Patrice came up alongside her.

"One question. You owe me that, Mags."

"What is it?"

"You said your husband is a geneticist in Boston. What's the name of his company?"

It was the last thing Mags had expected. She was so surprised, she answered without thinking.

"Edgegen Technology. Goodbye, Mr Martino."

After clearing security, Mags bought a portable phone charger and plugged it in. The flight was boarding. She checked her phone every ten seconds, but it only flickered back to life as she reached her seat. Economy this time. Squeezed between two strangers. As soon as the phone had booted up, she called Kit.

No answer.

The plane taxied to the runway, and a stewardess asked her to turn off the phone. The third time of asking, when Mags was praying Kit would pick up, she gave her the choice of turning the phone off or having the aircraft turn around and go back to the gate where she would leave the aircraft before being arrested. She turned it off, while her fellow passengers tutted.

The plane's engines rose to a scream and it lurched forward.

Eight hours and five minutes until she reached London.

CHAPTER TWENTY-THREE

In her early twenties, Mags had once smoked a joint at a party, not knowing it was far stronger than the weed she tried years before at the sixth form disco. This was hydroponically grown skunk, and it made her a passenger in her own body for twenty minutes. She remembered waves of panic, while a tiny part of her brain insisted that it would pass, that she just had to ride it out and she would be all right.

The plane journey from Atlanta to Heathrow was worse than an eight hour, skunk-induced psychotic nightmare.

As the 767-400 climbed to its thirty-five thousand feet cruising altitude, Mags knew there was no way she would get through the journey without a plan. If she wasn't careful, her thoughts might trigger another severe panic attack. If that happened, the crew might sedate her—best-case scenario—or divert the flight to get her to hospital. She couldn't let that happen.

There were earplugs and an eye mask in the bag they handed out. Mags ripped the bag open, put the earplugs in, and pulled the mask over her eyes. After a second, she pulled the mask up again and pressed the button above her head. When the stewardess appeared, her smile was a little forced after the phone incident. Mags spoke deliberately, avoiding giving vent to the scream threatening to break through.

"I will sleep for the whole flight. Please don't wake me for food."

"Of course, Madam." She looked relieved.

Mags was in the middle seat of a row of three in the centre of the plane. No one would have to climb over her to go to the toilet. She was certain she wouldn't sleep. For the first hour, images of Tam, Kit, and David kept coming into her mind. She wished now she hadn't read the news stories about the Bedroom Killer. He had murdered every adult with something the police described as a home-made garrotte. This was, they thought, constructed from very strong fishing line tied to wooden handles. He either approached his victims from behind, looping wire over their heads then pulling it tight, or—if they were lying down—he slipped the wire behind their heads as he knelt astride them, pinning their arms down. A sob wrenched itself out of Mags' tormented body. She followed it with a series of coughs so as not to make her neighbours suspicious.

She couldn't rest, but a lack of light, combined with the constant white noise hum of the engines leaking through the earplugs brought on a strange, semi-conscious state. It wasn't sleep, more a series of short blackouts, punctuated by nightmare images and waves of dread.

When, at last, the plane began its descent, Mags lifted her mask, blinking. She wouldn't have been surprised to have found her fellow passengers replaced by demons, the plane gone, her surroundings obscured by the roaring, spitting flames of Hell. Her sense of time was distorted. To the left, through an open blind, the sinuous Thames sparkled in the morning sun as it wound through the centre of London. She licked her lips. They were dry and flaky.

The woman on her right—young, dip-dyed pink hair, each ear pierced multiple times, handed her a small bottle of orange juice. "Saved it for you," she said. "Thought you might need it."

Mags took the proffered bottle and burst into tears.

"Thank you." She drank it as the young woman watched, her expression a mix of sympathy and wariness Mags might have found amusing under different circumstances.

The moment that the plane's wheels squealed and bumped on the tarmac of the runway, Mags turned on her phone. The old man on her left looked over. He was about to voice his disapproval when he looked into her eyes. Whatever he saw there, it made him shut his mouth so fast it made a sound like a clap. She watched the phone come on, and the mobile signal appear in the top left corner of the screen. It buzzed in her hand as a message came in. She held her breath, but it was a generic text advising her of the cost of UK calls. There were no other messages. She called Kit. The phone rang and rang. She tried David's number. It went straight to voicemail. There were three missed calls from the same unknown number.

It wasn't until she was through customs and heading for the taxi rank, that she gave up trying to call, another idea occurring to her. She stopped walking, looked at her phone, suddenly unwilling to do it. But she had to know. Mags opened Google on the phone, typed in *Camden Lock* and pressed *News*.

She waited.

CAMDEN KILLING: POLICE APPEAL FOR WITNESSES. She scrolled down. The police tape used by the British Constabulary was blue-and-white, not the gaudy yellow of their American counterparts. The photograph showed it pulled across the gate in front of 273 Aubrey Terrace.

"Tam." Her knees buckled. She hit the pavement hard. A turbaned man rushed over and helped her to her feet. "Are you okay? Do you need help?"

"Slipped. No. Fine." She had to get there, had to know what happened. "Need a taxi." The man insisted on walking her to the car and seeing her safely inside.

She didn't remember telling the taxi driver the address, but she must have said something, because he pulled out, merged into the traffic, and headed towards North London.

Something is wrong. I should feel different. This is not what I was expecting. I'm not sure what to do next.

It was so clear up to now. The dreams made it clear. I am like Joseph in the old Testament. He had dreams that told the future. Not just Joseph. Other prophets had dreams that came true. I am no prophet, but I know the Universe is listening to me. The dreams are another sign that I am chosen. I must try to live up to that honor. But I failed this time.

The dreams started back in Ocala. The night after I first knew I wasn't alone, that someone, or something, watched over me. I didn't know the dreams were important then, didn't recognise them for what they were. I often dream during my micro-sleeps of two or three minutes. Vivid dreams. Strange. Scary, sometimes. Not these new dreams.

These are wonderful, and they are as real as anything I see when I'm awake.

In the dreams, I'm a kid again. But not back home in Florida. I see no one I know, go nowhere I recognise. In school I sit with kids who are maybe ten, eleven years old. They all wear the same dark blue sweater. When I look at my arms, I'm wearing it too. The teacher is a woman. There are no sounds in the dreams, so I don't know what she's saying. When I look outside, everything is strange. The trees, the buildings, even the color of the sky. All different, all wrong.

The dreams don't repeat themselves, but they have an atmosphere, a flavor. When I'm not in school, I'm in a house I don't know. I'm in a bedroom with a poster on the wall, bookshelves, a laptop on the desk. It's tidy. I've never seen so many books in one place outside of the library. Who wants to read so much?

It's the dream after the trailer park that gets me moving. Maybe the signs were clear before but I didn't know how to read them. Maybe this feeling of failure is a punishment for being so slow to understand. I don't know. But two things I see in my dream send me to the airport. First, I look out the window. The street is narrow, cars parked on both sides. It's only after I wake up that I know what was wrong. The cars. They were driving on the left-hand side of the street. My dreams are in a different country. Then I remember a poster in the bedroom. Five colored rings; 2012 in big numbers. A photograph of some skinny black guy kissing a gold medal. The Olympics. The cars. London.

I take the bus to the airport and hang out until I see someone my build with the same color hair at the check in desk. I don't have to kill him, just follow him into the bathroom and lift his passport right out of his bag while he dries his hands. Some things are meant to be.

It's the first long-haul flight I've ever been on, and it's tough. Everyone falls asleep. I start wondering if maybe I could help some of them. Crazy. I would get caught for sure. But the urge is so strong I pinch the skin on my forearms to stop myself. Soon I have a line of bruises, real peaches.

I figured it would be easier once I got to England. The dreams would get clearer, show me where to go. But they don't. Not at first. I can't rely on them. Sometimes two or three days go by without a single dream. Sometimes, I dream four times in a day.

If I learn how to do it, I think I could dream while I'm awake. If I am being led, I must learn how to follow.

I checked my savings today. Not much left. But the signs are so much clearer now, and there are more of them. It's the end times. If I play my part, I will find peace.

Yesterday, a new dream. This time I see the name of a street, and a number on a door. I buy a map and go there. It's a difficult place to check out - the street is too busy. I stand opposite the house, watching for as long as I dare. It's strange. The people passing by don't look at me, don't care about what I'm doing. But still I feel I'm being watched. The feeling is stronger than ever here.

And, for a while, standing there, I know she's there, inside that house. It's the first time I'm clear about my purpose.

Coming to London was the right move. I am being guided by an unseen hand, and someone has led me to this exact location.

I'm tired. Soon, real soon, I will have rest. I, too, will sleep.

I am here because one soul needs me more than any other of the billions in this world. I do not know her name, but I know we are bound together. Sometimes my dreams are her dreams. Sometimes, when the excitement builds before I begin my work, she is with me, like an angel by my side.

I am here to free us both.

A few hours later, I go back to the street, watch the house, but my certainty is gone. A ghost of it remains, like the smell of stale beer the morning after a party.

Maybe it's better if I wait.

Then I see a light go on in the house, my stomach tightens, and I make my mistake.

I walk across the street when there's a gap in the traffic. I open the gate. My bag contains everything I bought since coming to London. Underpants, socks, towel, toothbrush, toothpaste, sledgehammer. I place it on the front step.

I lift the sledgehammer, take aim, and swing like I'm in my own Olympics.

My aim is true. The hammer drives the lock through the wood and the door swings open. I check the street, then step inside.

Stairs. I head up. A man's face above me. He yells, "Hey!" and disappears.

I run. He will not be thinking clearly yet. He will panic.

At the top of the stairs I see him. He has a cellphone in his hand. He's quick. I reach into my pocket and pull out the device. I used wooden handles from a jump rope to make this one. It feels different in my hands.

He runs but I'm faster. He has his back to me now, which makes it easier. I jump when I'm close, looping the wire around his neck and snapping it tight. He does what they all do. His hands go to the wire, try to loosen it. Folk don't think clearly when they are under attack. They should reach for me, not the wire. But they never do, and those few seconds are all that it takes to weaken him.

He crashes into a wall, slides to his knees, pivots, and

ends up face down on the floor. He fades quickly, feet tap-tap-tapping on the hard wood. I hold the wire in place until I'm sure.

I sniff in disgust. He has soiled himself.

Un-looping the wire, I tug it out of his fleshy throat. He is bleeding. I used too much force, but I wanted to be fast. The dreams have not led me to him. I have seen his face, but I am not here for him. It's someone else I'm looking for. There is a kitchen ahead of me, a corridor to my left with two doors. One, half-open, reveals a bathroom.

The second door is closed. Bedroom, I guess. I have seen this house in my dreams. He doesn't live here alone. There must be others.

I roll him over and take one last look. He is peaceful. "You can sleep now," I whisper.

I walk towards the bedroom.

CHAPTER TWENTY-FOUR

When the cab turned left into Aubrey Terrace, Mags opened the door before it stopped. As the driver cursed her, she fumbled in her purse for cash, finding only dollars. She stared at her credit card, forgetting what to do next, before muscle memory took over and she jammed it into the machine. When she got out, the taxi didn't move away. The driver honked the horn, and she looked at the open door in confusion, then dragged her case out. When she shut the door, the taxi jerked away from the kerb with one last long blast of the horn.

Across the road, a policeman guarded the shattered front door of 273. Twenty feet of road, another ten feet of garden path, a policeman and a broken door lay between Mags and finding out what had happened. Mags didn't move. She couldn't move.

Her phone rang. Unknown number. She brought the phone to her ear, said nothing.

"Mrs Barkworth? Margaret? This is Detective Sergeant Harrison. Can you hear me?"

When Mags spoke, her lips could only form one shape. "Tam."

"Your daughter is safe, Mags. She's safe, and she is unharmed. Where are you?"

Mags tried to speak again, but it was beyond her. Tam was alive. She was okay. She stared at the blue and white tape, the young policeman in front of the door stroking the suggestion of a moustache.

"Mrs Barkworth? I can take you to her. Where are you?" A pause. "Never mind. Are you opposite the house?"

Shocked, Mags looked up. A woman's silhouette raised a hand in the upstairs window, and Mags automatically did the same. The voice came back on the line. "Stay where you are. I'm coming down."

DI Harrison insisted Mags call her Hilary. As the Detective Inspector crossed the road, a police car drew up. Hilary Harrison put Mags' case in the boot and Mags got into the back. Instead of getting into the passenger seat, Hilary opened the rear door, slid inside and took Mags' hand. "Tam is fine, but she's had a terrible shock. I'm afraid I have some very bad news for you."

———

Three days later

———

The family liaison officer's name was Florence. This was the fourth time she'd visited since David's murder. Bradley had excused himself and gone to his office as soon as she arrived.

"Do people make jokes?" said Kit.

Florence raised her eyebrows. "Jokes?"

She was older, mid-fifties, perhaps. Her greying hair was cut short and she used no make-up. Florence always wore the same expression: a disconcerting mixture of compassion and professional distance. Mags supposed that was her job, in a nutshell. Florence offered support and passed on what information she could about the ongoing police enquiry into David's death.

"Your name," he said. "Florence. Often shortened to Flo. F L O. Family Liaison Officer. Do people make jokes?"

Florence blinked. "Oh. No. Not usually."

Mags looked at her brother. He was trying too hard. His timing was all off, his voice flat, his body slow. Mags sometimes walked into a room and found him standing there. More than once, she had taken his arm and guided him to the kitchen, or—if it was the middle of the night—back to the spare room, where he had slept since David's death.

Florence drained the last of her tea. They were drinking tea because that was the appropriate British response to a violent murder in the family.

Mags looked around the kitchen. Clock, sink, fridge, table, chair, Florence.

"Thank you for the tea." Florence stood up. "You have my number. If there are any more questions, call me."

"Any more questions?" Kit's voice was emotionless. He spoke as if he were reciting a shopping list. "Just the usual, Florence. Who killed my husband? Why would anyone kill him? Why, in three days, haven't you found the sick murderous bastard who did this? With DNA evidence and CCTV on every fucking corner, why don't you have the first fucking clue who wrapped wire round the neck of the only man I have ever loved, and strangled him? Those questions, Florence."

The FLO nodded, the same expression still on her face.

Mags tried to imagine a different expression. Happy, disappointed, angry, aroused. No. It was impossible.

"As soon as there are any developments, I will be in touch. If not myself, one of my colleagues. I promise."

It was only people in authority or young sales people trying to impress who used the word *myself* in that context. As if suggesting there was another version available, a superior, more helpful version, perhaps. *I am incompetent and untrustworthy, but myself is just the opposite. You'll be in safe hands there.*

Mags put the extra cup in the dishwasher and turned to her twin. Grief hadn't aged him. If anything, it was the reverse. He looked like a little boy.

She had tried talking to Kit about America, why she had called to warn them. How she had known. Each time, her brother had waved her into silence, or walked away. He couldn't process it. Not yet. David had gone back to Aubrey Terrace to pick up his laptop, and had never come back. Dealing with that was as much as Kit could handle, and he wasn't handling that well. But Mags knew they had to talk, and that she needed Bradley to be part of that conversation.

She had told Detective Inspector Harrison she was sure the killer was American, that he had flown to London in the past week, leaving behind two bodies in an Atlanta trailer park. She told her about her trip, and about Tam's pictures. Even as she had spoken, she could hear how crazy it sounded. No one said so. DI Harrison pressed record on the tape player, asked questions, and took notes. But when they called Mags in next day, it was a junior officer who sat down with her. Early in the interview, the policewoman asked about her mental health. She went home.

At least they were watching the house. Unable to establish a motive, but knowing David's death wasn't because of a botched robbery, they were protecting Kit, in case he had been the intended victim. Two officers in an unmarked car at the front of the house, and regular patrols checking nearby streets.

Tam was upstairs, reading. Her grieving process was the most natural and robust of all. She burst into tears several times a day, and at night, would come to Mags like a toddler with a scraped knee, climbing into her lap and sobbing. A meaningless mumble of reassurance while Mags stroked her hair was enough to send her back to sleep.

Mags described everything, from the moment Kit had seen the photo in America until the phone call when she discovered Tam had drawn their house.

Her twin and her husband listened in silence. She had asked them not to interrupt. Kit watched her from somewhere inside a haze of prescription drugs and alcohol. Sometimes, his eyes lost focus and his gaze drifted around the room before settling back onto the drawings spread out on the table. Bradley was the opposite: so engaged with what she was saying it became uncomfortable. As instructed, he didn't ask questions, but he made notes.

Of all the reactions she had expected from Bradley, this one hadn't made the list. It was the look on his face that threw her. She had expected scepticism, perhaps, or disappointment at her secrecy. Maybe even pity, if he didn't believe her story. But this. This she couldn't understand. When she said Tam was drawing murder scenes, he had looked up at her so sharply, eyes widening, that she had stopped speaking. It was only later that Mags remembered when she'd seen that look before. It had been at the first scan, when they had discovered she was pregnant with twins.

She downplayed Patrice's involvement, mentioning a reporter had given her a lift to Hinesville, and leaving it at that. Martino's role changed none of the essential facts.

When she had finished, she poured herself a glass of wine. Kit mumbled. He cleared his throat and tried again.

"Tam? Is she okay? She's okay, isn't she?"

There was a pleading look on his face, a desperate need for reassurance.

"She's fine, Kit. She'll be fine."

Kit poured more vodka into his glass, not bothering with tonic water. Mags said nothing.

To her surprise, Bradley closed his notebook, gathered the pictures into a pile, and stood up.

"Well?" said Mags. Why wasn't he asking any questions?

"Well," he echoed. "You know how this sounds, right? You told the police the same thing. What did they say?"

Mags took a gulp of wine. She was allowing herself one glass; she wanted to be alert if Tam needed her, but she wished she could chase oblivion, like Kit. "They think I'm crazy. They've assigned my case to the tea boy. The theory that an American serial killer has travelled to London because our daughter is drawing pictures of his crime scenes..."

"Quite. It sounds insane, Mags. But I know you're not crazy. Just scared, and vulnerable."

He scooped up the drawings and walked away. Mags called after him.

"Where are you going? We need to talk about Tam. What are we going to do? Do you believe me? How else can we explain what's happened? I need you. Don't walk away."

Bradley stopped in the doorway. "I'll scan these and

send them over to Dad. He has high-level contacts he can call. We'll find out what's going on. You really think Tam has a telepathic link with a psycho in Atlanta?"

He might have just described her as scared and vulnerable, but he wasn't being reassuring, or caring.

"Don't you think it's more likely this sicko posts photographs on some dark website before he kills, and Tam has found them? Come on, Mags, did you think this through at all?"

Again, Mags avoided bringing Patrice into the conversation. "Yes," she said. "Of course. I'm not an idiot, Bradley. So explain, if that's true, how he found us? The killer is in London. He wasn't looking for David, or Kit. He was coming for Tam. She was there until I told them all to get out. If David hadn't gone back... "

"Listen to yourself." Bradley sounded angry. His words were angry. But it was like watching an angry character in a movie, when you'd seen the same actor in a romantic comedy the night before. She didn't buy it.

He pointed at her.

"For the sake of argument, let's say this serial killer posts on the dark web. If he's good with technology, he could trace the IP addresses of people who visit his website. Maybe that's how he picks out his victims. Have you considered that?"

"No. No. I mean, I suppose..." She couldn't think fast enough to find a flaw in his argument, but there had to be one. Then she had it. "But if you're right, why did he go to Kit and David's house? The IP address would have brought him here."

Bradley was silent for a few moments as he thought it through. A brisk shake of the head signalled his rejection of her suggestion. "You're right. He would have come here first.

But I'm guessing Tam took her laptop with her to Uncle Kit's."

Mags felt her skin prickle. She took another swallow of wine. He was right. He must be right. She wanted him to be right, because the alternative was too terrifying. But she couldn't quite bring herself to accept it. "If you're right, we must take this to the police," she said.

"No. I'm calling Dad. If we give this to the local cops, they'll hand it to some underpaid geek on a trainee scheme. If they take us seriously, they'll need to contact the FBI, or Homeland Security. They'll have to set up a combined operation, share intelligence, do everything by the book. How long will that take? No, Mags. Edgegen has connections with the government and the military and they owe us. If this sick bastard has a website, they'll find it, and they'll trace it back to him. Once we have a name, we can find him."

Mags knew Edgegen was a successful, well regarded company, but the influence Bradley was talking about was way beyond anything she had imagined. He had always been tight-lipped about his work, citing non-disclosure agreements and security concerns, but she had never guessed at anything like this. "How... " she began, and stopped. She focused on one question and started again. "Even if Edgegen has these connections, what can be done that isn't already being done? The American police, the FBI, all those agencies, surely they are already looking for the serial killer? What can you do that they can't?"

Bradley waved Tam's pictures at her. "They don't have these," he said. "I'm gonna do everything to close this asshole down so we can all sleep at night."

With an obvious effort, he softened his tone.

"Mags. I don't know why you didn't come to me straight

away with this. I'm sorry you felt you couldn't. That's a conversation for another time." He held her gaze for a moment, kissed her forehead, then headed for the basement.

Mags picked up the open wine bottle, put it down again, rinsed her glass, and went to bed.

Regular glances at the bedside clock punctuated a restless night, alone in the double bed. 12:15, 2:04. 03:10. It wasn't until 03:45 that Bradley crept into bed and she drifted back into an uneasy sleep.

CHAPTER TWENTY-FIVE

Mags was awake at five-thirty. Through an inch-wide gap in the curtains, she looked for occupants in the parked cars outside. Whether it was budget constraints, or the police thought the threat had passed, their protection had gone.

She looked in on Kit. He was asleep, twitching and mumbling, wearing one of David's shirts. Closing the door, she crossed the landing to Tam's room.

"Tam?"

Tam was sitting upright in bed, eyes open, her head moving from left to right.

"Tam? Honey? You awake?"

No response. Mags recognised the same expression she had seen the morning Tam produced the Atlanta drawing. If this was what absence seizures looked like, it was an apt description. Tam was there, but she wasn't there. Her body moved, her eyes looked around her, but she wasn't seeing what was in front of her.

Scared to disturb her, but not wanting to leave her alone, Mags sat down and stroked her daughter's hair. "I'm here," she whispered. Tam didn't respond.

Mags said it again. This time, Tam looked at her. Mags jerked backwards in shock. It wasn't her daughter, it was a stranger.

"Mum?"

The moment passed and it was Tam again.

Her heart palpitating, Mags took a second to reassure herself that her daughter was back. Was that how a mouse feels when it looks up at a passing shadow and a silent owl drops from the sky?

"Tam. I'm sorry. Did I wake you?"

In answer, Tam hugged her mother. She spoke into Mags' hair. "I was dreaming. It was different, like I wasn't here. I dreamed I was someone else." She shivered.

"It's early," said Mags. "Everyone else is asleep. Fancy a fried egg sandwich?"

Tam straightened her shoulders and nodded.

"Rather."

My whole existence has led me to this moment. I am sorry for folk who go through life believing everything is random. I know better. There's a plan, and some of us know our part in it. I am grateful for that.

When I was a kid, I was angry. Angry my dad left us before I was born. Angry my mom wasn't cut out to be a mother. And angry about being sick all the time. As I grew up, I learned to dislike everyone around me, the so-called normal people. People who spend half their life asleep. I tried not to resent my condition, tried to accept I would never experience proper rest. But it affected everything.

At school they said I had learning difficulties. That's

what the teacher told Mom, anyhow. The kids used another word. They said I was retarded. They left me out of their games, didn't invite me to parties. So I hated them. I wasn't stupid, just tired all the time. And they were plain ignorant.

Mom wasn't a churchgoer, but she had a Bible, and she watched hellfire preachers on public television. I read the Bible because the people on TV—the politicians, the actors at the Oscars, even the president—all quoted from it, all believed it. They thanked God for their success. I wasn't sure what to thank God for.

I tried finding out more about what was wrong with me in reference books at the library. When I was older, I searched the internet. There were other people who struggled to sleep, but not many like me. Mom said I never slept for more than a few minutes at a stretch when I was in my cot. Nothing changed as I got older.

In my twenties, browsing a forum for the sleep-deprived, I found a post asking for volunteers. A research company offering decent money for drug trials. Their website listed conditions that qualified candidates for their program. Sleep disorders were on the list.

I called the number. I asked about money. The trial paid more than I made in three months pumping gas, so I packed my things and headed north.

There were over thirty of us at first. We met in a hotel conference room. The doctors talked about new drugs, we signed forms, we stayed for the weekend, giving blood samples and filling out forms. On Sunday, everyone was due to go home.

One of the trial doctors knocked on my hotel room door late on Saturday night. He asked about my sleep problems, but I could tell he didn't care about my answers. He was leading up to something. Finally, he asked if I would *consider a more serious procedure. An operation. Experimental, but it might cure my disorder. There were risks. He named a figure. I did some calculations, figured I wouldn't have to work for a couple years. Before I signed, he asked about family and friends. I told him Mom was drinking herself to death, and I'd never had a friend. I signed.*

The next day they collected me in a private ambulance. They sedated me on the way to the hospital.

Time passed. I don't know how long. That's a side-effect of never sleeping normally, I guess. I can't tell how long I was unconscious for. When I woke up, the same doctor asked me how I felt. I remember touching the bandage on the shaved part of my head. The hair on that side was rough stubble. After a lifetime of not sleeping, I had been unconscious for over a day. But it wasn't the same. I wasn't rested. I didn't feel the peace I hoped for.

They gave me the use of a small apartment. I'm sure they watched me. The doctor came by every day, ran tests, asked me how I slept. He asked me to be patient, said it would take time. He always had a list of questions. Some of them were plain weird. He wanted to hear about my dreams, and asked if I ever dreamed during the day, or saw visions.

One day, weeks later, I decided it had all been for nothing. The operation had given me nothing other than the scar on my head. It was my lowest ebb. I imagined ways to end my life.

That morning, I got on my knees and prayed. I never had religion like Mom did, but it seemed the right thing to do if I was about to die. And that's when it happened. At the foot of the bed, hands folded, my left eye twitching the way it does at times. I mumbled words and phrases I remembered from the Bible. My prayers were dry, mechanical. I guess that's how it is for most folk, most of the time. I thought no one was listening. But someone was.

I didn't hear a voice, saw no blinding light. Nothing like that. It was more like something unfolding in my mind. A flower, maybe. Petals opening, looking for the sun.

The words I had been praying stuck in my mind during this unfolding, this new sense of another presence. I repeated the words, and they had meaning now. The peace of the Lord. The peace of the Lord be with you.

I thought about the money, but only for a second. I had saved everything, since they were feeding me and the apartment was rent-free. The research guys could keep the rest of their money. Their operation hadn't worked, so I owed them nothing.

I packed the few things I owned, left the apartment, took the first bus without knowing where it was heading. As I looked at the faces around me—on the street, in the bus station—I saw pain. I saw exhaustion. They needed peace just as I did. The peace of the Lord. And I could bring them that peace.

The bus headed south. Two days later, I was back in Florida. As I got closer, I made plans. I had been given a purpose, and nothing would deflect me from my path.

Since then, I've followed it through the United States and, finally, across the Atlantic.

It ends here.

I'm standing on a sidewalk in London, and the blood is singing in my veins. I was drawn to this place as surely as a fish on a hook.

The sky is getting lighter. This city wakes early. I feel the other presence in my mind bloom. It's not faint. It's burning me up. I am about to meet an angel. She is here, and it is time. No more planning. No more waiting.

I smile, step off the sidewalk, and walk towards the house.

It's laughable, what happens next. Or it would be, if it didn't nearly end me.

I look left as I step off the curb. When you grow up with a sleep disorder, you learn to take care when crossing the street.

But I forget I'm in the wrong country.

The van brakes before it hits me—the tires scream—but it's too late. Everyone says time slows in a crisis like this, but not for me. For me, it's two explosions of pain, one straight after the other.

Bang. The van hits my hip. It shatters a split second before my body twists and my cheek smashes into the windshield.

Bang. I'm on the ground. My arm smacks the street with a sound like fast-twisted bubble wrap - a rapid series of pops. My skull flares with new light, red, liquid, wrong. Needle-stabs of pain. Something gives way a few inches under the scar from my operation.

I am still conscious when I see her.

The woman gets to me first. I recognise her, but I can't speak. I can't even move my eyes to look at her. Behind the woman is a smaller figure. It's her. I've come all this way. Thousands of miles, and there she is, a few feet away. I can't move. Something mutes my hearing, everything is confused.

Don't die. I latch onto this and clasp it to myself, this thought, this belief, this vow.

Don't die, don't die, don't die.

When I black out, it's not like the movies. The sky doesn't tilt, there is no dark tunnel. I don't lose focus, or see blackness coming in from the edge of the frame.

I'm there one second. Then I'm gone.

CHAPTER TWENTY-SIX

Tam's scream and the sickening impact of the van hitting the pedestrian outside happened at exactly the same moment. Eleven years of therapy had taught Mags to interrogate her own thought processes, question her conclusions. She mentally rearranged the facts to make sense. The crash must have happened first, followed by Tam's scream a fraction of a second later.

Mags was out of the door first. The driver of the van—young, with a wispy beard and dreadlocks—was only just exiting the vehicle. He was shaking, and could barely bring himself to look at the man lying on the ground.

Mags took charge. "Sit down." She pointed at the kerb, and the young driver did as she said, putting his head in his hands and moaning.

At first, Mags thought the man was dead. His body was twisted, his jeans bloodied and torn. One of his arms was bent the wrong way, and a piece of bone had pierced the skin just below the elbow. He had a head wound. Mags couldn't tell how bad it was, but blood was seeping from the back of his skull, matting his hair, glistening like an oil spill in the morning sun.

When she got close, she saw his chest move. He was breathing. A bloody bubble emerged from one side of his mouth as he exhaled, and she couldn't help looking away when she caught sight of his ruined cheek. Then pity overcame squeamishness, and she looked back, kneeling in front of him.

He was focussing on something behind her. There was a strange intensity in his expression, a tension around his eyes, as he clung to the last shred of consciousness. Mags looked over her shoulder.

Tam stood there. In the middle of the road. Staring. Not moving. Looking at the injured man.

"Wake Dad up," shouted Mags. "Tell him to call an ambulance. Bring a blanket. Tam!"

At first, she wasn't sure Tam had heard. Her daughter was still staring. Then she blinked, looked at Mags, and moved, sprinting to the house.

Mags turned back. The man's eyes were closed now. He was still breathing. Each breath brought with it a distant gurgle, like the water tank in their attic when she ran a bath. In this context, it was a shocking sound. Mags thought his lungs might be filling with blood. He must have internal injuries along with the obvious broken bones and lacerations.

She leaned down and put her face close to his. He smelled of cheap shampoo mixed with the dark, pungent, iron stench of fresh blood. "We've called an ambulance. You're going to be all right. Please. I don't know if you can hear me, but if you can, my name is Mags. You're not alone. You will be looked after. The hospital is close and they will take care of you."

The gurgling sound was worse, and his lips—where they weren't wet with blood—had taken on a bluish tinge. Mags found part of his head that was uninjured and stroked his hair. There was an old scar there. She could feel the ridge of hard skin.

Tam brought the blanket, and Mags covered his prone body.

"Is he...?"

"He's still breathing. Is the ambulance coming?"

As if summoned by her words, a siren cranked into life in a nearby street, sending a dozen hedge sparrows into the air from the privet outside number twenty-eight. Blue lights flashed in the windows opposite before the ambulance appeared.

She stood up as the paramedics approached and let them do their work.

Bradley came out of the house. While Mags answered questions, and directed a paramedic to the van driver, who was still moaning, her husband put an arm around her shoulder. One of the paramedics moved, putting her head flat on the road to examine the head injury. Bradley's hand squeezed Mags' shoulder so tightly, she yelped and twisted away.

She looked at him. His face was set, rigid. "What's the matter?"

He said nothing, staring down at the broken figure, the shocking red splashes of blood sprayed across the street.

"Bradley. What is it?"

He turned his back on the scene, put his hands on his knees. "Oh," he murmured.

Mags led him away. She turned back to the paramedics. "Is it okay if I...?"

"Of course. My colleague will nip in to get your details in a minute."

In the kitchen, she made Bradley drink tea with three sugars. Her mother had always insisted sweet tea was essential in a crisis.

Bradley pulled a face, but he drank it.

"You're the last person I'd expect to be squeamish," she said. "In your profession, I mean. Genetics. And your degrees in medicine."

"One of the many reasons I didn't go into that line of work," he said. "The only time I see blood in the lab is when it's on a slide. It's hardly the same thing, is it?"

When Bradley had recovered his poise, he retreated to his office. An hour later, he emerged, took the car keys, and picked up his jacket from the back of a chair.

Mags stopped him at the door. "Where are you going? What did your dad say? Talk to me."

Bradley put a hand on her arm. "We traced him."

"What? You traced him? Who is he? Have you told the police? Has he been arrested?"

"I told you we would deal with it. I said our contacts would get results. They did. But I can't give you details."

He opened the door. Mags slammed it shut with the palm of the hand. "The fuck you can't. Tell me what's going on, Bradley."

"I can't. Officially, what I did, asking Dad to use the company's contacts... it never happened. I don't even know everything myself. Trust me. Let me go check what I need to check. If I'm right, then Tam is safe. Now let me go."

"Safe? Safe? How can you say that? How can you know if she's safe? David is dead, Bradley. Murdered by a man who has killed at least ten people in America. How is anybody safe from him if he's not locked up?"

"That's what I'm trying to tell you."

Mags felt the strength drain out of her, her shoulders slumping. "He's been arrested?"

"If the information is correct, then he is on his way back to America. They will arrest him before he gets off the plane."

Bradley was giving her that confident, in-control, getting-things-done schtick. Mags knew it well. It had been attractive in her late twenties. Now she was nearer forty she often wondered if it wasn't—sometimes—nothing but show and bluster. She tested the theory.

"I have a google alert set up. I'm looking forward to seeing the news reports when they get him."

"Ah."

Ah?

Bradley's hand was on the handle. "It won't happen like that, Mags. There's insufficient evidence for a warrant, but certain anti-terrorist laws are flexible enough to allow Homeland Security to bring him in. Not strictly legal, so you won't see it reported. Sorry, Mags. He'll be incarcerated. That's what's important here. We can relax."

He left without another word. Mags went back to the kitchen. Tam put the kettle on when she saw her.

"Any news on that poor man, mum? Will he be all right?"

"I'll call the hospital later."

Mags sat down and while Tam bustled around the kitchen, Kit gave her something that almost resembled a smile. She smiled back, but her thoughts were elsewhere.

She wasn't sure she believed a word of what Bradley had told her.

CHAPTER TWENTY-SEVEN

For the longest time, everything is just plain wrong.

I wake up slowly. This is a new experience. Normally, I wake up a few minutes after I go to sleep. If sleep is an ocean, I've just been bobbing along on the surface all my life, rarely dipping my head under. When I had the procedure, the anaesthetic let me dive under the surface. But this... it's like they sent me down in one of those little submarines you see on the Discovery Channel. Down to the bottom of the ocean where there's no light, and the fish are nightmares, all goggling eyes and luminous fangs.

They put me in my submarine and sent me down, down, down. They left me there, just me and the nightmare fish. For days, weeks, months.

When I wake up, I'm in a hospital bed, and I don't know why. I don't remember. Not straight away. I don't know what city I'm in, or even the country. My name I do remember, but it has no meaning at first. The concept of a name confuses me. I look at the glass of water on the table beside me. I know the word water describes the colourless liquid, and glass means the receptacle that holds it. Glass is also what the *skylight above me is made of. I know what a skylight is, too. But my name comes without a definition attached. I've returned from my solo expedition in the deep, and they've stitched me inside this sack of skin and bone.*

I know enough to keep quiet. I remember I have secrets, but not what they are.

Thoughts appear in my mind along with images. Some are blurred, fogged, unclear. Others are more vivid, with edges, corners, beginnings and endings. These, I begin to recognise, are real. These are memories. Some are violent. Some involve death. These are my favourites.

The first time the doctor talks—or, at least, the first time I remember him talking—he tells me I've been sick for a long time. He says I will have to put myself together again. Like the nursery rhyme, he says. When I just stare back at him, he says my mind is a jigsaw puzzle I will have to assemble without a picture to help me.

It's not like a jigsaw puzzle. Even without a picture to work from, at least I'd have all the pieces of the puzzle, and could keep trying to put them together until I found the right ones. No. This is more like walking in the dark in a room the size of a football stadium. I stumble around this space and— every so often—I bump up against another part of myself. I absorb it and carry on walking. When I absorb a new piece, it gets a little easier to find the next. Slowly, I am taking shape. Slowly.

Besides the nurses, there are two doctors, an American and a Brit. The Brit answers questions. The American asks them.

The Brit—Doctor Stokely—tells me they kept me in a medically induced coma for seventeen weeks. He says they nearly lost me a few times during the first forty-eight hours. If they hadn't moved me to this private hospital, I would be dead. I wonder who's paying. Nothing comes for free. I remember that much. He tells me the holes healing on my left leg came from pins that were holding the bones in place for the first six weeks. He shows me a photograph. I only know it's my leg because of an old scar on my knee. In the photograph, there's a bicycle wheel around it, the spokes stabbing into my flesh. Stokely says it's called an external fixate. They used it because my left leg was broken in four places above the knee. Above the fixate is a fresh scar where they put in my new, plastic hip. My left arm was broken up even more than my leg. I lift it off the sheet. I can barely manage it.

"The most painful stage of healing happened while we kept you asleep. The nurses removed the pins in the fixator three times a day and rinsed the wounds with hydrogen peroxide. It can be uncomfortable, I'm told."

I wonder about Stokely's definition of uncomfortable. That's the word he used to describe how I might feel when Nurse Ratched manipulated my legs to prevent what he called 'flexion contraction'. I screamed and blacked out the first time. Uncomfortable. Sure.

I study Stokely's face while he talks. His eyes are dark, and he yawns. He's tired. A thought slides across my consciousness. I picture Stokely on his back, eyes bulging as the light inside them dies.

My face feels different. One morning, they bring me a mirror, and I find out it looks different, too. They've patched up my cheekbone and repaired the left side of my face. I guess it's pretty good, but it doesn't look like me. Nurse Ratched holds the mirror so I can see myself. That's not her real name, but I saw a movie once with a nurse I didn't like, so that's what I call her. She doesn't care either way. I think Ratched expected a bigger reaction from me when I see my reflection for the first time. She doesn't realise it doesn't matter what I look like. I remember enough to know I am an instrument of the universe. The fact that God didn't take me, the fact I'm still here proves my work is unfinished.

I wish I knew how. How I'm supposed to do my work. I don't remember what the work is, but I know I was close to the end. So close. That thought brings the sting of tears. Nurse Ratched notices, and dabs at my face with a tissue. She shows no emotion, but I think she enjoys this. She reminds me of Mom.

I ask her to hold the mirror to one side.

Tilting my head to the left, I watch the mirror with my right eye. My left eye is closer to my nose than it used to be. The skin below is shiny and pink. The eye still works, just not so well. I get few details, not much more than light and shade. I try to see the back of my skull, but I need two mirrors. I won't ask Nurse Ratched. Stokely will show me. It's his work I want to admire, after all.

The head injury was serious. When they took me out of the local hospital and brought me here, I went straight into surgery. Stokely says I'm his greatest triumph. Eleven hours cutting into my skull, fishing around inside, picking out fragments of bone from my brain. Repairing damage where possible. Stokely likes to talk about the procedure. He asks if I ever played that game when I was a kid—Operation—the one with a guy who had holes in his body containing his organs. You needed a steady hand.

"It's just like that. Only if my hand shook or slipped, your nose didn't light up and there was no buzzer, just some fresh bleeding and the risk of permanent brain damage."

He's cheerful in his work, Stokely. Not like Ratched. Or the American. The other nurse, Simon, is the only one who tells me his first name. He's young, and he talks like Dick Van Dyke in Mary Poppins. A little like him, anyways. Only

Simon talks faster and the accent isn't quite the same. I understand little of what he says, but I like the fact he talks to me at all. He doesn't care if I answer or not. I bet he talked the same way when I was unconscious. I bet he talks the same way to his dog.

About a week after they bring me out of the coma, Simon stops on his way out the door, looks back at me and whistles.

"I wasn't sure even Doctor Stokely could bring you back," he says, shaking his head. "I mean the man is good, do you get me? The best. But I've never seen anyone come back from where you'd gone. You were dead, for sure. Nice one, though. Amazing. You are one lucky, lucky bastard."

Lucky. He had no idea. None of them did. That was the day I remembered what my work was.

That afternoon, Stokely shows me the back of my skull. He takes a picture on his phone. Then he fetches the x-rays and shows me the damage, and his repairs. I look hard, but I'm no doctor, and can't see what he missed.

I wish I hadn't come back. Shoulda stayed in the submarine until my oxygen ran out. Better dead than this; this half-life, this nothingness.

When I see Stokely yawn, there's no urge to bring him peace. I can imagine it, but there's no passion. Nothing at all. There are no more signs. No guidance. The angel has left me. She isn't here.

I am alone.

The American sits in the only chair, after dragging it closer to the bed. He stares at me, says nothing. I glance at him and look away. But that glance is enough. I know him. I've seen him before. I'm good at remembering people. I search the parts of my memory that have returned, trying to find him. Then he speaks, and I have it. It's like when the fourth wheel of a combination lock swings to the right number and the whole thing clicks open.

"We almost lost you, Scott. And that would have been a tragedy."

He doesn't say Scott. He uses my real name.

He was there that night at the hotel. In the conference room. He was the one who told us about the drug trial, before we were interviewed.

He leaves the room, comes back with a large canvas bag. My bag. I look at the key on the table beside me.

"You were in a coma for four months," he says.

He pulls the device out of the bag, stretches the wire between his hands. I feel a dull ache of anger at that. It's not right that he should touch it.

"Interesting choice of souvenir," he says, wrapping the wire back around the handles. "You're a riddle, Scott. We've been running trials for over a decade and, over the years, we've learned how to choose the most appropriate subjects. We're better at performing the procedure. Only certain kinds of brains can accept the grafts at all. In the third year of trials, when a graft held for a week, we threw a party. By the time we operated on you, our best subject had given us three months. You're here a year and a half after the grafts. You are a pioneer, Scott."

I don't like the way he looks at me. Then he drops his little bombshell, and watches to see how I will react.

"I know what you did in Florida and Georgia. And I know why you came to London."

CHAPTER TWENTY-EIGHT

W hen they reconstructed my face, they had nothing to go on. No photographs. Not even the tiny photograph on the stranger's passport I stole at the airport. That's in the bag with a change of clothes, a sledgehammer, my Bible, and the device in a locker in King's Cross station. The locker key was all I had on me that morning. Funny. I've lost everything that matters, but my memory of a locker number is untouched.

The first few weeks after I open my eyes, I wonder if I should kill myself. It would be difficult, but not impossible. I could make a noose from the tube plugged into my wrist. I think I could. But I know I must not.

Simon brought in a Bible when I asked for one.

I remind myself that prophets are tested. Abraham almost killed his own son. Jesus himself had to spend forty days and nights in the desert, and—on the cross—he thought his Father had abandoned him. I will not give in to despair.

I ask Stokely how badly my brain is damaged.

"The brain is still the undiscovered country as far as medicine is concerned," he says. He talks fast, but pronounces *every syllable. Like listening to a tape running at the wrong speed. "Take your brain, for instance, Scott." I said he could call me Scott. It's not my name, but it'll do. When I told the American to call me Scott, he gave me a nasty smile like he knew something I don't.*

Stokely uses his fingers as he talks. He doesn't wave his hands in the air, he holds imaginary scalpels and makes precise incisions into the brains of invisible patients. "There was significant trauma to the back of your skull, and the initial cleanup and removal of all fragments took hours. Current thinking still holds that parts of the brain do particular jobs. Decades of neuroscience tells us that the signals to sustain life are sent from the brainstem. Breathing, heart rate, body temperature, and so on. Even when to sleep and when to wake."

I look up at him when he says this, but he shows no sign he thinks it's significant.

"The cerebellum controls muscles, coordination, balance. Yours was bruised, but I expect you to make a full physical recovery. Physiotherapy will help your cerebellum to restore those connections. It's the cerebrum which gives me more cause for concern. There was some bleeding. Your brain took quite a knock. However, there have been cases where the brain has circumvented a damaged area and duplicated its functions elsewhere. Or, sometimes, brain injuries have repercussions no one can predict. We will have to wait and see. That you have already undergone brain surgery makes your case even more fascinating. I'd never seen work like it. Pioneering. An experimental procedure of the nature—"

Stokely stopped talking. He looked over at me and apologised. "Sorry, got carried away. Not my place to... that is, shouldn't really discuss... ah. Anyway, the important thing is that you're awake, and there are—touch wood—no worrying signs of debilitating brain damage that might affect your quality of life."

I almost laugh at this. I have no quality of life. Not yet. But I must be strong. If I am to be God's instrument, forged in his furnace, then I must be prepared to be tested.

Stokely is using an invisible saw to remove the top of an imaginary skull.

"People with your injuries used to end up with a metal plate in their heads. It's all much more sophisticated now. We use a mesh to hold fragments of your skull in place until they begin the healing process themselves. Wonderful apparatus, the human body. Whenever I peer inside a patient's head and see a living human brain, I'm reminded of a poem. We had to learn it at school. Can't remember the title now. In fact, I only remember two words. Which is why I pursued the sciences rather than the humanities, I suppose. Those two words sum up the brain for me: fearful symmetry. That's what I was thinking when you were lying there, your scalp peeled back and your brain exposed. Fearful symmetry. Ironic really, as the brain is asymmetrical."

He chuckles, makes some notes on the chart hanging on my bed, and leaves.

One way in which I am prevented from restoring myself is the fact I am awake during the day and asleep at night. This is the first time I have experienced this pattern. It's drug-induced. While my body is healing, they send me to sleep every night. For most of my life, until my surgery, I wanted to be like other people. Funny. I looked at them and I assumed they were rested, alert, awake. Because they close their eyes every night and go somewhere I never go, I thought they lived at an elevated level of consciousness I would never experience. Shocking to discover how wrong I was. I sleep now from ten o'clock at night until seven-thirty in the morning. Three times during that period, a nurse checks me, changes my dressings. I barely stir, then I sleep again. And yet, when daytime comes—signalled by a light-ening of the square piece of sky beyond the skylight—I am conscious, but I would not describe myself as awake. I was more awake before, when I couldn't sleep. Here, I am always tired, a dull, spaced-out, staring weariness. I see the same in the face of Nurse Ratched, and in the American's movie-star blue eyes. People aren't awake. They are sleep-walking.

Maybe this is part of the test. Showing me how it feels to live like others.

Memories return of some of those I helped find peace. I am satisfied I have done good work. I wait.

I don't count the days, so I don't know how much time passes between the end of my coma and the beginning of physiotherapy. I only know that after the first session, the pain is so great I pray for death.

One evening, the American comes to see me again.

The American brings in the pictures. My body is a torture chamber, nerve endings screaming, muscles spasming. He has Ratched help me sit down at a table. I grip the edge so I don't fall. It takes all my strength to stay upright. My head is full of rocks, my neck isn't strong enough to support it.

He spreads the pictures on the table without comment. At first, I don't look. The American smiles, leans back and crosses one leg over the other. He knows the longer I sit here, the more painful it gets. I'm sweating already.

"Nurse, do you have some painkillers for Scott? He appears to be in distress."

He shakes his head as she approaches. "Not now. When he's back in bed. I have some questions for him first."

"Yes, sir." I can't turn my head, but I hear her drop the pills next to my glass of water. I bet the sadistic bitch is smiling.

"The pictures, Scott."

I can already taste the bitter tang of the pills under their sugar coating, feel the numbness that will envelop my body. I'll do what the American wants. But I'll be careful what I say.

When I see what's on the table, I have to use what strength I have left to hide my excitement. It's hard to explain the shock and delight I experience at the memories provoked by the drawings. Like I've been living in a rundown house for months, and I've unlocked a hidden door, leading to a beautiful room, with light streaming through the window.

I show nothing, say nothing.

I recognise the subject of every drawing. I remember being there. The excitement at finding those who needed me. The anticipation, the dry-mouthed thrill of planning what would follow.

Ocala, Florida. Toys in the yard.

Hinesville, Georgia. Watching the clapboard house.

Along with the memories, pieces of myself I left down in the deep, in my lonely submarine, slot into place. I remember leaving home, riding the bus north, stopping where I was needed, bringing peace. And I remember the angel that watched with me.

Atlanta, Georgia. The trailer park. The weight of his body when I dragged it inside. I was strong then. I will need to be strong again.

London. The house where I expected to find her. Then despair. Something was wrong. She wasn't there.

I remember finding her again, days later, the connection between us so powerful, I was little more than an observer in my own body. When I found her, I knew it was time. My task completed, the purpose fulfilled, a life brought to its end.

I stare at the pictures. And I know. She drew them. My angel. And I came so close. So close I could have touched her.

I'm making a noise now. A growl, wordless. I can't stop myself. I want to scream but I don't have the strength.

"Stop it." The American scoops up the pictures and stands up.

The noise keeps coming, a howl of frustration. It could have all been over. She was yards away from me and I failed her. It could have all been over.

The American leaves the room and Ratched comes back with an orderly. They drag me over to the bed and hoist me onto it. She injects me with something. Seconds later the room, the nurse, and the whole day fall away. The last thing I'm aware of is my own howl.

CHAPTER TWENTY-NINE

The human body is an amazing thing, as is the human will. I've seen documentaries. That guy who cut off his own arm to survive a hiking accident. Plane crash survivors eating the dead passengers and making it out alive.

Some folk get lost in a forest somewhere and are dead in days. Others survive for weeks under the same circumstances. What's different about them? How can they when others give up, their bodies shutting down? I'm no scientist, but I think it's down to what you have to live for.

Over the past few weeks, as Doctor Stokely has reduced my medication, I have returned to my usual sleep pattern. Well, my lack of sleep pattern. I tell no one. I stay quiet at night, close my eyes when they check on me. It's funny, but getting my sleep disorder back gives me hope. If I can be who I was before the accident, my time in the wilderness might end.

Three weeks after the episode with the pictures, the American comes back. It's twenty minutes since Ratched watched me pretend to swallow the knockout pills. The

American has someone with him. Another American. Older, from the sound of his voice.

I'm awake when they arrive, but my eyes are closed. The older American speaks first.

"What about the girl? Are you sure there's been nothing? No repeat of the absence seizures? No pictures?"

"Nothing. Not yet."

"It's possible the connection will manifest in a new way. You should be there. Our friend here is going nowhere."

Interesting. The second American is senior to the first.

"I agree," says the younger one. "I fly back tomorrow."

"Good. We can't wait much longer before we attempt surgery."

"No. It's too risky."

"He survived the first procedure. He survived being knocked over. It caved the back of his skull in. He's stronger than he looks."

"Perhaps. But we haven't been able to repeat the success with anyone else. And we don't know what came first - the psychosis or the connection. One may have caused the other. We can't mess with his brain."

I thought the American hated me. Now he's defending my brain. Today is full of surprises.

"We may have to," says the other voice. "This is the break-through I've been working towards my whole life. If we can reproduce it, my legacy is assured. Yours too. Our funding is still under threat. They'll turn off the tap next June."

"What? You never said our funding was—"

"Why would I? That's my business. It doesn't matter now. The future of the company is lying in that bed."

"I accept that. But we can't risk another procedure. We just can't."

"You have a better suggestion?"

"What about bringing them together? When he was in England, he found her in days."

I almost give myself away when I hear that. I assumed I was still in England. If not England, where?

"How?" said the older American. "The subject can never leave this building again."

This doesn't come as a shock. I already figured they would never let me go.

I'm good at lying still. They think I'm sedated. And I'm relying on them underestimating me. My performance in physiotherapy suggests a slow, difficult recovery. My performance is a lie. I am working out every moment I can, even if it's just clenching and releasing every muscle in my body. I must get strong. I will only get one chance to escape. Once they realise my real strength, they will strap me to this bed and I will spend the rest of my life in hell, alone.

As I listen to the American speak again, my eyes fill with tears. I pray that—if they look at me—they will assume I'm dreaming.

They don't look. I am nothing to them. Neither is the angel. They know nothing, understand nothing. They are so far from the light, they have lost their way. To them, I am the subject and she is the girl.

"You don't understand, Dad. No need for him to go anywhere. I'll bring her to him."

Dad? Interesting.

"What about the mother?"

"She won't know. I told her the killer's in a deep, dark hole someplace. She even quit therapy."

"Okay. Try it. Bring them together again. The connection might re-establish itself. If not, we've lost nothing."

They leave, still talking, and I do not hear the rest.

I can hardly believe it. Although I no longer sense a presence, something still guides me, and those around me. He will bring her here. A second chance.

I weep as I silently mouth my gratitude. I will not fail again.

CHAPTER THIRTY

"I have a surprise. How do you feel about spending Christmas in Boston?"

Bradley's smile was unforced, and Mags was glad to see it. Although the last four months had been hard, she now felt happier than she had since Tam produced her first drawing. There hadn't been a picture now since the killer's capture. Well, nothing out of the ordinary, just the usual woodland creatures and unicorns, plus Tam's attempts to draw a comic-strip version of Jeeves and Wooster. The only traumatic event had been the accident outside their house, but the hospital told her the poor man had been moved to a private facility where he was expected to make a full recovery.

She glanced at Kit. Bradley noticed and added, "It wouldn't be a proper family Christmas without Kit, would it?"

Kit's smile was still a little forced, but he was getting better. He was underweight, but not dangerously so.

He had lived with them for six weeks after David's murder. The first viewer of the underpriced Camden Lock house bought it. Kit moved into an apartment on the South-bank. Mags hoped that was a sign he would be okay. He wasn't hiding away from people, he was putting himself in the busy heart of the city. But it also gave him the gift of anonymity. Christmas had been worrying her, and she had been unsure how to bring the subject up with him. Now Bradley might have solved the problem.

Mags and Kit had only talked once about her call on the day of the murder. Kit asked why she told them to leave the house, how she knew they were in danger, and what Tam's picture had to do with it. Mags explained Patrice's theory about the killer posting photographs of his intended victims' houses online, and that Tam found them somehow. When she said it out loud, it sounded ridiculous, and Tam had flatly denied it, but she could offer no better explanation. Well, none she wanted to say out loud. Kit took a long time to consider the implications.

"You think he—the murderer—was coming for Tam? That he traced her somehow?"

Mags put both hands on the mug to stop them shaking, only trusting herself to nod.

"Fuck." Kit had a gift for finding the right word. When Mags looked at him, he was crying, silently at first, then crouching, his whole body convulsing. She knelt beside him, wrapping her arms around him while he rocked on his heels. When he could speak, he took her hands in his and looked in her face.

"Do you see? Do you see what this means?"

Mags had thought of nothing else for weeks. What did it mean? Was Tam the reason David was murdered? Would Kit ever be able to forgive her?

"I thought David had died for nothing." Her brother's voice was hoarse. "But he didn't, did he? He saved her. The evidence they found in our house, that's how they caught him, right?"

"Yes. Yes, of course."

It wasn't an outright lie, but it was close. She hugged her twin more tightly, glad he couldn't see her face.

That conversation had taken place over a month ago. It was December now, and they were celebrating Thanksgiving late, as Bradley had been in Boston for most of the previous month. He was working harder than ever; Edgegen was close to a medical breakthrough. She couldn't begrudge him the time away. He had been as good as his word. The Bedroom Killer had gone. Most of the US news sources speculated that he was dead, as serial killers didn't often stop, especially when the gaps between murders were getting shorter. Bradley and his father had saved not just Tam's life, but countless others. Mags wouldn't forget that.

She looked around the table. Tam was bouncing in her chair with excitement.

"Christmas in America, Dad? Brilliant. Can I learn to ski? You said you'd teach me to ski. Can you take me this time? It will snow, won't it? And you'll come too, won't you, Uncle Kit?"

"I can't."

Tam's face fell. Mags raised a questioning eyebrow.

"I was going to wait until the show was definite to tell you," said Kit. "But, well, it's pretty definite."

"What is?" said Tam and Mags at the same time.

"*Cheshire Cats.*"

Tam gasped. "No way. Wait until I tell Rose at school. I could text her if I had a phone. Mother, you are stifling my social progress."

Cheshire Cats was one of the most popular shows on TV, starting as an internet series before being snapped up by an international production company. An addictive mixture of documentary and semi-improvised soap opera, it followed the lives of a group of young, glamorous, moneyed women. Mags tried watching it once, but ten minutes in the company of the self-obsessed, self-important narcissists was more than enough.

"They're taking the show out to Germany for six months. *Cheshire Cats in Alexanderplatz*. It's huge there."

Mags didn't doubt it. German toilets often had a display shelf built in, so you could appreciate your own shit. *Cheshire Cats* no doubt fulfilled a similar purpose.

Kit laughed at his sister's expression. "You're not a fan. Don't pretend."

"True. I'm not. But I'm happy for you. That's wonderful."

They all toasted Kit's news. He'd be away over Christmas, helping set up the show for filming in January. Mags couldn't stop herself hoping her brother might meet a nice Berliner.

———

Mags let Tam have the window seat, and her nose was pressed against the glass as soon as her belt went on.

While the jet climbed above the clouds, banked west and headed towards the Atlantic, Mags took stock. This was a habit adopted during her years of therapy with Ria. Sunday morning was the regular stock-taking slot, but this trip marked a significant moment at the end of an awful year, and she needed to recognise there were positives to be thankful for. The therapist had advised her not to ignore the negatives, but to acknowledge them alongside more life-affirming moments. She balanced a notebook on her knee and chewed the pen. Writing things down always helped.

David's murder. It had been the worst moment of their lives; an unthinkable, unspeakable act perpetrated on a man they loved. Her brother lost a husband, Tam lost an uncle, Mags lost a good friend. But David had lived well and loved well. Eighteen years older than Kit, he had never been slow to point out how much he loved him. Kit admitted that David made him swear, should he die first, that—after a six-month period wearing black, wandering the streets of London ringing a bell, and reciting *Stop The Clocks*—he would get back out there.

Kit's temporary relocation to Berlin would help. Mags knew her twin.

Bradley. Her marriage was in better shape than she expected. She could look back on the years of paranoia with fresh eyes. Logically, she had always hoped her darker thoughts, her suspicions about Bradley, were down to her depression and anxiety. Now the evidence supported this. It had all been in her mind. When she needed him, Bradley came through in the most convincing way possible. He protected Tam, and he protected her. Over the months, the familiar distance between them returned, but Mags wasn't threatened by it anymore. She and her twin were huggers, quick to show affection. In her teens, she assumed the same intimacy would go along with marriage. That it didn't was not a bad thing, just an indication she shouldn't judge every-body by her own limited experience. People showed affection in different ways. Bradley showed it by making his family secure, financially and otherwise. Writing that down made it sound cold, but their passionate encounter on the kitchen floor hadn't been a one-off. There had been two or three more occasions since. She had suspected him of planning that spontaneity, then pushed the thought from her mind. It might not be the most exciting, sensual relationship in the world, but it was solid, and worth working to maintain. Bradley was a good man.

The picture on the fridge. That was how Mags labelled Tam's frightening few months. There was no easy psychological answer for what had happened to her. Mags researched the subject as thoroughly as an amateur with an internet connection could. She also asked Ria. The absence seizures common to some forms of epilepsy fitted the bill. When Tam drew the pictures, she phased out, she wasn't there. Tam was as surprised as anyone by the drawings. The mystery of where Tam had seen the original pictures was never cleared up. Early on, when Kit moved out and life was returning to normal, Mags broached the subject. She did it circumspectly, watching her daughter for signs of distress. It was clear that Tam, with the natural resilience of a child, had moved on. She preferred to forget all about it. After some thought, Mags couldn't help but agree.

Healthy daughter, solid marriage, Kit on the road to recovery. Yes, it had been a terrible year. Mags had always found the expression *time is the greatest healer* trite, at best. In the early days after Clara's death, it sounded cruel. She never wanted to forget her baby, never wanted to stop thinking about her daughter. As the months stretched into years, she saw she had been wrong. Time didn't bring forgetfulness, it brought ways of dealing with unimaginable pain. That was how it healed. The pain would always be there, but it was woven into her being. She carried Clara with her. She could never forget her. The same for David. They all carried David now.

The captain's announcement broke into her thoughts. Seven-and-a-half hours to Boston. Bradley had booked club class. A frosted panel blocked her view of Tam. As Mags closed the notebook, there was a tap on the glass.

"Yes?"

The panel slid down, Tam holding the button on the other side. They smiled at each other as their faces came in to view. Mags felt a wave of hope as she looked at her daughter's face.

"Do you want anything to drink, honey?"

"What a delightful idea, mother." Tam still sometimes spoke like a Wodehouse character. "A mint julep would hit the mark nicely, don't you think? Be a sport and order one for me, won't you? Thanks, old chap."

As the glass slid up again, they both snorted with laughter.

Mags pulled out her phone and made a note on her calendar. After this trip, she would call Ria and cancel her future therapy sessions. Maybe send her a bunch of flowers and a bottle of wine.

Everything would get better from now on.

CHAPTER THIRTY-ONE

M ags had expected Boston to be cold. Just not this cold. She'd visited half a dozen times, but this was only her second winter trip. Despite bringing a decent overcoat, she shivered as she and Tam made their way from the arrivals hall to the pickup point.

To her surprise, it wasn't Bradley meeting them, but his father. She couldn't recall Todd Barkworth ever putting family before work. Mags sensed he saw her as an unfortunate distraction for his son.

Barkworth senior was a big man, with the same pale blue eyes as his son. If Bradley aged as well as his father, Mags expected the envious looks from other women to continue well into his dotage.

"There you are, Mags. I'm sorry you're stuck with me. Bradley was in the middle of something in the lab, so I offered to pick you up. Wonderful to see you both."

He *offered*? Something had changed. Mags expected, and received, a firm handshake and a pat on the shoulder. The Barkworths didn't hug.

Tam stood shyly beside her, her usual bluster gone for

the moment. It had been two years since she had seen her grandfather; a long time for an eleven-year-old. When Todd smiled, she stepped forward, sticking her hand out.

"Absolutely charmed, old sport," she said.

Todd shot Mags an amused glance, then looked back at his granddaughter. "I heard you were getting precocious."

He leaned down and wrapped his powerful arms around her. Mags couldn't quite believe what she was seeing. She flushed as she acknowledged she might have misjudged the old man. Tam was his only grandchild, Bradley his only child. It couldn't be easy, seeing so little of her. Todd never denied being a workaholic, but still. It was his son's little girl, and she had changed, as little girls do, in the twenty-six months since he and Irene had last visited London.

Todd helped them with their luggage and held the car door open while they slid onto the back seat. He didn't take his eyes off Tam until he started driving. He looked delighted to see her. Excited, even.

Mags held Tam's hand as the car pulled away. Fat white flakes drifted past the window, lending a magical sheen to the snow-covered city.

Mags stayed conscious long enough to acknowledge Irene Barkworth's formal greeting at their palatial house in the moneyed district of Boston. Then she went to bed and insisted Tam did the same.

Bradley got in late that night, and Mags surfaced from a deep, jet-lagged sleep to kiss him, before turning on her side and snoring. She woke up to a note promising he would be home early that evening.

On their first full day in Boston, Irene Barkworth announced she was taking Mags and Tam shopping in the city. Mags enjoyed shopping, Tam wasn't a fan. If it had been a mother and daughter trip, they would have alternated the shoe and clothes stores with books and toys. Tam had pronounced herself too old for toys on her eleventh birthday, but couldn't walk past anywhere with a giant teddy bear in the window.

With Irene leading the way, poor Tam didn't stand a chance. Irene was a stick thin, brittle-haired woman whose dark, even, tan was far too good to attribute to Boston summers. She and Mags had little in common, and their conversation was amiable, stilted and tedious. Irene had appointed herself tour guide for the day, but her commentary was weighted towards which fashion outlets had opened, moved, or closed in the last few years. As the morning wore on, Mags had to stop looking at Tam, because every time she caught her glance, her daughter would go cross eyed, or slump as if falling asleep.

Despite knowing how bored Tam was, Mags couldn't help herself stopping in wonder outside a window which displayed the biggest selection of upmarket shoes and boots she had ever seen.

"Mum..." Tam warned. Mags knew how much of a cliché it was for a woman her age to be obsessed with shoes, but she couldn't pretend she didn't enjoy buying them. She was a feminist through and through, but no one could deny the absolute pleasure of slipping on a pair of slingbacks, objects of beauty untouched by human hand since their manufacture. She could admire the elegance of their design, couldn't she? Feet were not the prettiest part of a body, but Jimmy Choo could fix that in no time. Well, in an hour or two and a few hundred dollars time.

She felt a hand tugging at her sleeve. "Mum." Tam's voice was louder and carried a tone of mock-horror.

"You're not going to... you're not thinking of... oh, God,

it's too late, isn't it? You're beyond help. Please, Gran, help me drag her away before she spends my college fund."

Irene Barkworth looked from daughter to mother. "Tell you what. There is a place two blocks away does the most amazing hot chocolate you've ever tasted. Great waffles, too. How about Tam and I go there for a treat, while you try on some shoes?"

"Granny, whose side are you on? We must try to break Mum's cycle of shoe buying, leaving said shoes at the back of wardrobe, then taking them to a charity shop a year later. She needs help, can't you see? Medical help. Hang on. Did you say waffles?"

Tam took her grandmother's arm.

"I release you, Mother. Run free. If it's possible to run in heels."

"I'll join you in an hour," said Mags, optimistically. "Don't eat all the waffles. Shoe shopping makes me hungry."

She watched them turn the corner, Tam chatting with her grandmother. It was a rare talent, putting members of any generation at ease. Maybe she'd grow up to be a politician. Hopefully not.

When Mags turned back to the shoe shop window, she collided with a passerby. A man in a dark brown overcoat and scarf, a battered hat on his balding head.

"Excuse me—"

"Mags. How are you?"

She gaped at him in disbelief. Patrice Martino smiled and removed his hat. He wasn't dressed for the weather, his only concession a thin scarf. Mags folded her arms, making an effort to recover her equilibrium.

"Mr Martino. You look well."

"As do you, Mags, as do you. And please, it's Patrice."

"I think I'll stick to Mr Martino, if you don't mind. I'm guessing this is no coincidence?"

"You're guessing right."

"Mr Martino, there's a reason I stopped replying to your emails. To be honest, I don't even open them anymore. It was a terrible time, but we've moved on. The serial killer has stopped killing. Dead, probably. Whatever happened with my daughter is over. I don't want to drag any of it up again, ever. Please understand."

She frowned. "How on earth did you know I was in Boston?"

Patrice Martino shook his head. "Not here. There's a coffee shop around the corner. I'm buying."

Mags shook her head. "You didn't answer my question."

Martino spread his arms in a gesture of surrender. "One coffee. Please. I wouldn't ask you if it wasn't important. I'll explain how I knew where you were. Come on, Mags, I'm freezing my ass off out here."

Mags thought of that drive to the airport in Atlanta, and the way Patrice Martino had talked her down from a panic attack. "One coffee."

CHAPTER THIRTY-TWO

The coffee was good. It had to be. No one would dare serve sub-standard coffee in Boston. Bostonians were caffeine connoisseurs, and they liked it strong and flavoursome. Martino took a sip and sighed his appreciation.

"Now that's what I'm talking about," he said. Then he shook his head. "I never understood that expression. I assume it first came into use as a reference to something under discussion. Not anymore. It's become stand-alone. And it makes little sense. I'm sorry, I'm talking too much, I do that when I'm nervous."

Mags didn't ask why he was nervous. Patrice Martino had emailed her several times in the months after David's death. As the press never connected the Camden Lock murder to the Bedroom Killer, Martino hadn't known about it. He wrote asking what happened after Mags left Atlanta. Mags lied. She hadn't felt good about it, but the truth would lead to more questions. Answering those questions risked exposing Bradley's part in removing the killer from the scene. Not information Mags wanted to hand to a journalist. She didn't trust herself to speak to him on the phone and ignored his calls. She wrote one email telling him that Tam's picture, the one that sent her rushing back to London, was nothing out of the ordinary. That there had been no more pictures. That the killer was probably dead. For a few weeks, the emails stopped, and she thought Martino had moved on to a new story. Then they began again. She only read the first. Martino was following a lead on Edgegen Technology, Todd Barkworth's company. He had uncovered some scandals in the nineteen-seventies and eighties, when the company were pursuing a secretive line of research funded by the US military. He mentioned cover-ups and out-of-court settlements and promised to send more information. Mags wrote back asking him not to bother. Any unethical business practices in Todd Barkworth's past had no relevance to her family now. And she couldn't condemn Todd Barkworth's connections if they led to the capture of David's murderer. Mags sometimes wondered what had happened to the Bedroom Killer. He had never seen the inside of a court of law, never had a fair trial. When she thought of David, she decided she could live with that.

When Martino's emails kept coming, Mags moved them into her trash folder unread. She blocked his number on her phone and hoped she had done enough. His surprise appearance in Boston suggested she hadn't.

"You said you'd tell me how you found me," she said. Patrice dropped his hat onto the chair next to him, and squeezed the bridge of his nose. Mags remembered the gesture from the day in Hinesville.

"I bribed someone at the airport," he said. "When your name popped up on the passenger list, she called me."

"That's an outrageous violation of privacy," she said. She stood up, but Martino grabbed her wrist.

"Mags."

She looked down at him. Her reluctance to hear him out wasn't that she didn't trust him. It was because she did.

"Sit down, please. It's important."

He released her. She sat down.

"You haven't read my emails, have you?"

"Mr Martino," she began. He gave her a look. "Patrice. I'm not ungrateful for what you did in the summer. I don't know what I would have done without you."

Patrice offered no modest rebuttal. He didn't even shrug. His expression was level and unreadable.

"And, and... I know you're a good journalist and a good man. I have nothing but respect for you. But for Tam, and for me, it's over. No more pictures, no more murders. She's doing well at school, she's happy. She's growing up too fast but, every parent thinks the same, don't we?"

Patrice still made no response. Now he was in front of her, he seemed reticent to speak. Mags felt as if she were on the back foot, having to justify herself. She stopped talking, met his gaze. "If you have something to say, Patrice, you might as well say it."

"It's too complex to blurt out over a cup of coffee."

Mags looked down at her half-finished cappuccino. "I have to get back to Tam."

Patrice took a piece of newspaper from his jacket pocket, putting it on the table in front of Mags. It was faded yellow, the edges brown.

"Nineteen eighty-three," said Patrice. "Edgegen have never been much for publicity, but they couldn't avoid it when they built their new lab in Boston. Some of the money came from local politicians. They posed for the whole cutting the ribbon bullshit. And this was the only photo-graph of the research team I could find."

Mags studied it. The mayor of Boston shaking hands

with a much younger Todd Barkworth, who looked so much like Bradley she did a double take.

Patrice pointed. "Second from the left at the back."

There were six people lined up behind Todd and the mayor. The caption identified them as research scientists. They wore white lab coats with the Edgegen logo embroidered above the breast pocket. Todd wore a suit. Second from the left was a small woman: unsmiling, not looking at the camera. The scientists were unnamed in the caption.

"Ava Marston. She had been working there three months when that photograph was taken." He put the clipping in his pocket.

"So?" Mags took another mouthful of cappuccino. She wanted to find Tam and forget this had happened. She didn't want Patrice to keep talking. But he did.

"I just wanted you to see her face and know she is who she says she is. She was a scientist at your husband's company."

"Why should I care who she is?"

"Because I want you to meet her, Mags. Tomorrow morning."

Mags finished her drink. "I made it clear I'm not interested. You may consider me naïve, turning a blind eye to the fact that my father-in-law's company was involved in some shady business deals decades ago. Maybe I am. But if this year has taught me anything, it's that family is everything. I won't do anything to jeopardise that."

She stood up. Patrice Martino closed his eyes. His head dropped a few inches. When he looked at her again, she saw such pity there that she wanted to grab her bag and run before he said another word. Instead, she waited.

Patrice put a business card on the table. "I guess you blocked my number. I understand. But if you decide to meet Ava tomorrow morning, call me tonight and let me know."

"I've already told you I'm not interested. Now, if you'll excuse me—"

"I have a question for you, Mags. It may upset you. I don't expect you to answer right away. If I'm wrong about this, it will mean nothing, and you can forget this conversation. But if it means something, you need to call me, and you need to meet Ava. Because I'm not sure your family *is* safe at all." He paused. When he spoke again, his voice was flat and colourless. The words came at Mags like the heavy tolling of a distant bell. She had a curious sensation of being alive and enmeshed with the present moment, while looking at herself as if out of her body, far away, disconnected, and numb.

"Is Tam your only child?"

Mags willed her legs to move. She couldn't look away from Patrice's face.

"Did she have a twin?"

Mags didn't remember leaving the café, but she found herself outside, walking past the shoe store in the direction Irene and Tam had taken. She didn't remember picking up Patrice's card either, but it was in her hand, squeezed between thumb and finger like a crucifix to ward off vampires.

In the first clothes store she came to, she picked up a jacket three sizes too big and walked through to the fitting rooms, pulling the curtain behind her.

She sat on the hard bench under the harsh lights and she wept.

Patrice was a good journalist. When their lives had dovetailed in Atlanta, she had handed him a thread of a story. Since then, he had pulled that thread and begun to unravel her life.

"Oh God, oh God. What am I going to do now?"

The question was rhetorical. Mags knew exactly what she would do.

She would meet Ava Marston.

CHAPTER THIRTY-THREE

Mags wasn't sure how she would get through the rest of the day, but somehow she did. She made conversation, laughed at Tam's jokes, asked Irene about her charity work. At dinner, she listened to Bradley and his father, noting they never mentioned their work. She wondered what Martino had uncovered at Edgegen Technology. Several times during dinner, she thought of Patrice's words and fell silent, only rejoining the conversation with an effort.

Soon after Tam had said goodnight, she blamed a persistent headache for an early night. When Bradley joined her later, she feigned sleep.

She passed a restless night, waking well before dawn. Using the light from her phone, she picked out some clothes without disturbing Bradley and crept downstairs.

At 5:45, Mags called Patrice.

"All right. I'll meet her."

Patrice sent her the address and ZIP code of a neighbourhood on the far side of the city. Mags took the keys to

Irene's SUV. Her mother-in-law had said she could borrow it, never expecting Mags to take her up on the offer.

She scribbled a note and left it on the kitchen table.

I have some errands to run and I couldn't sleep. Borrowed the car. Back for lunch. See you later, Mags.

The satnav in the SUV was programmed for the Barkworth's ski lodge on Mount Sunapee. Mags punched in the new ZIP code and drove away.

The display showed an outside temperature of minus twelve. She was glad of the heated seats and the snow tyres. The sky was an ominous slate grey. The blue line on the satnav drew her northwest, and the time to her destination ticked down.

Ava Marston's house was a detached brick building in Burlington, a small town just outside Boston. Patrice answered the door when she rang the bell, Mags followed him through a hallway into a larger kitchen-diner. Pill boxes and pharmacy bags covered the table.

Mags had expected a younger woman. Ava Marston had been in her twenties in the photograph, but the woman sitting in front of her was surely in her eighties. Her skin was sallow and lined, her hair wispy. Her eyes, when she raised them to look at Mags, had a yellow, jaundiced tinge. As if reading her mind, Ava Marston took a sip from a glass of water and cleared her throat.

"It's not just my liver." Her voice was as dry and cracked as her skin. "Lungs, lymph glands. Stomach. And, in the next month or so, brain. There's no elegant way of treating cancer. In the very early stages, we zap it with radiotherapy or poison it with chemotherapy. If that fails, we grab a knife and slice it out. But, if we're not quick enough, we miss our chance, and cutting out the diseased cells would kill the patient. Many doctors would consider that outcome a failure."

She nodded towards the pharmaceutical display on the table. "We can prolong life, and we can help with pain, but we are pissing into a hurricane."

Patrice pulled out a chair for Mags before sitting down himself. After a moment's hesitation, Mags joined him. She didn't know how to respond. She could say she was sorry, but Ava Marston's humourless smile suggested she wasn't fishing for sympathy.

"I get tired, and I can't speak for long. Mr Martino called me back when I could still take a shit without someone wiping my ass for me. We recorded the interview and I let him transcribe everything I said, as long as he did it right here, sitting at my computer, with the Wi-Fi turned off."

Ava popped a pill out of a blister pack and swallowed it. "I gave Mr Martino a hell of a story. He can publish it when I die. After Edgegen pays out. I never had children myself, Mrs Barkworth, but my sister did. Good kids. I can be their fairy fucking godmother. I like that. When they have the money, Mr Martino can publish, and name me as his source. They'll deny it. But this time, some shit will stick. After we finished the interviews, Mr Martino told me about you."

The house was too hot. Sweat pooled at the base of Mags' spine. Her mouth was dry. "Me?"

"You. Martino here says his story will protect people. Once they know what's going on. But he said some folk need protecting now. Specifically, you and your daughter."

Mags opened her mouth. Ava Marston shook her head and wagged a bony finger. "Please, Mrs Barkworth. Don't say a word. Go read the document. It can't leave the house."

She pointed at an open door leading off the kitchen. "It's in the study. We'll be in here when you're done."

Mags stood up and looked at Patrice. He wouldn't meet her eye. She walked towards the door.

The old woman coughed and called after her. Mags guessed Ava was in her fifties or early sixties. Cancer had made her ancient.

"Mrs Barkworth." Was there a tremor in that acerbic voice? "Are you a religious woman?"

"No."

"Me neither, but I get an urge to pray these days. Always the same prayer. I pray there is no God, no judgement. You're gonna judge me, Mrs Barkworth."

Mags let her speak.

"And you'll have every right."

She stood up, unhooking a stick from the chair. She stepped towards the back of the house. When she stumbled, Patrice stood up, but she snarled like a feral cat.

"Mr Martino will show you out. I'm too much of a coward to face you after you've read my confession. You want to know the biggest lie I ever heard? The ends justify the means. *That's w*hat all monsters tell themselves. Goodbye, Mrs Barkworth."

She shuffled away, shutting the door behind her.

In the study, a single folder lay on the desk.

Mags sat down, opened it, and began to read.

CHAPTER THIRTY-FOUR

This transcript is an abridged compilation of conversations between Patrice Martino and Ava Marston in September, 20**. The original recordings and transcriptions are available on request.

PATRICE MARTINO

Ms Marston. When did you join Edgegen Technology in Boston, and when did you leave?

AVA MARSTON

I joined when the new lab opened in nineteen eighty-three. I worked there until two thousand-seven. When I joined the team, I was a junior research assistant fresh out of college. By the time I left, I was a senior researcher. They offered me management positions, but I was only happy in the lab. Maybe happy is the wrong word.

Ava, when we first met, you mentioned Edge-gen's military contracts. You worked on these projects, correct?

Yes. Yes, I did. It's no secret these days that the CIA and US military were interested in psychic phenomena during the nineteen-sixties and seventies. Folk laugh at it now. Different times. I remember some Texan millionaire flew that Israeli metal-bender over, paid him a fortune to find oil. If telepathy, clairvoyance or telekinesis were real, the government wanted to be the first to find it. Remember, this was during the Cold War. We didn't know what Russia was doing, and no one wanted to fall behind in any areas of research. Todd Barkworth saw an opportunity, and he took it. Genetic research was an exciting field, and his cutting-edge knowledge impressed the politicians. If there was any truth to psychic phenomena, Barkworth said it was down to genetics. If we could find people with testable abilities, we might isolate the gene that made them special. It wasn't much of a stretch to suggest that—given enough time and money—we might stimulate similar abilities in people without that genetic advantage.

Yeah, I remember documentaries about the CIA exploring remote viewing. Asking someone to

draw images transmitted from the mind of a subject hundreds of miles away, right?

Yes. Our initial research rejected most psychic phenomena. We could find no proof of telekinesis, the ability to affect matter with the mind. The same with clairvoyance. As much as astrology believers want it to be true, no one can see the future. It's bullshit. Lucrative bullshit. With all the advances in science in my lifetime, people still call premium phone lines so a con artist can tell them crap they want to hear. Fifty bucks, please. Jesus.

So, you ruled out much of this phenomena as impossible. What was left?

Well, this is where it got interesting. Although much of the evidence was anecdotal, there was a ton for telepathy. The most compelling reports suggested links between siblings, even over large distances. There were thousands of cases. And they were even more convincing when they involved twins. That's where Barkworth directed Edgegen's research.

On twins?

Yes. And our early studies won us a lucrative military contract. Barkworth sent researchers all over the country, running tests on twins. It was a long-term programme. Twins, triplets, quads and quins were interesting for research, but the data were tainted. The twins grew up together, went to the same schools. They adhered to identical value systems. Their genetic heritage and their environments may have produced a decision-making process so similar to their siblings that it seemed like telepathy. Like I said, much of the anecdotal evidence was compelling, but it was just that - anecdotal. There was only one area of research where laboratory-condition results were above average.

And that was?

Remote viewing. With one sibling kept under observation and the other sent into the field with an Edgegen observer. The lab subject might sketch a particular tree, or a distinctive building in a city he or she had never visited.The hit-rate was way above average. And we had our star performers, Waldorf and Statler.

(Laughter and coughing on recording)

That wasn't their real names. But even Barkworth called them Waldorf and Statler. They were in their late eighties. Brothers from Cincinnati. Farmers. In his mid-forties, a tractor rolled on Statler, pinned him to the ground. It was market day, and Waldorf was on his way into town. Halfway there, Waldorf drove like a maniac to the hospital and demanded they send an ambulance. He rode in it himself, directed them to the field where his brother was bleeding, his leg broken. Saved his life. Their history was full of similar stories.

And they could reproduce this under laboratory conditions?

To the extent that we couldn't find an alternative explanation for their abilities. They were unlikely cheats; god-fearing, gentle old men. But we operated on the assumption they were colluding somehow. We made the tests harder and harder. One day we sent Statler up in a light aircraft. Didn't tell Waldorf. When we started the test, Waldorf stared at the wall for a good long time. I thought he had dozed off. He was in his late eighties. But then he started drawing. Waldorf sketched a blanket of clouds as seen through a small square window.

Todd Barkworth brought in a bottle of champagne that night. The military contract was extended, and we had a few visits from men in suits who didn't introduce themselves. We got a raise. Barkworth moved to Beacon Hill. The atmosphere was febrile. We were pioneers. Half the team was sleeping with the other half. It's hard to explain how exciting it was. God, I should have left then. I was too caught up in it.

What went wrong?

Statler died. We knew it was gonna happen sooner or later. Guess we were banking on later. Neither of them were in great health. That's one reason they helped us out. We gave them the best medical care. But when it's your time, it's your time. Statler had a massive stroke in his sleep. Waldorf knew it had happened, of course. He woke up in the early hours, at the moment his brother died. They were in an apartment owned by Edgegen, a block away from the lab. They didn't know it, but we placed cameras and mics in every room. We saw the tape of Waldorf sitting up, reaching for the phone. He never recovered from his loss. Died a month after Statler.

They were our stars, our performing monkeys. Without them, we had little to show Edgegen's paymasters. Then Barkworth started the second stage of the research project.

Which was?

Stage Two was when we crossed a line. And we knew it. Barkworth called us in, and we got a big raise. That was all it took. Amazing how flexible my personal moral code turned out to be. My income was good, the healthcare was the best, and the retirement plans were very generous. We signed NDAs and military gag orders. The government was involved, and a scary Washington lawyer flew in for a day to explain our new contracts. We were now working for our country, and if we loved our country, we would keep our mouths shut. No one made any threats, but we knew there would be consequences if a single detail of our work ever leaked. I slept badly for weeks afterwards.

What did Stage Two involve?

Stage Two was a long-term study. It involved the artificial insemination of volunteers to produce multiple births. Within two years of the project's inception, we had four sets of twins, and two sets of triplets to study. We separated them after birth, placing them in foster homes all over the United States. No one was told they were siblings.

They never met their brothers or sisters?

It would have interfered with the integrity of the study. By separating twins and triplets, we could ensure they were brought up in different environments. Some foster families were religious, others were atheists. While none were dirt poor—because of the payments from Edgegen—there was still a large discrepancy in income across the families. One of our boys had a senator for a foster mother. Another had an alcoholic ex-con foster father who'd never held down a job.

And how often did you study the children? If they were spread across the country, it must have been a huge project.

It was. We used local researchers. Told them it was a nation-wide psychological study of children in foster care, paid for by the government. They filmed the subjects and recorded interviews, asking questions we provided. As the children got old enough to draw, we began the real tests. We make sure the twins or triplets were interviewed on the same day, even if they were thousands of miles apart. At a specified time, one twin would be shown a photograph chosen from a selection by the researcher. The other twin was given paper and crayons and told to draw whatever they liked.

The early years weren't encouraging, but the children's brains were still developing. The researchers tested them once a month. For over a decade, results were inconclusive. There were coincidences, behavioural similarities between separated siblings. Nothing more.

Things got interesting at puberty, but not for everyone. The hormonal changes only improved the results of some children. And only one set of twins showed significant progress. Molly and Jason. In their early teens, their remote viewing results went crazy. They scored a hit in over eighty percent of tests.

I can't tell you how exciting that was. It was twelve years since Waldorf and Statler's successes. Our military and government backers had signed up for the long haul, but that didn't mean there wasn't pressure. They wanted a return on their investment. For years, Barkworth had nothing to give them. So we latched onto the twins as our ticket for future funding. The problem was, none of our other subjects showed any abilities like Molly and Jason's. If it wasn't for our star twins, we would have had nothing.

Did you find out what was different about Molly and Jason? Why they showed psychic ability, and the others didn't?

Yes, we did. It was a priority. We brought in those poor kids and ran every test we knew on them. Barkworth told the foster parents that a rare genetic disease had been found in their birth parents, and the children might die if they weren't treated. Molly went to a private hospital in New York, Jason was in Los Angeles. I was with the team assigned to Molly. Hair, saliva, and blood samples. Lumbar punctures. Angiographies, brain scans, biopsies, EEGs, ENGs. If we could think of a test, we ran it. If we could take anything from their bodies to examine, we took it. And we found nothing out of the ordinary. We sent the kids home after three weeks and ran more tests on every sample. Still nothing. Barkworth was as close to despair as I'd ever seen him. He knew we were onto something–we all did—but one positive result from multiple case studies wasn't enough. If we couldn't pinpoint the reason they were special, we were finished.

Then we found the correlation. It changed everything. A junior researcher had been looking into the family histories, comparing the twin's birth mother and sperm donor to those of every other subject. It was a long, tedious, piece of work. When she brought me her findings, I checked and double-checked them before going to Barkworth. The correlation was the surrogate mother. We had chosen the mothers for their physical and mental health. We checked their family history to avoid common genetic abnormalities. But the junior researcher discovered Jason and Molly's mother was the only surrogate who had a history of natural multiple births in her family. She was a twin. Her mother was a twin, as was her grandmother.

Mags stood up, resting her hands on the desk. When her fingers started to ache, she realised she'd clenched her fists. She walked to the window.

The last thing she wanted to do was to read more. Not only was she a twin, but so was her mother, grandmother and great-grandmother.

Mags looked outside. The winter sun bounced off the

snow-packed street, making it hard to look at. Three black cars slowed as they approached the house. Mags moved away, not wanting a neighbour to see her.

Back at the desk, she put her phone where she could see it, and turned the page.

How much worse could it get?

CHAPTER THIRTY-FIVE

There's a camera in my room, pointed towards the bed. The chair in the far corner, where visitors sit, is out of range. That's where I work out. I've developed my own circuit training over the weeks. I get out of bed, making sure I look weak and unsteady as I walk around the room, and I head for the chair. Once I'm out of view, I start my first set of dips, using the arms of the chair. I kneel to do bicep curls, lifting the chair by its armrest. Push-ups are next. When I started, it took all my willpower to manage one. Now, even with my toes on the headrest, I manage three sets of thirty.

They trust me to take their pills. I rarely see a needle these days. At first, I took the pills, then I kept them under my tongue, flushing them away later. Whatever they are, they keep me slow, confused. I keep up the act. They take my dazed condition for granted, and they're getting sloppy. Good.

Today, something unexpected upends my routine. Something glorious. Something so beautiful, it makes me ashamed of my doubts. After today, I know I am not alone; the universe has not deserted me. I am part of a greater plan.

The pills they give me this morning are the strongest.

Yellow, oblong, bigger than the others. Last time I took them, I was unconscious for over an hour. So I know what to do. Five minutes after pretending to swallow them, I let my head slump against the pillow and close my eyes. Ratched comes in. Simon is with her. She seems nervous. Hard to tell, but there's a tightness in her voice, and she's double-checking everything. Her behavior, plus the stronger sedative, puts me on my guard.

"Check him," she says. I sense Simon at my side. I stay limp and relaxed. He checks my pulse, lifts one eyelid. I roll my eyes back in my head. I'm not sure I can fool him. Ratched saves me.

"Hurry," she snaps.

When Simon speaks, it takes everything I have not to sit up and stare.

"I don't think he'll be breakdancing anytime soon. The drugs he's on, he can't tell me what day of the week it is. Poor sucker doesn't even realize he's in Boston."

Boston. Back where it started. It makes sense now. This is where I came for the drug trial and the procedure for my sleep disorder. So the American didn't come to me, I came to the American. And his father. I'm probably in the same building where they operated on me. And they know who I am. Those pictures, the ones she drew. They know I'm the Bedroom Killer. That's what the TV guys call me. They can't understand that what I do is not killing. Nobody understands it. I have to get out.

Ratched and Simon leave me. I'm still holding my breath, so let it out as softly as I can. If I am in America, how can I reach her? How will I get back to England, to London?

I have no answer. It's the lowest I've felt since the connection broke. I lose my last hope.

Then it happens. At my worst moment. When I'm on the brink of giving up.

The door opens. I don't dare open my eyes even a fraction of an inch. I cannot let them discover I'm not taking their drugs.

It's the American. He is not alone. His voice is different. He's talking quietly, as if not wanting to disturb me. This considerate behavior is new. It's for the benefit of his companion. Not his father. Who, then? I assumed the American's father was in charge. Was I wrong? Is he here with the real boss?

"Sometimes we look after people here. This man suffered an injury to his brain. We have studied the human brain for a long time, so we agreed to help. We hope he might make a full recovery."

A second voice. A child's voice. What is a child doing here?

"Is he asleep?"

"We give him special medicine to help him sleep, honey. He won't wake up. Don't be shy. Let's take a closer look."

Honey? Was this his daughter? But her accent was wrong. She sounded British.

Footsteps, then her voice again, closer.

"Dad, I know him. He's the man from the accident outside our house. I fetched a blanket for him. A van knocked him over. Mum called an ambulance. It's him, it's him."

"He looks like him, doesn't he, Tam? I thought the same at first. But it's not. That poor guy is in London. I checked on him a few times. Last I heard, he was out of hospital and expected to recover."

"How odd. He really looks like him. Uncanny, what?"

"Sure, Tam. Uncanny."

I hardly hear what the kid is saying. My life has been

turned upside down. She was there—the kid—at the accident. She came out of the house. It's her. The American is her father. That's how he had the drawings. She's the one who's calling me.

She's here.

I won't have to escape if I move now. Can I risk it, with her father here? I hesitate and decide to try. There may never be a better chance.

I tense my muscles, open my eyes a fraction to get an idea of where she is. She's half-turned away. She has short dark hair, her neck pale. I cannot see her face. Her father is about to take her hand, lead her away. I brace myself.

The door opens. "Sorry, Mr Barkworth. There's a call for you." It's Simon. "They said it was urgent. Something about your wife."

Too late, I'm too late. Three seconds later, I'm alone.

I lie back, try to take in what this means. As I think about it, there's an unfolding in my mind, a tiny flower of awareness. I know what is, and I weep with gratitude. Then I think of the danger. If I feel it, maybe she does too. She might say something to her father. I turn my attention away from it, do everything I can to ignore it. I can't let it unfold. Not yet. I have to find my moment, make my move when it's quieter.

But it has to be today. I cannot hide what's happening inside me for long, and she is close by.

I will not lose her again.

Today.

CHAPTER THIRTY-SIX

Transcript continues. Ava Marston, September 20**

When we discovered the link with families who produced twins naturally, Barkworth jumped on it. He wanted funding for a fresh study; we would focus on women from families with a history of twins. But the answer was no. Governments had come and gone, supporters had retired or died. There was no more money available for a project which had become a joke in Washington. We expected to be closed down.

What changed their mind?

Luck. One lucky break changed everything. Jesus. I still think of what happened as a piece of good luck. I never considered what it meant for Jason. Poor kid. He wasn't a person to us, just a name on a report.

He had a skateboard - one of those long ones. I don't know what the kids call them. He used to ride the hills in LA. One day he didn't come back. They found him beside the road. In hospital, they drained fluid from his brain. There was swelling on the cerebellum, and that kind of damage makes recovery unpredictable.

He regained consciousness and was released. During the months of recuperation at home, our local teams showed up as usual, asked their questions. The parents didn't complain. They still believed we'd saved him from a fictional genetic disease.

In the remote viewing part of the interviews, Jason failed every time. It didn't matter if he was the sender or receiver; the ability had disappeared. We had scans of his brain before the accident and compared them to the scans afterwards. Barkworth had one of the country's best neurologists working at Edgegen by then, and they pored over the data together. They identified damage to a specific part of the brain on the right hemisphere. Barkworth was convinced he had identified the area of the brain that provided the telepathic connection with Molly. That was when we moved onto Stage Three.

(*crying sounds*)

Ms Marston? Ava? Do you want to take a break? Here let me, let me, hold on a second. Here you are. I have tissues. Would you like something to drink?

A glass of water, please. I'm sorry. It's just... I mean... I persuaded myself it was justifiable. I let myself drift into it. We said Stage Three was in the interests of science and progress. The greater good. What a fucking joke.

Are you okay to go on?

Yeah, sure, I can go on. Twenty years too late, but I can go on.

Stage Three moved from theory to practice. From observation to interference. From interpretation of data to playing God. Barkworth reminded us of the contracts we'd signed. Then he tried to inspire us, talking about the next generation of scientific research, the new frontiers we could explore. We were the architects of the next stage of evolution, he said. Stage Three of our research would pave the way. He didn't sugarcoat it. There was no point. We were all scientists, we all spoke the same language. Experimental surgery, that's what was next. Not to heal anyone, but to reproduce Molly and Jason's connection.

In the weeks that followed, as we digested what we

were expected to do, the research team stopped pretending we were friends. The excitement of the eighties was long gone, but now we didn't even want to socialise outside the lab. No more Friday night drinks. The company Christmas dinner didn't happen that year, or any other year afterwards. No one in the team was sleeping together anymore.

No one quit. At least, that's what I thought. Now I'm not so sure. Tony, who'd lost his kid to leukaemia, didn't like Stage Three. He didn't like it at all. He was careful to hide his disgust, but we all saw it. I wondered if he would confront Barkworth, or if he'd walk away. A month after Stage Three began, he died in a car crash. An accident. Yeah. Right. The worst thing is, I believed it. Poor Tony. He was the best of us.

Stage Three involved invasive surgery on human subjects. There was no way anyone would agree to this at government level, but Barkworth had found a new source of funding. He may have lost the faith of a new generation of politicians, but a few believers from the early days were now running departments in the military, CIA, or other agencies. The money came back, that's all we knew.

We looked for subjects. We wanted people with existing neurological conditions. Mild epilepsy, narcolepsy, aphasia, Parkinsons, sleep disorders, Alzheimer's.

Ms Marston? You mentioned experimental surgery. What was the nature of the surgery?

Brain surgery. We operated on their brains.

There was a thorough process to find ideal candidates. It was important they had few living relatives. It was best if they were loners. We knew the procedure might leave them with permanent damage. Some wouldn't survive. Barkworth played that possibility down. But it was better if they were the people no one would miss. There was a generous fund available as compensation for any family members who asked questions.

So this was experimental brain surgery? What does that have to do with twins?

Okay. Okay. To answer that, I need to back up a little. Can we take a break? I need a break. Turn that off, would you?

Level check. Six-forty pm. Are you okay to continue, Ms Marston?

Yes. Let me talk. No questions. If I miss anything, you can ask me later, okay?

Yes. Go ahead.

Barkworth and his neurology team developed an experimental brain graft procedure. It involved a tiny amount of material, a sliver of cells. A thin slice of the cerebellum was removed from the subject—from the part of their brain active in Molly and Jason—and new cells were grafted to replace them.

God help us all.

By this time, we had two Barkworths to deal with. Bradley had joined Edgegen in his twenties. He was bright, capable, charming. If he'd gone into politics, he'd probably be president by now. But he was in the shadow of his father. Bradley never had quite the same drive, or vision. What he had was an intense desire to please Daddy. It's a common enough story. I feel like I'm making excuses for him, to explain what he did. What I think he did. Which no one could forgive.

Organ transplants are commonplace these days. We forget the early attempts, the failures, the deaths. A human body is prepared to protect itself. Introduce a foreign object, and it will fight the invader. Transplant surgery relies on convincing the body to accept that invader, welcome it. Barkworth expected this problem. The best chance of success—perhaps the only chance of success—depended on using genetic material the human brain would be the least likely to reject. Stem cells.

Potential subjects came to Boston, where we gave them a battery of tests. We shortlisted nine candidates.

Once we had our shortlist, we waited. Barkworth never told us where he would find the stem cells we needed. They couldn't be just any stem cells. They had to be those of a twin from a family with a history of multiple births. We didn't know where he would find them. We didn't want to know. I stopped thinking about it. That's the truth. I stopped thinking about it.

In most workplaces, parents bring their infants in to show them off. They pass them around, and everyone gets a turn holding a newborn. I sometimes dream about that, about holding a baby at Edgegen. It's not a dream, though, it's a nightmare. I wake up shaking, sweating, crying.

Around that time, I heard a newborn baby's cry at work. It was during one of Bradley's visits. He was spending half his time abroad. Barkworth told us he was working on a separate project. Nobody minded. As charming and good looking as he was, there was something I didn't like. An emptiness. Maybe I'm projecting. If I can make him more evil in hindsight, can I make myself less complicit? No. I don't think so. Too easy.

It was so short, that cry. Tiny. Piercing. Unmistakable. I was in a corridor near the operating theatre. I stood still, hoping to hear it again. Dreading to hear it again. I told myself, as I stood there, that I'd imagined it. I counted to ten, but there was no second cry, so I walked away. I walked away. But I know what I heard. There was a child in the theatre that day.

The first procedures took place a week later. Three, over the course of a week. Every procedure failed. The brain rejected the graft, or it accepted it with no discernible result. No one could have predicted how the brain would react. It was a setback, but Barkworth scheduled in the remaining six candidates, anyway. Their procedures took place over the next two years. We learned a little more from each one.

Stage Three was put on hold while we examined what we had learned from the subjects. The neurology team improved the procedure and made suggestions for the selection of future candidates.

After the initial failures, Barkworth was cautious. Two or three procedures a year, and we kept the subjects under close observation. Barkworth was convinced the procedure would work with the right candidate.

He was right.

Subject twenty-two—S22—was in his late twenties. He was fit, but he suffered from a rare disorder meaning he had never snatched more than a few minutes sleep in his life. He also suffered from delusions, probably because of the sleep disorder. Many of his delusions were harmless, but he had a fascination with death. He envied those who could sleep, and he thought of death as the deepest, most peaceful sleep of all. His childhood had been troubled. Heh. That's an understatement. Never knew his father, mother was an alcoholic who committed suicide when he was thirteen. Hanged herself with fishing line. He was the one who found her. He talked about her as if she were still alive. I remember there was some debate whether to accept him as a candidate. But Barkworth insisted.

The procedure went well. We transferred S22 to the Edgegen apartment after his initial recovery period and watched him through hidden cameras as the weeks went by. His physical recovery was faster than any of the others, and we became optimistic. No one saw what was coming. We were paying well, and he was not a wealthy man. But, one day, he disappeared. Walked out, never came back. We told him he needed to see us for drugs essential to his recovery, but he ignored that. We spent months trying to track him down, but he was a drifter, and he knew how to exist under the radar. We never saw him again.

The atmosphere in the team changed afterwards. Or

maybe it was just me. Barkworth pressed ahead with new candidates, but he was furious. According to him, S22 was his golden ticket. We weren't so sure. Okay, if the graft held, what then? If he was trying to duplicate the connection between Molly and Jason, he needed two subjects with functional brain grafts. Who was the other candidate?

If anyone in the team found the answer, I never heard about it. A year after S22 disappeared, my annual medical came back with some anomalies. Two biopsies later and I was given the prognosis. Funny. It was a relief. Karma. Punishment.

I'm tired. I need a break. You can ask me questions later. Have I given you enough to bring Barkworth down? I hope so. It's the only way to stop Edgegen. Make it public. Take this to the police, and they'll bury it. They'll bury you, too.

I wish you luck, Mr Martino. I told you I'm not religious, but sometimes, in the middle of the night, the pain driving me crazy, I wonder if there's a higher power. But if there is a God, a heaven and a hell, then I know where I'm heading. And hell will be familiar. It will be the cry of a baby. Only this time, it won't stop, it'll go on and on, and I'll be standing in the Edgegen corridor, not doing anything to help.

I'm going to bed.

End of transcript.

It was strange, but when she discovered all her worst fears were true, Mags could handle it. Maybe it wasn't the same for everyone, but she surprised herself with her reaction. For a while, she could barely bring herself to read what was in front of her. The sickening dread that built as she read on was physical, a weight settling on her shoulders. But not inanimate; worse, the weight was alive, clammy, cold and moist, sliding its heavy limbs over hers, wrapping dark sinuous tentacles around her shoulders, chest, and stomach. Entering her body like black smoke, swimming through her bloodstream, whispering a message of death. Then, with a cold splash of clarity and decision, she refused to yield. The weight lifted. The monster evaporated.

Mags could not afford to lose her mind, to surrender to the horror. She was a mother. And her daughter needed her.

The future narrowed until she could only see a chain of events, a sequence to follow. Find Tam, drive her to the airport, leave. For now, Mags couldn't see beyond that. But it was enough. Get Tam. Get away from the Barkworths. Go home.

She closed the folder and stood up. The small study was just as it had been when she first walked in, other than the angle of the sunlight slanting in through the small window.

With no idea what she would say to Patrice Martino, she opened the door and walked into the kitchen.

The man sitting at the table looked up. It wasn't Patrice Martino.

It was Bradley.

CHAPTER THIRTY-SEVEN

"Where's Patrice?" said Mags.

"It doesn't concern you anymore, Mags. Forget about him." Bradley stood up. His expression, as ever, was hard to read. "Come on. I'll drive you home."

Mags looked at her husband and saw a stranger.

"Not until you tell me where he is."

Bradley stood up. "Give me the keys."

She shook her head and gripped her bag.

"No one's gonna hurt him, Mags. But he can't publish his story. Sooner or later, he'll see it's best to drop it. Sooner would be better, for him."

A man and a woman, both wearing suits, walked through the door Ava had used earlier. They stood in the middle of the room, their posture reminding Mags of a documentary she'd watched about animal predators. They looked relaxed, bored even. Their arms hung loosely by their sides, legs planted in a wide stance, and their eyes never stopped surveying the surrounding space.

She swallowed.

"The keys," repeated Bradley.

The woman moved, took a step towards Mags and held out her hand. Mags gave her the keys, and the woman tossed them over to Bradley.

"Come on," he said. She looked back at the strangers. They were entering the office. The man paused on the threshold and looked at her. He didn't move until Mags had gone.

Outside, Bradley was waiting. She stopped outside the door.

"Where is Tam?"

"With Mom. Making cookies."

Mags fumbled her phone from her bag and called Irene Barkworth. "Irene, it's Mags. Is Tam there?"

"Yes, honey, she's right here. Wait up. Tam, wash the flour off your hands. Your mom wants to speak with you." Irene lowered her voice. "Are you okay, Mags? We were worried."

Mags wondered how much Mrs Barkworth knew about her husband's business, and her son's role in it. Irene Barkworth's whole demeanour was that of a woman who had stopped asking questions a long time ago. If she ever had. She had a lifestyle many would envy; prying too closely might jeopardise that.

Tam was on the phone. Mags pressed it to her ear. Her daughter's voice reminded her the world wasn't all darkness and despair.

"Hi, Mum. We're making peanut butter cookies. They smell divine. Where are you? I missed you."

"I missed you too. I'm coming home soon. Save some cookies for me."

"I will. Did Dad come to get you? He said he would. Did he tell you where we went this morning?"

Mags glanced at Bradley, then away again. She focused

on her daughter. "No, he didn't. Where did you go?"

Tam sounded excited, and more than a little proud. "He took me to work with him. I had a tour of the whole lab. They've got those fridges with test tubes in them, and microscopes, and loads and loads of computers. And there's an operating theatre just like in a real hospital. It's amazing, Mum"

Mags felt her stomach lurch. Tam had been to Edgegen Technology. While she had been reading Ava Marston's confession, her daughter had been walking those same corridors.

The world tilted and she stepped to one side, stumbled. As her knees buckled, Bradley was beside her. He took her weight, lowering her onto the stoop. He pulled the phone out of her fingers.

"Hey, honey, we're on our way. See you soon."

Tam's tinny voice answered, "Top hole!" before Bradley thumbed the phone off.

"Let's go."

They drove for five minutes without exchanging a word. Mags watched the cars, and she watched her thoughts. Who had she married? What had Bradley done?

Her body was reacting as if it was a fight-or-flight scenario, pumping adrenaline into her system. She was alternately hot and cold, her skin becoming first hypersensitive, then numb. When she tried to deepen her breathing, she found she couldn't, concentrating instead on not letting her rapid gasps turn into an attack. She thought of Tam.

At the end of the five minutes, as they were about to leave the I-95 for the 93 back to Boston, she pointed at a half-empty business park.

"Pull over."

He made no move to obey, so she grabbed the wheel.

The car left the road and bounced across the dusty shoulder.

"Jesus! Okay, okay."

Bradley pulled into the lot and turned off the engine. He shifted in his seat and looked at her. Mags forced herself to look back. She tried to spot the monster behind those movie-star blue eyes and failed, despite knowing it was there. Her stomach lurched, and she looked away before she threw up.

"This is not the time or place," he said. "We need to talk, but not now. I'll give you five minutes."

She gasped. "You've ruined my life. You've done nothing but lie. You, you—" She couldn't find the words. "Five minutes?"

"Four-and-a-half now. You've caused enough damage today."

"Me? *I've* caused damage?"

"Yes, you. This is a critical time for our research. We're on the brink of the scientific achievement of the century. No one can jeopardise that. No one."

"What have you done to Tam?"

"Nothing. You wouldn't understand. Jesus. As long as you have your therapy sessions and a bottle of white wine every other night, you're happy. You don't have the first idea what Dad and I have achieved. You're small-minded. It's all about you and your little family. You were useful for one reason. You're not useful anymore. When you stayed out of my way, you didn't matter. But now you're interfering with my work. Jesus!"

He smacked the steering wheel. Then he let out a long sigh. "Look," he said. "I don't mean that. It's just, well, this couldn't have come at a worse time. You don't understand the importance of..." He frowned. "You just don't understand, okay?"

Mags looked out at the parking lot, the snow, crusted with ice until the next fresh fall, reflecting the low sun. A playground chant was running round her head.

Sticks and stones may break my bones, but words will never hurt me.

If she asked him, if he told her the truth, she thought it might kill her. There are some words no one should ever hear.

I'm stronger than I think. Sticks and stones.

"Did you kill Clara?"

He answered. At least he would not torture her.

"No. No, Mags. Of course not. Honey,—"

Mags brought her hands up as if to attack him without knowing she was doing it. "Don't call me honey, you sick bastard. Don't you ever call me that."

"If that's what you want, Mags. Clara,—"

She interrupted again. Mags couldn't bear to hear him say her name. "No more lies. No more lies."

"I agree. No more lies, Mags. I've seen some of Martino's notes. What would be the point?"

He smiled. He actually *smiled*.

Mags bit the inside of her cheek to stop herself ripping the skin from his skull with her fingernails.

"Mags, I couldn't tell you about Clara. I'm sorry. But now... well, I guess we're way past that. Hon—" He stopped himself saying it. "Mags. Clara isn't dead."

CHAPTER THIRTY-EIGHT

M ags dug her nails into her thighs. When she spoke, her mouth felt as strange and numb as it did after a trip to the dentist. How could Clara be alive?

"What do you mean?"

Bradley turned away and looked out at the half-empty parking lot. His eyes were unfocused.

"Okay," he said. He spoke without turning towards her. "I don't know everything Ava Marston told Martino, but I guess it makes us look pretty bad. Wouldn't be a good story if there were two sides to it, would it?"

The question was rhetorical. Mags wasn't sure she could have spoken even if she wanted to. She waited for him to go on, and, after a time, he did.

"You need to understand something. You don't have a decision to make right now. You might think you do, but you don't. I guess you're already planning your escape, thinking about divorce, maybe criminal proceedings. It won't happen, Mags. It'll be easier if you accept that. Remember what happened to the Bedroom Killer. Disappeared without a trace after we pulled some strings. Martino will never publish. And you will never talk about this. Not if you care about Tam."

That was too much. Mags heard her own voice emerge, pushed through her teeth by a tide of hate. "Don't threaten my daughter."

"Oh, don't misunderstand me, Mags. I would never hurt Tam. She's my daughter too. Whatever you think of me, I love Tam. It's an unexpected side-effect of parenthood."

A side-effect. Right.

"There's no point making any trouble. Tam is staying right here in America. I have her passport. I have yours, too. You can go, if you like, I won't stop you. But Tam stays. If you fight for custody, if you file for divorce, you'll lose her. You can't hope to win. Think about it. I have everything to offer her. A great home with family nearby. I've been a model father, have provided well for you. You have a history of mental illness. You're unstable. You have no hand to play, Mags. Tam is staying in Boston. If you want to be in her life, you'll stay too."

Mags knew he wasn't bluffing. Everything was falling apart, and there was nothing she could do about it. He was dragging her into hell and taking Tam along too. All those times she had convinced herself she was paranoid for not trusting him. She should have paid attention to her instincts. Tears pricked the corners of her eyes.

"We looked for surrogates fifteen years ago," he said. "Edgegen's backers were getting jumpy. There had been a couple of scares, a leak to the press by a junior researcher. They killed the story, but they were only prepared to keep funding the project if it was secure. That's when I volunteered."

"Volunteered for what?" Mags' voice was a harsh whisper.

"Stage Three. We looked for women with twins and triplets in their family, but not in America. We concentrated our research on Britain and Australia. English-speaking countries. I admit I pushed hard for Britain when the initial results came back. I always liked London.

"Twelve candidates came back as possibilities. We eliminated five of them because of their age. Two of the remaining seven were gay. Of the other five, only three were acceptable."

"Acceptable?"

Bradley smirked. "I rejected two of them because they wouldn't have looked right dating me. I'm good-looking, Mags. People would have asked questions. Even you were borderline. Sorry, it's the truth."

Another piece of paranoia confirmed as a fact. He had been out of her league all along. Kit had been right.

"I dated three of you. One didn't work out. We weren't compatible. There's only so much pretending I can do. The relationship was never gonna work. I still tried to get her pregnant but I guess she wasn't very fertile. That left you and Joanna."

He looked across at her, as if waiting for a reaction. Mags said nothing. He was playing with her. She wanted to know about Clara. If he didn't tell her soon, she swore she would strangle the deceitful bastard.

"Joanna fell pregnant during your second trimester. I was going to move her to Boston after the birth. Better to have more than one option. In the end, it was unnecessary. The first scan showed a single foetus. She lives in Italy now. We arranged a lucrative job offer for her when the kid was two. Unlikely you and I would run into her in London, but better not to risk it.

"We had a team standing by on the day of your

caesarean. We had planned for months. I anaesthetised you to avoid any unforeseen problems. One baby was driven to City Airport and flown back to Boston. The other stayed in London with us."

"Tam," said Mags. She was crying now. She couldn't help herself. But her face was rigid as the tears ran down her cheeks, dropped off her chin, and splashed onto her lap.

"We harvested stem cells from the umbilical cord, and we placed the other subject with a foster family."

"Clara. Her name is Clara."

"Clara, yes. It's not her name anymore, though. It's Ellen, I think. Or Helen."

He took his phone out of his pocket, tapped on the screen a few times, and placed it on the dashboard. Mags leaned forward. It was a video of Tam. There was no sound. Her hair was longer. Mags didn't remember it ever being that long.

Then she spoke and Mags knew it was Clara. Even without sound, the way her mouth moved was different. Her physicality, her gestures, even her smile, were like Tam's, but everything was slower. She moved like Tam did when over-tired, on the brink of sleep. Everything was sluggish. Tam's sparkiness and quick reactions were missing.

Bradley spoke throughout the thirty seconds of footage. Any love she had ever experienced for the man next to her was turning to implacable hatred; but her heart was swelling with impossible love for a daughter she had never met.

"We told the foster family she had a rare genetic disease. We said we would pay for her care, so we could learn from her condition. The foster parents needed money. He had embezzled his company, and she was an accessory to his crime. We kept them out of prison, they didn't ask questions. The arrangement worked well. It still does. When we had subjects ready for Stage Three, we brought Clara in, and removed cells from her cerebellum to use alongside the stem cells we harvested when she was a baby. We've performed this procedure three times now. There was no way to prevent some damage to the brain. She is well cared for, and she has a good life, Mags, but she has some learning difficulties. If it were possible, I would want her name known to everyone, as a pioneer. It will happen, one day. She'll be the Neil Armstrong of human evolution, the—"

"You did this to her? She was healthy, and you did this? To your own daughter?"

Mags could no more have stopped what happened next than stop a hurricane. She pummelled Bradley's face with her fists, screaming, punching, reaching for his throat. She wanted to destroy him. There was no room in her mind for a single rational thought. In that moment, she was more animal than human.

Something hit the side of her face and she slumped in her seat. For a long moment, reality paused, and she heard a high-pitched whine. Then it faded, and she looked at the roof of the car, noticing a stain and wondering how it got there. For a few seconds, she didn't know where she was. It was like waking from an afternoon nap on holiday, confused by unfamiliar surroundings.

For a blissful second-and-a-half, she looked at Bradley and knew he was her husband, nothing more. Then her cheek throbbed, and she remembered. She brought her fingers to her mouth and winced. It was already tender, and the skin was swelling. Her teeth felt loose and she could taste blood.

"I'll break your jaw next time. Try me."

Bradley started the car and headed for home. He didn't speak again.

Mags fought to keep her focus on Tam. If she thought about the enormity of the lie she had lived with Bradley, of how she had been used, she wasn't sure she would be able to stop herself wrenching the steering wheel away from him and putting them both into the path of a truck.

What was she going to tell Tam? How could she live with the monster who had used his own children as experimental subjects?

But, if leaving him meant leaving Tam, what choice did she have?

CHAPTER THIRTY-NINE

I make my move at the end of Simon's shift. I'm sorry it's him. He has been good to me, in his own way, but I will do whatever I have to. If there was any other way, if I could escape without killing him... but there's no use thinking like that.

My best chance comes after physiotherapy. The nurses run these sessions in the room next door. There's only one other door on that corridor, and I hope it's the nurses' station. I'll find out soon enough.

I cut the physiotherapy session short today, faking a problem with my leg, a strained ligament after trying too hard. I've been underplaying my physical recovery for weeks, and Simon has become relaxed around me, thinking I'm weak.

He helps me back to my room and onto the bed. The adrenaline is making me sweat, but he puts it down to pain from my leg.

"You need some painkillers?"

I nod.

As soon as he leaves, I jump out of bed and go to the IV

stand in the corner. I reach up to to the dangling plastic bag and snap the tubing away. Moving as fast as I can, I wrap it around my hands and pull, testing it for strength. It holds.

The door opens. Simon takes two steps inside before he realises something is wrong. He stops, confused by the empty bed. Before he turns, I'm on him. I jump, looping the medical tubing around his throat, pulling it taut and wrapping my legs around his chest.

He's a big man, but it's no real advantage when your opponent is clinging to your back. Given his situation—the blood can no longer flow to and from his brain and he is losing consciousness—he thinks fast and falls backwards. He's hoping to crush me under his weight. I react, letting go with my legs. As he hits the ground, I jump onto his chest and continue pulling. Blood vessels burst in his eyes and he makes jerking motions with his head. Then he is still.

The doors open with an electronic key fob. I unclip Simon's from his belt, open the door and look outside. Everything is quiet.

I duck back into the room. Simon was wearing a thick canvas belt. Far better than the tubing. I undo the belt and pull it through the loops, snapping it tight between my hands. Later, I will make a new device. For now, this will do.

In the corridor, I hurry to the door I spotted before. The key fob beeps and it opens. Inside, an automatic light flickers on. My guess was right. It is the nurses' station. There's a table and chairs, three lockers, a coffee machine, a water-cooler and a TV screen showing my room. Simon's body is clearly visible. I could go back and move it.

For a moment, I'm frozen with indecision. Then I gasp as the petals of connection unfold in my brain. She is not far away. I know I can find her. Speed is important. More important than covering up the body.

A white jacket hangs behind the door. I take it, and open the nearest locker. Lucky first time. I pull on a pair of sweatpants, a T-shirt and a hoodie. The shoes are too big, so I'm stuck with the hospital slippers.

I put on the white coat over the hoodie. I find what I hoped for on the wall: a map showing the fire exits. The building is on two levels. The top level, where I am. The lower level has more rooms. Offices, perhaps.

There are car keys in my pocket. I study the map again. The car park is on the lower level. At least it's at this end of the building. I memorise the route, pull the coat tight around me, put my head down and walk out of the room.

I walk as if in a hurry, but I don't run. If someone sees me, I want them to see a nurse on duty.

The corridor turns left, then ends in front of a large door. I hold the key fob to the panel and it clicks open with a beep. I step through and turn right, entering the stairwell. No one has seen me. I jog to the bottom and the lower level.

It's a long, exposed corridor with doors leading off on both sides. The parking garage is at the far end.

I estimate the distance and count down the yards in my head as I walk.

Twenty yards. Fifteen. Ten.

A door opens behind me. I keep my pace steady and don't look back.

"You! You there! Stop!"

I recognise the voice. I think fast. If I run, get outside, I have to find an unfamiliar car, get to the exit, and leave, by which time he will have raised the alarm. If the authorities know the car I'm driving, they might stop me.

I turn around. The man facing me is the American's father.

CHAPTER FORTY

B y the time they arrived at the Barkworth's house, Mags appeared calmer. She wasn't sure how long she'd be able to keep up the act, but—for Tam's sake—she hoped she could manage until bedtime. She needed time to think. There must be a way out of this nightmare. Surely she wasn't condemned to stay with a man who sacrificed his own daughter, after separating her from her mother, to further his scientific career?

She used the car's mirror to apply foundation, cover the bruising on her face. It wasn't perfect, but Mags hoped it would be good enough to avoid awkward questions. She wasn't sure she could hide the horror of her day from Tam. But she had to try. Later. Later. She could think it through later. She repeated it to herself like a mantra.

Bradley's phone had been buzzing for the last five minutes of the journey, and the display showed six unanswered calls from his mother.

"She probably burned the cookies," he muttered. Mags didn't respond.

As their headlights swept across the front of the house,

the front door opened and Irene Barkworth ran out. Her immaculate hair was in disarray and she was shouting.

Bradley and Mags opened their doors at the same moment. Mags was nearer to the house, so it was her arm that Irene grabbed, pulling her out.

"It's Tam," she said.

"Is she hurt?" Mags felt fresh pain lance through her.

"No, no, nothing like that. It's, it's, well, I can't get through to her. She can't hear me. And she's, well, come and see. Help me, please."

Inside the house, Irene dragged Mags to the dining room. A strange sound reached them from inside, a squeaking and scratching. Mags heard Bradley hurrying to catch up.

She walked into the dining room and stopped. Tam stood facing the wall. In both of her hands she held sharpies. The cream-painted wall was now a canvas for Tam's drawings. Mags put her hand on the nape of her daughter's neck.

"Tam? Can you hear me, sweetheart?"

Just as she had feared, there was no response. Tam hadn't heard, she was somewhere else. Her eyes stared straight ahead, not seeing the wall in front of her. Mags looked at Tam's hands in disbelief. They moved independently, filling in details of the pictures. She had just begun a third drawing. Her body obscured it, so Mags stepped back and looked at the rest of the wall.

At the far end, the first drawing showed a hospital room. There was a single bed, some monitoring equipment. In one corner was a chair. In another corner, an IV stand with a bag hanging from it.

The second drawing showed another room. This one had a table, lockers, a water cooler. The most detailed part of the picture was a diagram on the wall, like the ones you find in hotels showing the fire exits.

Bradley was in the room, standing behind Mags.

"Fuck, no."

Irene Barkworth was in the doorway. "There's no need for that kind of language, Bradley."

Bradley pointed at her without looking away from the wall. "Shut the fuck up, Mother."

Irene Barkworth shut the fuck up.

Bradley looked over Tam's shoulder at the third drawing. He gasped, put his hands on her shoulders and pulled her away. Tam didn't protest. Bradley breathed fast as he took in the details of the picture.

It was an office. A luxurious office with furnishings that exuded status. There were certificates on the wall, a huge desk with a large leather chair. Long shelves lined with books. Three large computer monitors.

Mags had never seen it before. But Bradley had.

"Dad." The word was a whisper. He ran from the room. Seconds later, he was back. He tossed the SUV keys to Mags, who caught them, looking at him in surprise. Tam was back at the wall, both hands moving.

"He's escaped," Bradley said, his face haggard with fear. "I'll take my car. Take Tam to the lodge. The address is in the satnav."

Mags ran after Bradley as he left the house, heading for his BMW. The cold air was a slap in the face. The temperature must have dropped five degrees since they had arrived. Snow was falling from a silent yellow sky.

"Wait!" Bradley ignored her, getting into the car and starting the engine. She ran over and yanked the door open.

"Who's escaped?"

Before Bradley spoke, she knew the answer. Her knees buckled, and she braced herself against the roof of the car.

"The Bedroom Killer." Bradley slammed the door shut, and Mags stumbled backwards as he accelerated away, the back of the car sliding on the icy drive before the tyres bit onto the road.

CHAPTER FORTY-ONE

H e might be old, but he's fast and he thinks on his feet. That moment in the corridor, when I decide to kill him, he sees it in my eyes. He runs back to his office.

I sprint, covering the distance between us before he can shut the door. He slams it in my face with his weight behind it. It's almost enough to keep me out.

I lose momentum, and by the time I'm in, he's thrown himself over the biggest desk I've ever seen. Paperwork goes flying. So does the phone. But he wasn't reaching for the phone.

He lands badly on the far side of the desk, falls and cries out. He fumbles for a drawer, pulls hard at the handle. The whole drawer comes out, spilling its contents over him.

By that time, I'm vaulting the desk. He's on his side. I spot a gun on the floor by his shoulder. He sees where I'm looking and sweeps it up, bringing the barrel towards me.

I see why he cried out. He can't hold the gun, shouting in pain as he forces broken fingers onto the trigger. I land on my feet and kick the gun out of his hand. He shrieks in agony and frustration.

My hands are on the desk behind me. I saw something when I ran in. I look now. A statue, like an Oscar, but darker. I smash it into his skull.

He stops moving the third time I hit him. I do it twice more to be sure. Then I look at the statue.

For contributions to the pursuit of knowledge. 2002.

I put the statue back on the desk. It's a handsome piece of work. Then I leave the way I came.

No one challenges me this time and I make it to the parking garage. There are only four cars in the place, and when I press the key, the lights of a small Honda flash.

I get into the car. There's a remote control for the garage door in the cup holder.

I'm about to start the engine when the shutter rolls up. I duck as headlamps roll across the windshield of the Honda, then straighten up again.

A BMW rockets across the space and comes to a tire-squealing stop next to the door into the building. The American gets out and runs inside.

I sit in the car for a few seconds. I guess he will check on his father. When he finds the body, he'll call 911. If he doesn't do it from the office, he'll call from the car as he goes back to protect his family. His family. His daughter.

I put my trust in God's hands, cross the garage and slide into the rear seat of the BMW.

Then I wait.

"Mum? I don't feel so good."

Tam dropped the sharpies a few minutes after Bradley left.

Irene Barkworth opened the good scotch and sat at the

dining room table, drinking, facing away from the newly illustrated wall.

Mags put the back of her hand on her daughter's forehead. "Are you sick, honey?" Tam, always pale, was as white as the ploughed snow at the side of the road.

"No, it's not that. It's like a headache. But not a headache. More like something pushing, inside my head." She rubbed the side of her skull. Mags brushed Tam's dark hair back and stroked the side of her face. She sent up a silent prayer to whoever atheists were supposed to pray to. Whatever Bradley had done to her daughter—her *daughters*, she reminded herself—please don't let it be permanent. At the thought of Clara, a surge of love and rage threatened to burst through, and she pushed it away, hard. There was no time for it now.

She pulled Tam into the kitchen, took down her coat from the peg, and put it on her as if she were a toddler. Tam didn't protest, holding Mags' hand as they went out to the SUV.

They made good time out of Boston, and headed north as a fresh snowfall began.

In the car, Mags thought fast. She was confused, betrayed, and terrified. She and Tam were in the car, alone. They were not far from the Canadian border. Bradley was certainly capable of following through on his threats, but his world might be about to come crashing down. This was their chance to escape. Even if Bradley and his father covered up their involvement with the Bedroom Killer—and she didn't know the extent of that—she had to make the most of this opportunity. What was the alternative? Canada was a four-and-a-half hour drive away in normal conditions. In a snowstorm, it might take double that. Her hands tightened on the steering wheel.

Tam moaned and slumped in her seat.

"Tam. Tam, what's wrong?" No response. "Tam, please answer."

Mags was looking for somewhere to pull over when Tam sat up, staring ahead. Mags recognised the expression in her eyes. She was seeing something else. That was why the diagnosis of absence seizures had been so compelling. It was as if Tam had gone. But there was a difference this time - she wasn't drawing.

Tam's eyes widened, and she slumped again.

Mags indicated, slowing the car as they pulled into a layby.

Tam was awake. And it *was* Tam. "Mum? Where was I? Where did I go?"

"What do you mean? You were right here, honey."

Tam shook her head. "No. I was in another car. I was waiting for something. It was dark. What's happening to me?"

If the drawings meant Tam could see through the eyes of the Bedroom Killer, what on earth had she just seen?

Mags was exhausted already. She brought up the map on the car's touchscreen and changed their destination to Montreal. The live map was littered with red triangles and warnings to the north.

It looked as if the weather was conspiring against her. The snowflakes which had drifted slowly in front of her as she drove out of Boston were coming thick and fast now. Visibility was dropping by the minute.

"We're not going to the lodge, Tam. We're going as far away as we can get." She looked up at the sky. Night time looked like it was arriving early, bringing with it a swirling cloud of fresh snow.

"Shit." Mags accelerated, and the SUV slid sideways

before the tyres found purchase and bumped back onto the interstate.

Tam wasn't asking questions. That was unusual. She hadn't even asked about her father. Mags looked at her. She was asleep.

Mags twisted the windscreen wipers to their highest setting and drove on.

I don't have long to wait. I picture the American running along the corridor to his father's office, imagine him throwing open the door, seeing the body. I allow enough time for him to check the pulse and discover he is too late. A few moments of confusion, perhaps. But the American is a decisive man. If he doesn't come back through the door of the parking garage in the next ten seconds, then I've made the wrong choice. He might be calling the police right now. My hands tighten around the belt. I'm grinding my teeth. I haven't done that since I was a kid.

Even though I'm expecting it, I jump when the door to the garage bursts open. I duck behind the driver's seat and wait. The car moves as he drops into the front seat. He guns the engine and we move forwards. He brakes sharply in front of the shutter. I have my heels braced on the floor to stop me knocking into his back and betraying my presence.

He waits until the shutter is halfway up then skids out onto the street. I see Boston for the first time. It's snowing.

When he comes to a halt at a stop sign, I make my move. I sit up and loop the belt around his throat and the headrest, pulling it tight. His hands go to his neck, and I lean forward until my mouth is an inch from his ear.

"Put your hands on the steering wheel." I loosen the pres-

sure. Able to breathe again, he sucks in the air desperately. He's listening.

"Take me to her."

"I don't know what you mean."

I prevent him lying by reminding him there's a thick canvas belt across his windpipe. I control whether he lives or dies.

"The girl. Your daughter. Take me to her."

He doesn't answer. He's thinking it through. I try to imagine what factors he might be considering, but I can't. It's something I've never been good at. That expression, 'put yourself in my shoes,' never made sense. How can I? How can I know what it's like to be someone else? How can anyone?

"All right," he says. "Don't hurt me. Let me breathe."

He's trying to trick me, of course. He knows who I am. And he knows what I've done. He thinks I will kill him whatever he does. So he's planning something.

"Drive," I say. It takes ten minutes to get to the interstate, and we head north.

"Where are we going?" I ask him.

"Sunapee. We have a lodge up there. That's where they'll be."

"Who?"

"My wife. And my daughter."

"Take me there. And don't do anything stupid."

I tighten the belt for a second to remind him who's in charge. We drive on.

The conditions were getting worse by the second. Mags had never been a confident driver, and she hated the way the car skittered, the steering vague on the slippery surface. She slowed to forty miles-per-hour, then thirty.

There were very few cars around them. At each junction, people were leaving the interstate to find shelter. The snow came thick and fast, swirling hypnotically in the headlights. Tam moaned and shifted in her seat. She'd fallen into a restless sleep. Mags checked her forehead again, but there was no sign of fever. Tam muttered to herself as if in the grip of a nightmare.

For twenty minutes, Mags stared grimly ahead, picking out road signs as they loomed from the swirling storm, keeping her vehicle in its lane, squinting into the narrow cone of light.

Tam sat up, opened her eyes, looked at Mags and said, "He's coming."

She only took her attention off the road for two or three seconds, but it was enough.

"What did you say?"

Tam repeated her words.

"Mum, he's coming." Then she looked out at the storm and screamed.

"Mum!"

Mags snapped her eyes back to the road in time to see a huge truck, stationary, its bulk blocking their path. It was on its side. The heavy vehicle must have jackknifed, its trailer pulling the cab after it as it overbalanced. All Mags could see at first was wheels - twelve of them looming out of the white and black night. They were still spinning. The accident must have only just happened.

Mags did precisely what drivers are advised never to do in icy conditions. She stamped both feet onto the brake and jerked the steering wheel hard to the left. Such a manoeuvre in a car manufactured when she had first passed her test would have been her death sentence, but the modern SUV had sophisticated computer-assisted safety features. Anti-lock brakes began a rapid series of actions and reactions. As soon as the tyres slid on the ice, the brakes released their hold for a few hundredths of a second before applying again, more gently this time. The rapid cycle of releasing, braking, releasing, and braking communicated itself to the vehicle's occupants as a violent juddering. Precious speed was scrubbed off in those few seconds, but nothing could stop the slide initiated by Mags' jerk of the wheel. The back-end of the SUV swapped places with the front.

There was a loud metallic bang as the rear corner of the SUV hit one of the truck's enormous tyres. The air inside the tyre absorbed some of their speed, and the SUV bounced away, shuddering. It came to rest parallel to the underside of the truck.

"Tam, are you okay? Are you hurt?"

The look in her daughter's eyes was a mixture of shock and fear, but it was nothing to do with the accident. She gripped her mother's hand.

"He's coming, Mum."

A figure in fluorescent clothing walked round from the front of the truck, materialising in their headlights like a ghost. On seeing their car he broke into a jog.

Tam's fingernails dug deep into Mags' palm. "We can't stop. We have to go, Mum, we have to go."

The engine was still running. Mags pressed the accelerator, and the car lurched forwards, all four wheels fighting for grip as it built up speed. The driver of the truck waved his arms over his head. He was shouting. Mags could just make out his words over the noise of the engine.

"Stop! It's too dangerous! You'll get yourself killed."

He stepped away from the truck and into their path. Mags pushed hard on the accelerator and leaned on the horn. She flipped the headlights onto full beam. The man's face went slack with shock. He dived out of the way as they passed him.

The truck lay across both lanes of the interstate, but there was just enough room for a single vehicle to get through. Mags breathed in as the side of the SUV scraped the front of the cab, a cloud of steam rising from its punctured radiator. She was shaking.

As they pulled back onto their side of the interstate, the car developed a worrying clunking noise. Within the next thirty seconds, Mags almost lost control twice, despite keeping her speed under twenty miles-per-hour.

When the sign for the next exit came up, she almost missed it. She slowed to a crawl as another sign appeared.

Motel. There was a motel half a mile away.

Tam whimpered. Mags held her hand.

"We have to stop, Tam. I can't drive in this. I'm sorry. It'll be the same for... for anyone who tries to follow us. No one knows where we are. We just need to lie low until the snow eases off. Okay?"

"Okay."

Mags risked a quick look at her daughter. Her voice sounded flat.

"What is it?"

Tam's voice was as emotionless as before. "It doesn't matter what we do. He's coming now. Nothing can stop him."

CHAPTER FORTY-TWO

A t first, as he drives, the American tries to make conversation. My guess is he heard about this somewhere; that it's a good idea to talk to someone who is threatening you, get them to see you as a human being, establish rapport. I make it clear it won't work with me. Every time he talks, I tighten the belt. He gets the message. He's a smart guy.

After we've been driving for just over two hours, he holds up his hand for permission to talk.

"Forget about it," I say. "Pee in your pants if you have to. We're not stopping."

He shakes his head.

"Okay, what do you want?" I tug on the belt to warn him.

"We're coming up to the Sunapee exit," he says. "Our lodge is on the mountain, so we need to head west and skirt the lake. But the roads, in these conditions... Look, I'm not sure we can make it. I'm already having a hard time keeping it on the road."

He isn't lying. We've had a couple of slides. But I can't

stop now. Not when I'm so close. I can't let her get away again. I have a second chance, and I'm not about to blow it.

"You let me worry about that," I say. He nods, and a few minutes later, we leave the interstate.

That's when I feel the change. Since leaving the parking garage, the whole time we've been driving, I'm like a fish on a hook being hauled in. No effort from me. I just relax and let myself be taken to her.

Not now. There's something wrong. Pain blossoms in the part of my mind where the new flower unfolded.

It's all wrong.

"Stop the car."

He does as he's told. He tenses as we pull over. I know he is thinking about making his move.

"Uh-uh," I say, pulling hard enough to close his windpipe this time. He gasps when I release him.

"Keep it down. I need to think." He wheezes more quietly. Keeping my grip tight, I let my attention return to that unfolding, that new awareness. It's her. This is the wrong direction. The pain began when we left the interstate, and it's getting worse as we sit here. I'm losing her.

"Turn around," I say. "Get back onto the interstate. Head north. Drive faster."

He raises his hand to speak again. I jerk his head back against the headrest.

"Yeah, there's a blizzard. I get it. If you drive too fast, you might crash. You might be killed. The thing is, if you don't drive faster, I'll lose control, and you will get killed. Do as I say."

He does as I say.

The moment we turn onto the interstate, I'm back on the hook, everything is right again. I am being reeled in.

I see the problem before he does. Flashing red and blues.

The American takes his foot off the accelerator, and we coast towards the police car.

The road is blocked by a truck on its side. A cop has pulled up alongside it. The cop is out of his vehicle, waving to turn approaching drivers around, sending them back the way they came. A pickup truck U-turns in front of us. The cop holds his hand out, palm facing us.

The American tenses again.

"Turn around," I tell him. "We'll use the smaller roads. Do it now."

The cop watches us approach. He acts like he knows something is wrong. One of his hands goes to the butt of his gun and stays there.

The American moves his hands on the wheel. I think he is about to obey and I relax. Only a little, but enough for him to seize the moment.

He accelerates, then slams on the brakes. I am thrown forwards, taking the pressure off his neck. He reacts, diving to his right, fumbling with the glove box. It drops open. I see a gun.

At that moment, the car—which has been sliding sideways ever since the American hit the brake—reaches the truck. We've slewed across two lanes, and the trunk of our car hits the truck's cab hard, sending us into a clockwise spin. I pull hard on the belt. The American jerks and flails.

I don't know what we hit next, but there's a bang, the world tips, and the roof of the car is an inch under my knees. The American is wearing a seatbelt, and the airbag has exploded, pinning him into his seat. All my weight is on the belt as I hang there. It doesn't take long for him to die.

I drop onto the roof, still trying to get my bearings. There's shattered glass everywhere. When I put my hand to the side of my head, it comes away wet. My vision blurs.

"You okay? Yell if you can hear me."

The cop. He's coming over. I blink, screw my eyes up, shake my head, hunt for the gun. I don't see it anywhere. Glass fragments bite into my palms as I stretch into the shadows, panicking.

The cop is close. I see boots, black pants, the holster on his hip.

"Are you hurt?"

Something cracks my shin, and I reach under my leg. The gun is underneath me. I pick it up, wipe blood out of my eye, and brace the gun with my other hand.

"Help is on the way."

He's so close I can see a streak of mud across the top of one boot. Glass crunches under his feet.

The safety. I thumb it off. I don't even know if it's loaded.

The cop bends down. He has green eyes and a brown moustache.

I shoot him in the face.

CHAPTER FORTY-THREE

The motel owner was bemused by the sight of two new guests turning up in the middle of the worst storm of the season. She looked up from a sudoku book and brushed cookie crumbs off her chest.

"You folks sure picked a night for it."

Tam clung to her mother's hand in a way she hadn't for years. Mags squeezed her hand in mute reassurance. Her gaze darted around the hotel lobby, as if the Bedroom Killer was hiding in the shadows.

Under different circumstances, Mags might have found the motel lobby amusing. Tam would have commented. "Jolly festive, what?" Something like that. Something carefree. Something a bright, happy, eleven-year-old would say.

The walls and ceiling were dark wood, the floor lighter, covered in thick rugs. There were two Christmas trees, one on each side of the desk, behind which was a plump woman wearing a Santa hat. Someone had covered every available surface with tinsel, baubles, or other festive decorations. Mags had forgotten it was nearly Christmas.

"Come in, come in. I guess you didn't book. Any port in a storm, eh?"

From her accent, the hotel owner was Canadian. As Mags approached the desk, she saw room keys on a rack behind the smiling woman. Only two keys were missing. Business wasn't good.

Mags forced a smile and waggled her cell phone. "I have no signal. Could I use yours?"

"Sure." The motel owner pushed the phone across the desk. Her name badge said *Theresa*. She smiled at Tam. "Hey, honey, cold enough for you? How does a hot chocolate sound?"

Tam stepped back, eyes wide. She nodded, a tiny movement of the head.

"Great. I'll be right back." As Theresa pushed through a door at the rear, Mags hesitated, the phone at her ear. Who should she call? The police? And tell them what? That a serial killer who disappeared months ago has returned, and he's hunting them through a psychic link with her daughter? She dialled the Barkworth's home number. There was no answer. She tried Bradley's cell phone. After six rings, it went through to voicemail.

The woman was back. "It'll be ready in two shakes. Twin room?"

"Yes. Just for tonight, please."

"Well, you have a wide choice of cabins. We only took over this summer, had the whole place renovated. We don't get busy until the New Year. Every cabin has a bedroom, bathroom, and kitchenette. The luxury cabins have two storeys and an open fire with—"

"Do you have any rooms in this building?" Mags had seen the cabins as they'd driven up. She would prefer to be nearer to other people. The woman shook her head.

"Sorry. It's just Bill and me in here. Guest accommodation is in the cabins. Would you like me to tell you about—"

Mags interrupted her again. If they couldn't be in the main building, it might be better to get further away from the road. Somewhere where they could see anyone coming. "The cabin up the slope," she said, pointing out of the window. "Is it free?"

"Sure." She turned and unhooked a key. Her smile was still there, but it was looking strained. Mags knew she was being brusque, but she didn't care. She needed to get Tam somewhere safe. Maybe she'd even get some sleep.

She handed over her credit card.

"Is there somewhere to park the car round the back?"

"There's an overflow car park back there. But you can leave it out front, it's no problem."

"I'd prefer to leave it round the back."

"Well. Okay, then." The smile was definitely faltering.

Mags walked away, Tam still holding her hand. The woman called after them.

"Don't forget your hot chocolate." She handed the steaming mug to Tam. Mags burst into tears at this simple display of human kindness. Theresa's expression softened.

"Man trouble?" She said it in a conspiratorial whisper, laying her hand on Mags' arm.

"Something like that."

They parked the SUV behind the main building, where it couldn't be seen from the road. From the car park, they walked up the slope, staying behind the cabin. No footprints would betray them in the snow at the front. Mags didn't believe this killer could find them, but a primal part of her brain screamed at her to take precautions. What harm could it do to listen to it? And Tam was terrified.

There was a log pile in an open-sided wooden building

at the back of the cabin. An axe hung on a hook. Mags lifted it by its rubber grip, feeling the weight in her hand. Then she pictured the killer finding it there and slid it between the logs on the ground until it was out of sight. The cabin was the last at the top of the slope. The front door faced the interstate. At the rear, beyond the log pile, was a well-maintained path leading through the trees. According to a signpost, the town of Havers was a two mile walk away. Snow fell harder, the wind whisking tiny flakes against their faces.

"Come on."

Mags turned the lights on as they walked in. Twin beds, an antique pair of skis displayed on the wall above them. A bathroom through one door, the promised kitchenette a tiny room through an arch. There was a microwave and a fridge. The largest window was on the far side of the beds, looking out towards the road, although all it showed was a swirl of snow and the lights of the motel reception. There were lampposts on the path outside, spaced at regular intervals, darkness pooling between them.

Tam reached behind Mags and flicked the lights off.

"This way we can see anyone coming, but they can't see us."

Smart kid. Mags kissed the top of her head. She wanted to tell her no one was coming, but she wasn't sure who she was trying to convince.

With the curtains open, enough light spilled in from outside to illuminate the room. Tam went to the bathroom. Mags opened the cutlery drawer in the kitchen. No sharp knives.

They shared the hot chocolate, sitting on the bed. It was a long time since either of them had eaten. Mags could hear her stomach complaining, but she wasn't hungry. Food could wait. Everything could wait. Their lives contracted to one small room, somewhere between Boston and Montréal. Time meant nothing. There was only tonight. Mags watched the wind lift great swathes of powder snow from the road in the fields, sending it skittering across the horizon.

Tam had been quiet for a while, her body pressed up against her mother's.

"I can feel him. In my mind." Tears ran down Tam's cheeks.

Mags grabbed at a crazy idea. "Can you block him? Think about something else? Shut him out?"

Tam, miserable with fear, shook her head. "I tried. In the car. I tried everything. I can't. He keeps looking for me. It's all he wants, Mum. He's coming."

Tam shivered. Mags pulled a woollen hat out of her jacket pocket and put it on her daughter's head. She could find no words of reassurance.

They sat close, arms wrapped around each other. They looked out into the night, and they waited.

CHAPTER FORTY-FOUR

The cop has a heavy jacket on. I take it, and his gloves.

I take his car keys and go back to his cruiser. I look at the keyring. It doubles as a bottle opener. It's in the shape of a fish and has 'Gone Fishing' printed on it.

I wonder.

I drop the gun into my coat pocket, go to the trunk and unlock it. It pops up to reveal three fishing rods and a couple plastic boxes. I pop open the bigger box and there it is. Four reels of sea-fishing line, the strongest kind. It's even the same brand I used for my first device. I find wire cutters and cut it to length, wrap it around my gloves multiple times before pulling it taut. The gloves are thick. The fishing line glints, reflecting the lights on top of the car. It's perfect.

The cop's body is lying a few feet in front of the flipped vehicle. The American's car blocks the only way past the truck. There's no way through.

How can I reach her if I have no car?

My face is ice cold, my cheeks stinging where the snowflakes hit them. I was asleep on my feet just then. Not sure how long for. Seconds? Minutes?

I blink. Lights slide sideways left to right, then back the other way. I shake my head in confusion, before I work out what I'm looking at. Two vehicles, coming this way.

I have to leave. I shouldn't have shot the cop in the face. He was wearing a hat. If I'd shot him in the chest, I could have taken it. I can't think straight in this cold.

The lights come closer. The snow in front of me glows blue, then red, then blue again. The cars are heading towards the flashing lights of the cop car. I'm standing next to it like a fool, blood on the side of my face where my head hit the car door. The gun is in my hand, and the dead cop is a few yards away.

Then, like an answered prayer, I taste chocolate. I'm not sure what is it at first. Warmth, sweetness, a powdery after-taste. I have her. She's there, in the unfolding, a hidden room in my mind. I am not finished yet.

That direction.

I walk away from the cop before the cars arrive. At the edge of the interstate, I don't hesitate, striding off the road and into the snowy fields. I dodge around the truck and keep to the fields, follow the road north. Even in this coat, I am cold.

After a few minutes trudging through the snow, there's a strange warmth in my feet. I look down. The thin hospital slippers have fallen off. Maybe when the car crashed. I'm walking in bare feet. But there's a numb warmth. Frostbite. If I don't get warm soon, I'll lose some toes, maybe even my feet.

I don't care. She's ahead, drawing me in.

It ends tonight.

When you have only one goal, life becomes simple. I keep going.

I think I'm back in Florida, or in the hospital in Boston. When I remember where I am, I become fascinated by my feet. They don't look like my feet any more. They are swollen, and there are patches of dark skin. The numbness has spread into my calves. My knees creak and there's a distant ache in my legs I know is dangerous. My body is failing. All those weeks in a hospital bed. Even with the workouts I've been doing, I am nowhere near fit.

Since lunchtime, I have killed four men. The nurse, the boss, the American, and the cop. So much death. I wasn't bringing them peace, I wasn't helping them rest. They were in my way.

I am tired.

I guess I may have covered a mile when I stop for the first time. I've been falling asleep every so often, between steps, snapping awake as the snow crunches under my strange feet. This time, it's for longer, and when I wake I have stopped walking.

It scares me, standing still. I reach out for her in my mind. She's there. I move again.

The nurse, the boss, the American, the cop. The nurse, the boss, the American, the cop. I step in time with my chant. The nurse, the boss, the American, the cop.

The second time I stop, I figure I sleep for a few minutes. It's hard to get started again. Real hard. My body protests. My legs are numb, but my hips, my arms, my chest, and my face are alive with pain.

The nurse, the boss, the American, the cop. The nurse, the boss...

I remember some Hollywood writer I saw on TV. He wrote dramas, thrillers, horror maybe. I forget. But I remember this: he said great drama needed two ingredients. Only two. Intention and obstacle.

I grab this idea. It makes sense. My intention is to reach her. The obstacles are many. The storm is an obstacle. My frostbitten feet, like wearing roller skates three sizes too small, are obstacles. The distance between where I am now and where I need to be is an obstacle. My body, the way it wants to shut down, is an obstacle. The wound on my head is an obstacle. I take off a glove and touch my face. The frozen blood is like plastic. There is no pain. My fingers still feel something, but the skin on my face doesn't. Not good.

Intention and obstacle. The nurse, the boss, the American, the cop.

I reach the top of a slight rise. The interstate sweeps left from here. A small road forks right. I follow it with my eyes and see lights, not far away.

There.

The snow is easing off now, the clouds above drifting away to reveal the moon. I draw a mental line between where I stand and the cluster of buildings less than a mile away.

I follow that line.

The nurse, the boss, the American, the cop. The nurse, the boss, the American, the cop.

The terrain slopes down to the road before rising again. When I reach the road, I see the source of the lights. It's a motel. One big building, and lots of smaller buildings all around it; bungalows or cabins. Four of them have two stories. Paths lead from the main building to the smaller ones. Lampposts line these paths, but their light is dim. Solar powered, I guess. One path heads up the hill to the right. The final cabin sits on its own, backing onto trees. No lights inside. No footprints leading towards it.

It's so still. So quiet. The occasional gust of wind lifts the newly settled snow from the ground and from the branches of trees, obscuring my view for a moment.

Although I already know she's there, my regular senses confirm my conclusion. A movement inside, lighter shadows among dark. Then a door opening. A whisper of voices.

I killed her father. She must be with her mother. I check the coat pocket, the loop of fishing line coiled there. It reassures me.

A promise brought me. The promise of peace. I no longer have doubts.

The steps creak as I climb onto the wooden porch of the cabin.

I twist the handle of the door. Locked. I rattle it, put my shoulder to it and push. It doesn't move.

I try sliding the window open. It's shut tight. There's a small table on the porch. Two chairs. Made for the weather. Made of iron.

I pick up the nearest chair. It's heavier than I thought, or I'm weaker, and I drop it. I take a breath, hoist the chair up to my shoulder and lurch towards the window.

The glass shatters, and I reach in to unlatch the window.

By the time I'm inside, I have two new injuries: a gash in my left hand and a long cut down my right shin. I feel nothing.

The room is empty. I take off my gloves and drop them on the bed. I am almost dizzy with her presence. She is so close.

Through the back window, I see someone run. I open the back door. A figure rises from behind a pile of logs. Her mother.

I speak to her. "You should go. I'm here for her, not you."

She has something in her hand. An axe. She is screaming at me.

"Come on, you fucker. COME ON!"

She is brave. She doesn't hesitate when she sees me. She lifts the axe over her head and comes at me. I see the intention in her eyes. She will kill me if I let her.

I put my right hand in the coat pocket, bring out the gun, and shoot her.

She pirouettes like a dancer. An arc of blood, black in the moonlight, sprays onto the snow. The axe drops to the ground and, half a second later, she joins it, face down.

A needle of agony stabs my brain. The gun drops from my fingers. I hold both hands to my head, and stagger into the cabin.

The pain disappears as I slump onto the bed. And there it is; a final unfolding of the flower in my mind.

I take out the fishing line and lay it beside my gloves. And I wait.

CHAPTER FORTY-FIVE

She didn't lose consciousness, but it was a close thing.

Like many people, Mags had wondered how being shot might feel. Like most people, she had assumed she would never find out. Unlike most people, her assumption was incorrect.

Being shot was a very similar sensation to being flicked by a wet towel, which is something Mags had experienced at school swimming lessons. An older girl—Fiona O'Toole, she remembered, despite not thinking about her for years— was an expert, often leaving marks on other girls' skin that lasted days. Fiona had once caught Mags with an expertly placed flick that made her scream in shock. Being shot was no worse. Not at first. A secondary wave of pain followed the initial shock, an insistent throb of discomfort that became agonising when she moved.

The problem was, she *had* to move. Mags was alive, the killer was near, and Tam wasn't far enough away. Not yet.

She managed not to scream as she rolled onto her left side. The bullet had hit her below the ribs on her right side. She suspected it had passed through, given the blood dripping down her back. She was scared to move again, knowing how much it would hurt. If she lay there, she supposed she would bleed to death. It might take hours, unless hypothermia did the job first.

Mags didn't intend to wait.

She looked around for the man who had shot her. Mags had only seen him for a few seconds and doubted she could describe him well enough for a police artist to produce an accurate picture. He was the definition of average. Average height, average build. Brown hair, cut short. A bland face.

Where was he? Tam's footprints led from the cabin to the path. No other prints had joined them. Mags looked back at the cabin, propping herself on one elbow. From that angle, she could see the top of the killer's head. He was sitting on the end of the bed, facing the door.

What the hell was he doing?

Mags decided she didn't care. He wasn't going after Tam. That was all that mattered. He was injured, she remembered. There had been blood on the left side of his face. Maybe the injury was serious, and he could go no further. The idea was tempting. If true, she could lie back in the snow and be done with it all, knowing her daughter was safe. But he might be gathering his strength for a final effort. She couldn't give up. Not yet.

Keeping her teeth clenched, she pushed her left hand into the snow and levered her body into a sitting position. She didn't scream. Good. She took a few fast, ragged breaths, and pressed her palm flat over the wound on her midriff. The pain made her gasp, and she froze for a moment. When she checked the cabin window, he hadn't moved.

The axe. It must be nearby. Mags scanned the snow,

finding it four feet away, but by then she had spotted some-thing else. Something better.

In the snow by the back door of the cabin, the gun lay where he'd dropped it.

Why had he left it behind? Mags answered her own unspoken question: *Who gives a shit?*

Mags had never fired a gun before, but she knew it was her only chance. A gun gave her a massive advantage.

What if it had run out of bullets? Was that why he'd dropped it?

Mags didn't know how to check. It was a risk she would have to take.

She didn't stop to wonder if she could kill another human being. She knew she could shoot this man. If she could hold the gun steady, if she could squeeze the trigger, she would squeeze and squeeze until there were no bullets left. She would save Tam, even if it meant dying herself.

Mags tried to stand, but blurred vision and a lancing pain in her skull dropped her back into the snow. She breathed hard, didn't scream, kept pressure on the wound.

The gun was ten feet away, but the journey towards it was the hardest she had ever made. Mags moved her left knee towards her hand. Then she dragged her right knee forward, her body sending desperate signals for her to stop. Mags ignored the signals, lifting her left hand from the snow, planting it a few inches in front of her head.

Progress was slow, but she was moving.

When Mags reached the gun, she couldn't pick it up. Her right hand still covered the bullet wound, and her left hand was all that stopped her tipping face-forward into the snow. If she did that, she might not get back up again. She considered crawling with the gun in her left hand, but feared she might accidentally fire off a shot. However badly injured the murderer was, she doubted he would ignore that.

Mags stared at the gun with a kind of dumb fascination. When the solution came to her, she realised how hard her body was working to keep her alive, leaving few resources for rational thought. She was wearing a jacket. A jacket with pockets. Pushing herself into a kneeling position, she picked up the gun and dropped it into a pocket.

The cabin door was half-open. Mags was now six feet away. She mentally rehearsed what came next. *Crawl forward until behind the door. Kneel without making a sound. Take gun from pocket and hold it ready, pointing towards the room beyond. Remove right hand from bleeding stomach, push the door open, use both hands to support the weight of the gun. Fire, putting as many bullets as possible into the serial killer sitting on the bed.*

It wasn't a complicated plan, but there was one serious flaw. Mags was already much weaker than when she had started crawling towards the gun. By the time she reached the door, she would be weaker still. Would she have the strength to push open the door and squeeze the trigger? Her body wanted her to remain still. The more she moved, the more she bled.

The storm was moving away. It was a beautiful night. Hard to believe the blizzard of only an hour before. So peaceful. Not a sound. Patches of cloud had cleared, and thousands of stars glittered. The snow was soft and pure, other than the dark trail of blood behind Mags.

I will not die here. I will not die.

Mags knew the longer she waited, the harder this would be.

She counted down from three to one. That's what she'd done with Tam, the first time she'd jumped into the swimming pool, or the day she'd gathered the courage to plummet down the steepest slide in the park. Even blowing out the candles on a birthday cake.

Three.

A sound in the stillness. Unexpected, somewhere behind her.

Two.

The sound getting closer. Footsteps.

Someone had heard the shot. Help was coming.

One.

Mags turned her head and looked back towards the path.

"No." Her mouth formed the word, but she made no sound. "No."

It was Tam. She was walking towards the cabin. She must have heard the gunshot, and come back to save her mother. Mags braced herself to stop her daughter. It couldn't end this way. It just couldn't.

When Tam was close, Mags saw something was wrong. Her daughter wasn't hurrying. Her steps were neither slow nor fast. She maintained a steady pace, head up, arms swinging by her side.

Closer still and Mags could see Tam's face in the moon-light. Her eyes stared ahead, but she saw nothing of what was around her. She was looking at something else. She was seeing some*where* else.

Mags couldn't prevent the groan of frustration and terror that escaped her then. It was a guttural, animal sound. She didn't care if the killer heard it.

"Tam. Tam. No. He's in the cabin, Tam. Call the police. Run. Please. Please!" Tam didn't pause as she passed her mother. She didn't even look at her. Mags put out her hand to bar her path, but Tam stepped to one side and continued. Mags slipped and fell to the floor.

Mags didn't even have the strength to crawl now. Instead, she pulled herself along with her left hand, pushing with her toes.

Sounds reached her from the room beyond, but the sofa prevented her seeing what was going on. It was worse than any nightmare. She whimpered, tried to move faster, and succeeded only in falling hard, the side of her face smacking the floor.

After a few seconds of silence, the sounds began again. At first, they made no sense. Material brushing against material, like someone pulling on a sweater. A creak from the bed as the killer shifted his weight. Another creak, then more silence.

The yelping breaths were next, wheezing, desperate. A staccato series of muffled shrieks.

A memory of her with Kit when they were kids, on the BMX bikes, the noises she had made when winded. The panic. This was worse. Instead of the strangled gasps being followed by a return to normal breathing, the attempts to draw breath decreased in frequency. At first, half a second between each breath, then a second. Three seconds. Five seconds. Ten. The yelps grew quieter until they were hardly audible.

The silence that followed was the worst of all.

Mags used her legs to push herself past the sofa, her face sliding along the polished wooden floor.

When she could see the room, her eyes filled with water. She struggled to make sense of what was in front of her. At first, the shapes were only suggestive outlines of reality.

She blinked away the tears, looked again.

One figure was kneeling in front of the bed. Another squatted behind the first. As Mags watched, the nearest figure twitched, spasmed, fell backwards, and was still.

The stench of death was reminiscent of a filthy public toilet. Piss, shit, and something undefinable, a sickly caramel sweetness.

Her vision clear, Mags pushed herself up on one elbow.

The Bedroom Killer was dead. He had died with his eyes closed. Tam crouched behind him wearing a thick pair of gloves too big for her. Coiled around the gloves was a length of fishing line. Where the wire was wrapped around the killer's throat, it had bitten into the flesh, leaving a line as clear as if drawn with a pencil.

Tam teased the fishing wire from the neck of the corpse.

She looked at Mags, her eyes shining.

"He can sleep now," she said. "He can sleep."

Eighteen months later

The phone chimed at 7pm, UK time. Thirty seconds later, it chimed again; the vibration making the empty champagne flute rattle. Mags picked up her phone, closed her eyes and counted to three before opening the message.

It's over.

There was a hyperlink underneath. When she tapped it, it opened the homepage of the Boston Globe.

EDGEGEN GUILTY - DIRECTORS AND EMPLOYEES FACE PRISON. JUDGE DESCRIBES PRACTISES AS 'AKIN TO TORTURE'

She skimmed the article until she found what she was looking for. Page 21: Read exclusive extracts from Patrice Martino's explosive new book Twinned With Hell: The Terrible Secrets behind Edgegen Technology.

Mags twisted the cork from the bottle and poured a glass, toasting Patrice silently.

It took ten minutes for the tears to end.

Closure. That was the word Ria had used, and she had been right about Mags needing it. Patrice's message was the final step from darkness to light. Bradley and his father were dead. Now Edgegen was finished.

To her surprise, Mags had mourned Bradley—or, rather, the idea of Bradley—recalling countless small, unguarded moments between them that had once seemed genuine. She tried to remember those moments whenever Tam talked about him. A young girl had lost her father, and it was healthier if her mother didn't snarl every time he was mentioned. Forgiveness was impossible, of course. Mags hadn't yet decided whether to tell Tam the truth one day. Some decisions could wait.

Tam had no memory of anything after they had arrived at the cabin. No memory of running through the woods in a blizzard, no memory of walking past a trail of blood to face the killer. And no memory of the ritualistic act that ended his life. Ria said the mind was capable of removing a chunk of time completely, if it was so traumatic it might otherwise cause severe damage. Mags woke up every morning grateful Tam didn't know what really happened that night.

The Massachusetts police had been efficient, but not unkind. DNA evidence established the identity of the corpse found in the cabin, and Mags experienced a brief taste of fame, when the story broke that a British mother had stopped the Bedroom Killer.

All through Christmas and the first few weeks of the new year, stranded in America, Mags had remained focussed on her daughters. It wasn't just her and Tam anymore. She pleaded with the police and lawyers to help her track down Clara, terrified that she might never find her, never know how it might feel to hold her.

She poured another glass of champagne and walked through to the kitchen. In the doorway, she froze, her smile faltering.

No. Not again.

Her daughter had her back to her. From that angle, Mags could see the top of a piece of paper. The scratch and slide of a pencil nib was the only sound, but the artist wasn't looking at her work. She stared straight ahead, her hand moving independently.

Mags moved closer on legs that no longer wanted to support her weight. She put the champagne flute on the table and forced herself to look at the picture.

It was a large hall, full of people. Children, Mags realised, playing a game, sitting in a circle. One girl had turned away from the game as if noticing the artist as she sketched the scene. Mags knew that face. It was Tam.

It was a picture of the Guide hall. Tam was there now.

"That's very good honey," said Mags, her voice less shaky than she'd anticipated. "Is it..."

"Tam? Yes. Tam. Guides. Singing songs."

Mags stroked Clara's hair. Her foster parents had promised to visit every year, but Mags wasn't convinced they would, and Clara barely mentioned them. All three of them felt the same, she knew; that they belonged together, that they completed each other. Despite the horror of the previous year, Mags' anxiety had lifted like sun-warmed dew, her spirits rising with it. This was her family.

She bent down, kissing Clara's cheek. With eyes shut, inhaling her daughter's scent, she couldn't tell the difference between the twins.

"Are you happy, Clara?"

Brown eyes fixed on hers. A small nod, a bigger smile.

"Tip top, Mom."

AUTHOR'S NOTE

For the occasional email about my books and an exclusive free story, visit The Las Vegas Driving Lesson.

Thanks for reading. The Picture On The Fridge (known as *the bloody fridge book* because the idea wouldn't leave me alone) has had a great response from readers, and went on to win the 2021 9 Kindle Storyteller Award.

You won't be surprised to learn I decided to write more thrillers. The first few chapters of my next book is over the page for you to try.

Bedlam Boy is a character with a strong moral centre, an aptitude for violence, and a list of people he wants to visit... at night...

It's not a list anyone would want to be on.

Meet Bedlam Boy...

1

The hot, bright, evening sun made the shadowed corners darker, and it was in the dusty gloom under the scaffolding that Tom saw him. Tom hadn't thought about Bedlam Boy for a while. Not much, anyway. He'd dreamed of him, but Tom's dreams were confusing, and often hard to remember.

How long had it been? Was it while Tom was working here, on the housing site in North London? Or at the last job, in Manchester? If Manchester was the last job. It might have been Cambridge. Cambridge had been the site near a river. Tom tried to think back. When he concentrated, the images that drifted through his mind didn't help. There weren't enough of them, and he couldn't sort them into the right order. He gave up. It might be weeks, or months, since Bedlam Boy last came for him.

The figure in the shadows nodded; wraith-like in the dust, insubstantial. Two men were laying an exterior wall in the shade of the planks. Neither of them had noticed that they weren't alone. Tom knew he mustn't acknowledge the Boy. He looked away, ducked under the wooden planks, squatted, and tipped the hod to slide its load next to Kev and Craig. They didn't pause, caught up in the rhythm of brick-laying, their movements out of time with the thin beat from a dust-caked, paint-splattered radio hanging on a ledger. Craig spoke without looking up.

"Two more of 'em, Tiny."

The men on the building sites used more than one nickname for Tom. On a good day, when they accepted his mostly silent presence, they called him Tiny. *Tiny* seemed strange until Tom's latest landlady, Myra, explained that sometimes people used the wrong word deliberately.

"You know, dear, like Little John. Robin Hood's friend. He was a big fella like you. They call you Tiny because you're huge." It made no sense.

The nickname Tom didn't like was Mad Tom, but he didn't react when they said it behind his back, and when they said it to his face, he blinked and ignored them.

"Mad Tom! What are you mumbling about?"

He looked up. He was still standing by the pile of bricks. Craig had stopped to roll a cigarette and now waved a hand in front of Tom's face.

"C'mon, pal. Shake a leg. Two more trips. Off you pop."

Tom picked up the hod and walked back the way he'd come. He couldn't see anything in the shadows, but he knew Bedlam Boy was there.

Tom Brown was thirty-two years old, maybe thirty-three; he wasn't sure. His real surname was Lewis, he knew, but he had to pretend it was Brown. The police lady, Debbie, had told him that. She had tried lots of other surnames for him, but Brown was the only one he could remember.

His childhood had been a happy one, he thought. Sometimes, when about to fall asleep, or during the confusion of waking, he would remember his mother's voice, or the roughness of his father's beard.

Trying to remember more didn't work. It was like picking up wriggling wet fish. Thinking about the future was equally pointless. Tom existed where he was, and when he was. Bedlam Boy took care of the rest.

Physical labour suited Tom best. Cash in hand, a few days here, a week or two there. This building site had kept him busy for more than a month without the usual restlessness.

In the building trade, there were few hod carriers as strong and as tireless as Tom. The hod, a three-sided box on the end of a rod, carried bricks from the pallets by the office to whoever needed them on site. Tom braced the wooden handle alternately against his shoulders. Brick hods usually held twelve bricks. Tom carried eighteen without a problem, and the first foreman to realise this built him a bigger hod.

Carrying more bricks than anyone else didn't make Tom any more popular with those who worked alongside him. He was a good, strong, reliable worker, but he was tolerated, rather than liked. The other men—and they were usually men—didn't like his silence; they were suspicious of his solitude. He didn't laugh at their jokes and turned away when they made fun of him. Tom frowned when they called him the Odd Carrier. Being odd meant not fitting in. The bricks he hefted hour after hour onto his shoulder slotted into the hod, each individual block nestling perfectly against its fellows. If Tom had been a brick, he would have been rejected before reaching the building site. He didn't fit with the others. Too big, roughly cut, unfinished, wrong.

It was Friday, so Tom joined the back of the queue leading to Mrs Hartnell's office. The creature in the shadows had gone, but Tom's hand went up to the hard, raised scarring on his skull. Bedlam Boy was calling him.

The men talked louder and laughed more easily at six on a Friday. A hard day's graft at the conclusion of a long week meant the brown envelope they picked up from Mrs H would travel less than half a mile before being ripped open and its contents depleted at the bar of the Coach and Horses.

Tom kept his head down and shuffled behind the rest. It had been Ken's birthday last week, and Tom hadn't been able to avoid being added to the invitation to meet for drinks. His lemonade tasted funny, and when the lads told him it was his turn to buy a round, it had cost eighty pounds. When Tom tried to protest, they all pretended not to understand.

He smoothed the black bandana over his shaved head. Kev had pulled it off when he'd left the pub last week, and everyone had laughed. When Tom asked for it back, and they all saw the front of his head, they stopped laughing. Stevo had even said sorry when he threw the bandana back to him, but, once outside, Tom heard their voices through the open window.

"Car accident, d'ya think?"

"Brain damage, I reckon."

"Explains why he's such a numpty, though, dunnit?"

Inside the office, Mrs Hartnell, a skinny middle-aged woman with a Jack Russell always at her feet, kept the wage slips and cash in a plastic box on top of her desk. Everyone signed for their pay, so Tom preferred to be last in line.

Mrs H pushed the paper across to him. Her husband, Les, the foreman, stood behind her, old, faded blue-green tattoos across his folded muscled forearms. He glared at Tom.

The only time Les Hartnell didn't glare was when asleep. The brickies described him as 'hard but fair', but Tom had never known Hartnell to be fair. He paid as little as possible, and he paid Tom less than anyone else, because Tom couldn't argue his case, and no one was there to argue it for him.

Bobby, the Jack Russell, darted out from under the desk, sniffed Tom's trousers, then lay on his feet, tail wagging. The small dog was infamous on the site for hating everyone apart from his owner, and for confirming his opinions with a bite or two. But, like most animals, he loved Tom, much to the disgust of Mr Hartnell, who muttered, "Get off him, you stupid little bastard." Bobby huffed happily and ignored him.

Tom made his mark on the paper. He drew something that looked like 'Tom' and added a squiggle. The squiggle changed from week to week, but if he looked at the letters for long, his head ached. Les added a smirk to his glare.

"There you go, love." Mrs H handed him the envelope. It felt even thinner than normal. He opened it. Four of the pinky purple notes. There should be many more. He looked back at the thin, brittle-haired woman.

"It's a government thing, Tom." She'd never used his name before. "It's your last week, I'm afraid. No more work. We've deducted your national insurance, your contractor's insurance, and your union dues."

"Mm, mm." Tom couldn't remember if the last time he'd spoken was today or yesterday. It took a while to get the first words out.

"But mm, but-"

"But nothing." Les Hartnell took a step forward. He stood a few inches shorter than Tom's hunched six feet, but his glare, his knotted muscles, and an old murder conviction he made sure everyone knew about, meant he wasn't shy about picking a fight.

"You're lucky I gave ya a job at all."

"Mm. Work hard." Tom pushed the words through his tight lips.

Hartnell seemed momentarily stunned at the interruption. He leaned across the desk and put a dusty, cracked and blackened fingernail on Tom's sternum. "You're a hoddie, pal. You carry bricks. I could train a monkey to do it, and it would be less of a bloody liability than you. What if there was an accident, an emergency? You couldn't find your own arse with both hands. What use are you if the scaffold collapses, or there's a fire?"

Les Hartnell talked too fast, and Tom struggled to keep up.

"Mm. Mm."

"Yeah, yeah, mm all you like. Mrs H's sister's boy gets out on Monday, so you're surplus to requirements. We don't need you anymore. That's your pay up to date. Now piss off out of it. On yer bike."

Tom rested his fingers on the scar under his bandana. "No bike," he whispered.

Les Hartnell's neck turned purple. Mrs H put a warning hand on his arm.

"He doesn't understand, Les. Look, I'll make it easy for you. Job is finished. You go home. Don't come back."

Tom looked blankly at her. She pointed at the door.

"Fuck off, love."

Tom looked at the few notes in the envelope one more time, then up at the hard-set faces of his former employers. Before leaving, he took a last look around the cramped office, and bent down to stroke Bobby's head.

The bus stop was a hundred yards out of the site to the

right, but Tom turned left, and headed downstairs to the underground, boarding the first tube south. He wouldn't be going back to Myra's bed-and-breakfast tonight, or ever again.

Bedlam Boy was waiting.

Soho was packed. Tourists from every nation jostled ad agency designers and office staff on their way to the pub. Actors, restaurant staff, and sex workers hurried to another paid performance. Motorcycle couriers darted through the traffic shoals, helmets flashing like silver minnows. Taxis inched forward, sweaty arms hanging out of their windows, leaning on their horns.

Tom moved through it all with his head down, shoulders hunched, following the sinuous progress of the masses, allowing the crowd to guide his route.

As he passed an alleyway, its entrance half-blocked with black and green bin bags, Tom joined a human tributary hugging the shopfronts. He left the flow, diverting into a passage just wide enough to accommodate a vehicle. A white transit van meant Tom had to turn sideways, folding its wing mirror to squeeze past. The van's owner, bearded and belligerent, registered his displeasure as he came out of the door at the end of the alley.

"Oi! What are you playing at? Hands off, unless you—"

Tom straightened, pressing his back against the wall to

ease his bulk through. The bearded man looked him up and down, registering his size. "Nah, don't worry, no harm done, mate. You coming in? I'll get the door for ya. Nice one."

Tom's gaze dropped back to the floor. The door slammed shut behind him. In the outer room, a middle-aged woman flicked through a magazine behind a counter. Shelves full of packing materials filled the walls; boxes, sticky-tape, bubble wrap, polystyrene pellets, all marked with a bright orange sticker stating Sam's Soho Storage.

The woman didn't look up. Tom entered a five-digit number into the keypad on the door. Tom remembered the pattern his fingers needed to make, and the door beeped. He pushed it open.

Inside, the bright orange theme continued on the roller shutters of every unit. The height of the ceiling suggested the building's Victorian provenance, and the birds in the rafters were far from the first generation to nest there.

Tom could count to ten, and he only needed to get to seven to find his unit. It was on the left side, the same as the scar on his head. He unlocked the metal grille, sending it clattering upwards. Inside, he yanked it halfway down again before clicking on the light. Then he pulled the grille shut and slid the bolt.

The unit was half the size of a standard garage. Big enough to accommodate a double cupboard, suitcases, cardboard boxes and a clothes rail. Chests of drawers of various sizes partially obscured one wall. Against the other, the most notable item was an old-fashioned writing desk with a red leather swivel chair.

Tom was, as always, drawn to the writing desk first; antique walnut, with three drawers on one side. He sat on the swivel chair, which creaked under his weight. His thighs, even with the chair lowered as far as possible, pressed against the underside of the desk. He slid out the felt-topped guide rods and lowered the writing lid on top of them. The writing surface was topped with the same red leather as the chair. It was a beautiful piece of furniture, marred only by the side blackened and scarred by fire.

Tom placed his hands on the stretched red leather surface, closed his eyes, and breathed in, leaning right to avoid the charred wood. The mixed scent of old leather and skin cream brought him a sense of peace, of *home*. There were no accompanying images, no comforting memories, but he knew this desk had been his mother's.

The sense of peace didn't last. Bedlam Boy was waiting.

The Boy didn't frighten Tom - but he could no more refuse his call than a starving baby could refuse the breast that kept it alive.

He shut the desk and opened an empty wheeled suitcase, propping the lid against the wall. He took running shoes, underwear, and a razor from a drawer, a black motorcycle helmet from one of the boxes. The clothes rail yielded designer jeans and two shirts. All of it went into the suitcase with a roll of bin liners, a MacBook, and a charger.

Tom's last stop was the cupboard. Each shelf held four mannequin heads. The hairpieces on the heads were blonde, dark, ginger, and many shades between. Half of the staring faces also sported facial hair, from sideburns, through moustaches and goatees, to a full beard.

Tom picked up a bag containing glue, double-sided scalp tape, and various bottles and tubes. He removed a shoulder-length black wig, putting it into a net. He couldn't have explained why he chose the items he did, only that they were *right*.

With the suitcase zipped up, Tom took one last look around the storage unit. Bedlam Boy had acquired this eclectic collection of odds and ends. Tom didn't know how long it had taken. His concept of time periods longer than a week or two was hazy.

Tom smiled. This unheated aluminium box, lit by a single fluorescent tube, comforted him.

He put his thumb on the bolt to slide it open. Something was different this time. Bedlam Boy's call had been stronger than ever. Tom thought back to the earlier glimpse, the Boy's insubstantial form twisting through the shadows, watching him. His head throbbed with the effort of assembling his scattered and amorphous thoughts. Something had changed. Something.

A rare sliver of memory: his father coming into his bedroom late one night, putting an object on the bedside table.

Tom, half-asleep, lifting this object, holding it up so the light from the street illuminated his prize. A book. A new story. He reached down the side of his bed, found the torch and—once he'd tucked the duvet back around him—clicked it on to read. It didn't seem strange that he could read. He accepted it. It was the way the book made him feel that was important. Tom was almost feverish with excitement. He'd been waiting for this a long time. It was the final story in a series. He was dry-mouthed with anticipation as he turned the first page.

The memory faded, but the excitement remained. Bedlam Boy's call was stronger because he was excited. This was the beginning of a story.

Or, perhaps, the end of one.

Tom flicked the light switch and the desk, shelves, boxes, and cupboard disappeared into the blackness.

Only the faintest scent of skin cream and burned wood remained.

The hotel was one of an increasing number of establishments trying to dispense with the need for human contact. Rooms were booked online, and the check-in process involved scanning a QR code to release each room's keycard.

Tom watched the lobby from the opposite side of the street. Only one member of staff on duty, but her role as hotel receptionist—besides answering the phone and greeting guests—also included running a bar and kitchen. Despite this, she still tried to help new arrivals with the check-in machines.

It was ten minutes before an opportunity presented itself. A group of Chinese students, led by a tired teacher, dragged their enormous suitcases into the hotel lobby.

Tom crossed the road, squeezing in behind the last student. The teacher stepped up to the first screen; the students flocked round her like needy ducklings, and the receptionist came over to help. As soon as she turned to the machine, Tom took his phone from his pocket, scanned his code, and was through the door to the rooms before the first student received their key card. The burst of concentration made his head ache.

Room 18 was small, but contained everything he needed. A bed, a bathroom, and a decent Wi-Fi connection.

Tom took off his bandana and stripped, stuffing his work clothes into one of the bin liners. He showered. Brick dust and dirt swirled around the drain. After drying off, he shaved his face and head.

Muted sounds from the neighbouring rooms provided a confused soundtrack: snatches of conversation, indecipherable dialogue from a television, the dull thump of dance music. Tom sat naked on the edge of the bed, slumped, his eyes on the brown and black carpet under the rough soles of his feet.

He waited for the first signs to appear. It didn't take more than a few minutes. The surrounding objects lost their names. The television at the foot of the bed was a shape with no purpose. The motorcycle helmet on the desk became neither familiar nor exotic, merely a reflective sphere. The bed underneath him was softer than the wooden desk. The light diffused by the thin curtains was different to that provided by the yellow glare of the lamp. But Tom forgot what made light different to darkness.

There was no panic. The opposite was true. The sense of peace fleetingly experienced in the storage unit flowed into the gaps left as identification and meaning dwindled. Tom looked back at his feet, his legs, his hands resting on his knees, but did not recognise them as his own.

His identity, and any awareness of being distinct from the television, the desk, or the last of the sunlight, followed the rest into obscurity. No thoughts. No body. Nobody.

Time may have passed, but as there was no Tom to

mark it, there was no way of knowing. A human being sat on a bed in a compact hotel room near Leicester Square.

The very last thing to dissolve was the sense of waiting. The room itself seemed to collude with the anticipation, the stale air like a held breath. Then that too was gone.

When only emptiness remained, Bedlam Boy arrived.

4

In any normal sense of the word, nothing *changed*. But, if anyone had witnessed what happened to the man in room 18, they would have seen a transformation.

It started with the bald man's eyes. For a while, unfocused, gaze fixed downwards, they saw nothing. Now the pupils moved from left to right, from the door to the darkening curtains. The big head moved next, as the man's posture altered, chest expanding, shoulders relaxing.

The body language of the man now sitting on the hotel bed was so altered, it was hard to believe it was the same person. There was confidence in the squaring of those shoulders, a latent energy in the previously indolent frame.

The man stood up and stretched, pulling one hand behind his head and holding it, then swapping to the other arm. He worked through a sequence of gentle yoga-like exercises, then stretched every muscle group.

He took the MacBook out of the suitcase, booted it up, and connected to the hotel Wi-Fi. A series of passwords opened hidden folders, and he accessed a program he had coded months before. He picked up his phone and tapped the screen, opening an app. Now the phone showed the same view as the laptop: Lo-Fi security camera footage of an end-of-terrace house, a Peugeot van parked on the drive.

The naked man got dressed, pulling the clothes out of the open suitcase on the floor. Jeans, shirt, running shoes.

In the bathroom, he cut six pieces of scalp tape into strips. He shook the black wig out of the net, sticking two pieces of tape onto it. He stuck the rest onto his head, peeling off the protective layer covering the sticky surface. In the gaps, he painted a thin layer of glue with a soft brush, avoiding the scars. The glue needed a smooth surface to stick to.

With the ease born of repetition, he pressed the front of the wig to his forehead before smoothing it back over his head. His natural eyebrow colour was light brown, but mascara enabled him to match the black wig. The eyes that stared back from his transformed face remained his familiar dark green. Contact lenses could alter their colour, but this was one feature he would not consider changing. For the four people on his list, those eyes would be the last thing they ever saw. He wanted them to recognise him.

He put on the leather jacket and scooped up the black helmet. When he put his hand on the keycard in the slot on the wall, he caught sight of himself in the mirror. Upright now, six-foot-three, with a heavy, powerful body.

Tom might hunch himself up to avoid drawing attention to his bulk, but not Bedlam Boy. Now that Tom's slack features were animated by intelligence and purpose, even without the wig he would be almost unrecognisable to his fellow workmen. His mouth twitched into a smile. His expression didn't offer comfort, empathy, or forgiveness. He had seen horrors most people never dreamed of. A boy who shouldn't have lived, but who had held onto the thinnest of threads, clinging to life with a tenacity that no doctor predicted.

He knew the secret to his survival. A junior nurse had put her finger on the truth the day Tom Lewis was discharged from hospital.

"No one thought you would pull through. You should have seen the look on the doctor's face when you first opened your eyes. You were saved for a reason, Tom. I truly believe that. One day you'll find that reason. No one comes back from an injury like yours. No one."

She'd patted Tom's shoulder when the car arrived for him. "Good luck. Find out why you were saved."

Poor Tom, poor, gentle, silent Tom, smiled up at her, but didn't understand.

Bedlam Boy understood. He wondered what the nurse would make of the purpose he had found after twenty long years. He remembered the crucifix dangling from her neck. She probably wouldn't be best pleased.

The Boy smiled at his reflection, noting the cold fury in his eyes, the commitment, the lack of fear.

Time for someone to die.

"Looking good," he said.

To read more of this book, visit Amazon here: Bedlam Boy 1

ALSO BY IAN W. SAINSBURY

Thriller

Bedlam Boy 1

Bedlam Boy 2

Bedlam Boy 3

Science Fiction

The World Walker (The World Walker 1)

The Unmaking Engine (The World Walker 2)

The Seventeenth Year (The World Walker 3)

The Unnamed Way (The World Walker 4)

Children Of The Deterrent (Halfhero 1)

Halfheroes (Halfhero 2)

The Last Of The First (Halfhero 3)

Fantasy

The Blurred Lands